THE SHIMMERING
BOOK 3

MICHAEL L. CLARK

Published by

Historic Traces Publishing

Pensacola, Florida

Paperback ISBN: 978-1-965756-00-3

Hardback ISBN: 978-1-965756-01-0

THE PROPHET

Ebook ISBN: 978-1-965756-02-7

Chapter I

April 4, 1962

A siren screamed as a man dressed in a white lab coat opened the glass door and walked out into the fading light of day. His sixteen-hour shift was ending, and he was looking forward to a long weekend. He ignored the ambulance as it pulled into the hospital emergency bay to unload its latest pickup. He opened the door of his baby blue 1955 Chevrolet Bel Air and then got in.

Morgan Turner was a twenty-eight-year-old medical resident finishing his final year at Vanderbilt University Hospital in Nashville. On June 1, he would accept a position in the emergency department at Maury General Hospital in Columbia, Tennessee. Ten years of college, medical school, and residency were finally ending.

He drove out of the hospital parking lot and turned onto Edgehill Avenue. He traveled a few blocks to the east before pulling into a Texaco station to refuel his ride. When he pulled up to the gasoline pumps, two young men dressed in clean white shirts and dark trousers came running out to greet him.

"Fill her up, sir?"

Morgan replied, "Yes, please. And please check the oil for me."

"Yes, sir," said one of the young men.

As the first young man pumped gas into the Chevy's gas tank, the other opened the hood to check the oil. He pulled the dipstick from its location on the engine block, then wiped off the stick and reinserted it. He pulled

"

it out once again and checked the oil level. He brought the dipstick over to let Morgan see and said, "Looks like you're about two quarts low."

Morgan said, "Okay, top it off for me, would ya?"

"Yes, sir," replied the attendant.

After fueling the automobile, the other attendant sprayed the windshield with window cleaner and wiped it away with paper towels. He then checked the air pressure in all four tires and ensured they were properly inflated.

Finally, the two young attendants approached Morgan, and the first asked, "Will there be anything else, sir?"

"No," replied Morgan. "How much do I owe you?"

The young man looked at the gas pump, which read $3.72, then added sixty-eight cents to the total in his head. "That will be $4.40, sir."

Morgan reached into his wallet, took out seven dollars, and handed them to the first young man. "Here!" he said. You two can split the change."

Their faces both showed the excitement they felt when they heard Morgan say, "Keep the change."

One dollar and thirty cents each was quite a nice tip for less than ten minutes of work. The two scampered back to the station office, questioning each other about how rich their customer must be to offer such a generous tip.

Morgan wasn't rich, at least not financially. However, he did believe in rewarding people for good service, good manners, and jobs well done. Morgan knew what it was like to work in the service industry. He did so throughout his years at Vanderbilt. He had earned a scholarship to attend Vanderbilt. But that was for tuition and board only. He sometimes worked three part-time jobs to make enough money to pay for books, clothing, and other essentials.

When he pulled out of the gas station, he turned south onto Highway 31 and drove for about an hour until he came to Carter's Creek Station Rd in Neapolis. Neapolis was a tiny community nestled on the highway between Spring Hill and Columbia in Maury County. Then, he turned west onto Carter's Creek Station and traveled on it until it ended at Carter's Creek Pike. Then, he turned south once again, and after a half-mile, he pulled into the drive of his family's farm.

The Turner farm was on four hundred acres of rolling pasture and timber bordering on Carter's Creek. It had been in Morgan's family for over one hundred years. Morgan's father, Bob, raised nearly one hundred head of beef cattle and row-cropped one hundred and twenty acres of corn and soybeans. The house on the property was adequate but meager. The white-painted outer walls needed new paint. Some of the window shutters were barely hanging. The metal roof was rusty and needed some repair. It wasn't much to look at, but it was home.

Morgan drove up to the house just as the April sun dipped behind the western hill. Two women came out of the house to greet him as he parked the Chevy in front of the house. The first was a special surprise for Morgan. Her long blonde hair curled around her shoulders and bounced upon her back as she ran to meet Morgan. Morgan smiled as he looked into her bright blue eyes while she quickly approached.

"Morgan! It's so good to see you!"

She wrapped her arms around Morgan and gave him a gentle kiss on the cheek. Maggie Riner had been Morgan's sweetheart since high school. She lived on the farm next to the Turner Farm. She was two years younger than Morgan and had always had a crush on him since the first day they had met.

"Hello, Maggie! How are your folks?"

"They are just fine," she replied.

"Morgan!" came a squeal from the other young lady.

It was Lacy, Morgan's younger sister. Her eighteen-year-old body came bounding across the front yard to meet him. Lacy was ten years younger than her brother. Their mother died while giving birth to her when Morgan was ten years old. Morgan had been heartbroken over the loss of his mother. He decided that, soon after, he would become a doctor. Morgan worked hard on the farm to help his dad but even harder at school. He was determined to be at the top of his class every year. He was also instrumental in helping to raise his younger sister. Morgan was a model son whom his father could always depend on for help.

Lacy had dark curly hair cut just shy of her shoulders. Her eyes were the color of jade stones, and her smile was contagious to anyone who saw it.

"Morgan!" Lacy screamed again. "I thought you'd never get here. What took you so long?"

Morgan responded, "Well, you know how it is. I can never get away from the hospital when I'm supposed to. There's always another patient to see."

The young ladies each grabbed an arm and led Morgan into the house. Just as they entered the front room, they all heard the screen door at the back of the house slam shut. They all looked at each other with smiles on their faces as they realized Bob Turner had entered the house just in time for supper.

Bob stood at the kitchen sink, washing his face and hands as the trio entered.

"Daddy? Look who's home!" said Lacy.

Bob turned halfway around to look over his shoulder at Lacy while replying, "Hmm?"

When he realized his son was standing between the two girls, Bob exclaimed, "Morgan!" while he reached for a towel and hastily dried his face and hands.

"When did you get here, Son?"

"Just now, Dad."

"Well, have a seat. You're just in time for supper."

They all sat down at the family table that had been in their family for over fifty years. Lacy and Maggie had prepared a meal of fried steak with rice and gravy, green beans, fried apples, and biscuits.

Morgan looked forward to having a home-cooked meal. Unfortunately, he was lucky most of the time if he had time to go to a diner in Nashville to have a hot meal. As a result, he often choked down a sandwich in between cases at the hospital.

Morgan forced himself to slowly chew and savor the food as he shoveled it into his mouth. He wanted to enjoy every morsel.

Bob asked, "They keeping you busy at that hospital?"

"Yes, sir." Morgan answered. "I barely have time to stop and relax. Sometimes they'll pull a double shift on me."

Bob then said, "Well, I guess you're looking forward to this weekend, then."

Morgan replied, "I can't wait to get started. I hope y'all don't mind if I head out early tomorrow. I need to get there before sunset."

Bob replied, "That's fine, Son. We'll see you when you get back on Tuesday. Then we can all catch up."

Morgan had been looking forward to this weekend for a long time. April 6th and 7th would be the one-hundredth anniversary of the Battle of Shiloh, which was fought in April 1862 and was the bloodiest battle fought during the Civil War to date.

Shiloh was located near Corinth, Mississippi, just across the Tennessee state line. The Tennessee River flowed right past the area where the battle was fought, and the river played a pivotal part in the war.

Morgan had been a Civil War enthusiast nearly his whole life. As a young man, he took part in many Civil War reenactments throughout the middle Tennessee area. As a young boy, Morgan would arrive at the reenactments as a drummer boy. When he reached his teens, he traded his drum for a rifle and fought with and against the other young men. Morgan had fought imaginary battles at Rippavilla Plantation just up the road from their farm and Stones River in Murfreesboro. He had also been to Shiloh several times, but this would be different. The one-hundredth anniversary would draw men in from all over the country. Thousands were expected to be there this year to participate in the festivities.

Morgan would be wearing a different uniform once again. He would no longer be a foot soldier. Instead, Morgan was trading in his rifle for a medical bag. He would now be Captain Morgan Turner, Surgeon of the Army of the Tennessee. Morgan had spent much of his free time and money putting together his costume for the event. His medical bag was as authentic as he could manage, including the instruments that it carried. Of course, he wasn't expected actually to perform emergency surgery on anyone. Still, he would be available to provide first aid to anyone who might become injured during the pretend skirmishes.

After supper, Maggie helped Lacy clean up the dishes while Morgan and Bob retired to the den to catch the end of the evening news on the television. Once the girls finished in the kitchen, they joined the men. Morgan stood as Lacy and Maggie entered.

"Can I walk you home?" Morgan asked.

"I'd love that," replied Maggie.

Maggie's home was about a half-mile down Carter's Creek Pike from the Turner's farm, but they wouldn't be walking down the road. Instead, they would cut through the fields. Morgan could have driven Maggie home, but it was a nice night for a walk, and it would allow them more time to be together and talk without prying ears to bother them.

The two walked hand in hand as they slowly walked toward the Riner's farm. The cattle could be heard nearby as they lowed to one another, preparing to bed down for the night. There was no need for a flashlight to guide them along the way. Although clouds were beginning to gather together, there was still enough open sky for the moon to light their way. A pack of coyotes could be heard off in the distance as they yelped and howled at one another.

As the young couple approached the pond in the western pasture, they paused to stare into the water at the moon's reflection. Frogs were singing to one another, and crickets were chirping. It was as if nature's symphony was playing its concerto just for them.

As they stood at the edge of the pond, Morgan released Maggie's hand, then wrapped his arms around her waist and pulled her close. He looked into her eyes, then reached down and caught her lips with his. The kiss lingered but was gentle. When their lips parted from each other, Morgan was satisfied to hold Maggie in his arms for a while. Their bodies swayed as if they were slow dancing to the orchestra of wildlife that played around them.

After a while, Morgan said, "I'd better get you home."

The two of them strolled hand in hand together until they reached Maggie's front porch. Neither Morgan nor Maggie was surprised to see her parents sitting on the front porch enjoying the night breeze that blew from west to east.

"Hello, Morgan," said Mrs. Riner. "It's so good to see you."

"It's good to see you, too." replied Morgan. "Good evening, Mr. Riner."

Mr. Riner nodded his head slightly and responded, "Howdy!" Then, he drew from his pipe and released the smoke into the air.

Morgan and Maggie lingered at the first step of the porch, continuing their small talk with her folks. Then, finally, Morgan said, "Well, I'd better be going. I've got to get an early start tomorrow."

Mrs. Riner said, "You best be careful drivin' tomorrow. A storm's movin' in tonight."

"Yes, ma'am.", Morgan replied.

He bent down and kissed Maggie lightly on the cheek, then released her hand and walked back home.

CHAPTER 2

April 5, 1962

A clap of thunder shook Morgan awake from a deep sleep. Yesterday's sixteen-hour shift had finally caught up with him. The rain pelting the Turner home's roof sounded like someone was throwing handfuls of marbles onto the tin roof. Morgan wiped the sleep from his eyes and then glanced at the clock on the bedside table. The hour hand was on the eight, and the minute hand was approaching the six. Morgan stared at the clock with confusion. Why had the alarm not gone off at six-thirty as he had set it?

He jumped from his bed, scrambled to put on his clothes, and then darted into the kitchen to find Lacy. There she was, scrambling eggs and frying bacon for their breakfast. Breathless, Morgan asked, "Did you turn my alarm off? I had it set for six-thirty."

"Hmm?" she asked. "What alarm?"

"The alarm clock in my room. Did you turn off the alarm?"

Lacy gave a little snicker as she responded, "No, silly. That alarm hasn't worked for months. Besides, what's your hurry? I'm just now finishing breakfast. Have a seat."

Morgan was exasperated as he said, "I wanted to get an early start this morning. I should have already left."

Bob walked in the backdoor and asked, "What's this? What's got you so riled, son?"

"Nothin', Dad. I was just upset because my alarm didn't go off as I expected."

Bob said, "Oh yeah, forgot to tell you that old alarm clock don't work right no more."

Morgan rolled his eyes as he said, "Thanks, Dad. I know that, now."

Then Bob said, "Well, sit down. Let's eat. I've got a lot that needs doing today."

Morgan tried to relax while he sat with his family and ate breakfast. Unfortunately, the sound of the rain falling against the metal roof of their house made their morning breakfast conversation seem more like a shouting match. Twice while they were eating and talking, thunder shook the house. Bob commented, "Looks like we got us a real frog strangler today."

After breakfast, Morgan packed up his weekend gear and loaded it into the Chevy. He had a haversack that he packed with a change of clothes and other items he would need for the excursion. His tent and other camping gear, along with his medical kit, were already loaded into the trunk of his car. Next, he donned his Federal uniform with its newly stitched-on captain's bars. Next, he pulled on his boots, grabbed his hat, and said goodbye to Bob and Lacy.

Morgan trotted out to his car, tossed the haversack into the back seat, started the Chevy, and pulled away from the house. At the end of the driveway, he turned right onto Carter's Creek Pike and began his journey into the past. Although he didn't get the early start he had hoped for, he was still excited to be on his way to Shiloh.

After about five miles, he turned south onto Highway 31, heading toward Columbia. When he reached Columbia, he turned right onto Highway 9 after crossing the Duck River Bridge. The water of the Duck River was swelling from all the rain that had fallen during the night and early morning. Morgan found it a little difficult to see out of the windshield while driving because the rain still fell at a heavy pace. His wipers ran at full speed but did little to help clear his view.

He continued his drive on Highway 9 until he reached Santa Fe (pronounced Santa Fee). Then, he turned off the highway just north of Santa Fe and entered the Natchez Trace Parkway. The parkway would be the straightest path to Waynesboro. Once he reached Waynesboro, he could jump on Highway 64, taking him to Shiloh.

The rain let up a little as he turned onto the Natchez Trace. Finally, he was able to turn his wipers on the lower setting. His wipers squeaked as they rocked back and forth across the expanse of the windshield. Morgan allowed himself to relax a bit and began to enjoy the drive down the Trace. There were no other cars in sight. He had the road all to himself. He took in all the sites and passed them without stopping. The Water Valley Overlook was on his left, but he continued to drive. A little while later, he drove by a field where the Gordon House once stood. John Gordon and his wife Dolly had built the house, raised their family, and operated a "Stand" and a ferry in the early 1800s.

Morgan drove as he passed Jackson Falls, Fall Hollow, the old Metal Ford, and Napier Mine. Then, just on his right, he passed what was once known as Grinder's Stand. In the early 1800s, this stand was once operated by Robert and Priscilla Griner. The locals kept mispronouncing the name, calling it Grinder's Stand. The name eventually stuck. This stand is where Meriwether Lewis met his death while traveling up the Natchez Trail to Washington, D.C., in 1809.

Morgan turned his head as he passed the area where Grinder's Stand was, trying to get a glimpse of it. It was no use. He could only see another road that turned off the Trace, which led to the field where Grinder's Stand had once stood.

He continued to drive down the Trace highway for another fifty miles or more. He looked to his right and saw the rubble of an old house off in the distance. As he looked forward again, a large buck deer ran out onto the road in front of the Chevy. Morgan panicked as he swung the steering wheel to the right to dodge the deer. He managed to miss the big buck but lost control of the car as it slid on the slick surface of the wet roadway. The Chevy spun clockwise, leaving the road surface and spinning onto the shoulder.

The car seemed to spin forever. Finally, the front of the Chevy collided with a large outcropping of limestone at the edge of a wooded area. The impact threw Morgan through the windshield like a rock from a slingshot. His eyes widened as he saw that behind the limestone was a large Hickory tree. He quickly realized he would not avoid colliding with the tree. He closed his eyes and expected that he would not survive. Maggie's face flashed into his mind. He instantly hated that he would never see his love again. Accepting the inevitable, he opened his eyes again and prayed, "Dear God, save me!"

Suddenly, he realized that the tree was blurring. He wasn't sure if the rain obscured his vision or if he was not seeing straight. Then, just as his face was about to collide with the tree, everything changed.

"Am I dead?" he thought to himself.

The tree was no longer there. Neither was the rain. The air was dry and warm. Morgan landed with a "thud." He passed out on the ground. His face and hands were bleeding from the broken windshield through which he had flown.

———◆———

April 5, 1862

Morgan roused from a deep sleep. His head pounded a beat: *boom, boom, boom, boom*. After a while, it became louder in his ears: *boom, boom, boom, boom*. Then, a high-pitched whistle rang in his ears that matched the booming in his head.

"*What is that*?" he thought to himself.

He closed his eyes, trying to relieve the pressure on his brain. It was no use. The booming beat and the whistle only grew louder. Then he heard voices in the distance. Singing! Men were singing!

When Johnny comes marching home again
Hurrah! Hurrah!
We'll give him a hearty welcome then
Hurrah! Hurrah!
The men will cheer, and the boys will shout
The ladies they will all turn out
And we'll all feel gay
When Johnny comes marching home.

Then Morgan saw them. Thousands of men were marching down the trail, singing their tune. All of them were dressed in Federal uniform costumes, much like his own. A general wearing a white beard while riding a white horse led the formation. The troops marched in time as they sang their song with the accompaniment of the fife and drum.

Morgan struggled to get to his feet. He stood, leaning over, looking at his feet while trying to gain his balance. Morgan saw his haversack lying next to him. He reached over and grabbed the strap, lifting the bag to his shoulder, then stood up straight as best he could.

Morgan slowly stumbled toward the marching soldiers. They were at least one hundred yards away. He waved his left arm in the air, trying to attract the attention of someone in the formation. No one could hear him. He was too far away, and the music and singing were too loud. He stumbled along, steadily moving toward the army. He struggled to walk toward them, but he could only manage a couple of steps at a time before needing to stop to rest. Had it not been for the fact that there were so many troops moving down the trail, no one would have noticed Morgan. But someone did.

A private noticed Morgan as he stumbled toward them.

"Sergeant!" said the private. "Look!"

The soldiers pointed to the left of the formation at Morgan. Many heads turned to see what Private Jeff Henry had seen.

The sergeant looked in the distance and saw where Henry was pointing.

"Henry, you and Hawlsey follow me. The rest of you men stay in formation."

Sergeant Bob Sikes and the two privates trotted out to see who was trying to catch up to their unit. Just as they reached Morgan, he tumbled to the ground, exhausted.

"Looks like he's bleeding, Sergeant!" observed Henry.

"Yeah, I can see that, Henry. See if he's been shot."

Hawlsey and Henry both looked Morgan over, thoroughly searching for bullet wounds.

"No, Sergeant! But he's covered in little pieces of glass."

"Glass?" asked the sergeant.

Morgan was able to speak now as he breathily said, "I had an accident. I went through my windshield."

"Windshield?" asked the sergeant. "What's a windshield?"

They all pondered momentarily, then Hawlsey offered, "Maybe he meant window."

Morgan again said breathily, "Yeah, window. Glass."

Then, Sergeant Sikes noticed the bars on Morgan's uniform.

"Captain, we'll get an ambulance up here to pick you up so we can transport you to our next location."

Morgan said, "No. I don't need an ambulance. Just put me in a car."

"A cart?" asked Henry. "I don't think we've got any carts. The closest thing would be the ambulance, Sir."

The sergeant told Hawlsey, "Jim, go back to the line and fetch the ambulance for the captain."

"Yes, Sergeant!"

Then the sergeant asked Morgan, "Sir, where were you going when you had the accident?"

"Shiloh. What day is it, anyway?"

Henry spoke up, "Saturday, Sir. April 5th."

"Oh good!" said Morgan. "I haven't missed it then."

"Missed what?" asked Sikes.

"The battle at Shiloh.", Morgan replied.

CHAPTER 3

June 21, 1819

Just before dusk, Tommy and Daniel had finished digging a grave for Gus. They laid him to rest just below the hill leading to the bluff on the valley's far side. There was a large Hickory tree there that would cover him for eternity. They all gathered to say one last goodbye to their old friend. Only Daniel knew the struggles that Gus had endured in his life. At such a tender age, he suffered hardships trying to survive in a wild and untamed world. Daniel held the diary as they gathered around the grave to honor Gus. Daniel said, "I thought I would read the last entry in Gus's diary to you rather than reading scripture."

He opened up the diary to the last page and read,

June 20, 1818

This will be my last entry. Daniel and I will be going home tomorrow. At least, that is the plan. We still don't know for sure if it will work or not. It is just a theory that Daniel has. I told him that Robbie and I came through on June 21, 1973. He came through on December 21, 2017. So his theory is that the Shimmering only opens on the summer and winter solstice. We will test it out tomorrow. Cross your fingers. I haven't seen my home in such a long time. I can't wait to get there.

All three of the women wept as Daniel finished reading. Daniel and Tommy held back the tears they felt welling up in their eyes. Once the grave was secured, they all returned to their homes. Amy and Tommy walked to their cabin, Daniel and Emily to theirs, and Susan climbed up into the wagon that served as her residence.

Gus Childers had been a good friend to Daniel in the few months that they had known each other. They shared similar experiences that had bound them together. Gus accidentally passed through the Shimmering in 1973 while he and his friend Robbie were foraging for berries and nuts along the Natchez Trace. Robbie was killed by the Black Hand, which left Gus stranded in an unknown place and time. Daniel had also passed through the Shimmering unwittingly in 2017. He, too, lost a friend to the Black Hand.

Susan lay in the wagon bed and covered herself with a blanket. She didn't sleep. At least not at first. She thought about all that had occurred over the past several days. She and her new husband had come to the Water Valley for medical assistance while traveling to New Orleans. How Daniel had recognized her husband as a wanted criminal and murderer and held him captive until the militia could come and claim him. Daniel had escorted her on the trail as they traveled to testify against Charles in New Orleans. But Charles managed to escape his bonds with the help of his fellow cohorts, only to be shot down by Daniel and the two militia who traveled with them. Now, she was back at the Water Valley. She didn't know what she would do next. Go home to Virginia and endure public humiliation when the community found out she and her family had been taken by one of the most notorious con men in the South. Maybe move to Nashville? But with what? She had no money. Only her Surrey and three Morgan horses.

Daniel and Emily had invited her to stay with them. Daniel told her he would build an addition to their cabin for her to stay in, which could also serve as a hospital for Emily's patients.

Susan liked Emily, Daniel, Amy, and Tommy, too. They made her feel like she belonged. Even though she was only sixteen, they treated her like an adult. Her parents never did. Charles Van Dusan took them in in his flashy ways. They were the ones who insisted she marry Charles. They were the ones who got her into this mess.

That settled it. She was not going back to Virginia. She didn't care if she never saw her parents again. She would have nothing more to do with them. With that decision made, she drifted off to sleep.

The next morning, Susan woke as the rooster crowed. She dressed and gathered herself before climbing down from the wagon. She had decided to pull her weight around this homestead from now on. She knew Emily was probably already preparing breakfast, so she took it upon herself to go and gather the eggs.

As she walked by the cabin, she grabbed a reed basket from the porch and carried it to the chicken coop. Most of the hens were already stirring around in the yard, searching for food. Susan found the burlap sack holding corn and untied the top, exposing millions of kernels of the yellow seeds. Inside the sack was also a small scoop. She scooped up some of the corn and flung it into the yard. The chickens scattered toward the morsels of grain, pecking and eating as quickly as they could.

Susan tied the sack back closed, entered the coop, and gathered the eggs from the nesting boxes. She found thirteen eggs. An especially protective hen well-guarded the last three, but Susan managed to get the eggs despite the hen's constant pecking.

Susan returned to the cabin and found Emily coming out to the porch. "Morning, Susan."

"Good morning, Emily.", she said with a smile.

Emily noticed the basket Susan was carrying and asked,"Well, what have you got, there?"

Susan replied, "I went ahead and gathered the eggs for you. I hope you don't mind."

Emily smiled and said, "Well, no not at all. Thank you so much!"

The two of them went inside the cabin to finish up breakfast.

Susan asked, "Has Daniel gone out already?"

"Oh, yes. He's looking after the horses probably. He'll be back in time for breakfast, though."

Emily fried a dozen eggs to accompany the fried diced potatoes and bacon she had already cooked. While cooking the eggs, she asked Susan, "Would you please check the biscuits for me?"

Susan took an iron hook and removed the lid from the Dutch oven that hung in the fireplace. She looked inside and said, "They're nice and brown."

Emily replied, "Good. Would you take them up for me?"

Susan found a hand towel and used it to grip the Dutch oven handle. She lifted it from the hook where it had been hanging above the fire. She placed the pot on another towel that rested on the wooden countertop. Then, she dug the biscuits out of the pot and carefully placed them on a wooden platter.

Just as she placed the platter on the table, Daniel walked into the cabin. He found time to milk the goat while checking on the horses, so he placed the bucket of milk at one end of the table and then sat down.

Emily could see that he was in deep thought. He hadn't spoken a word since he got out of bed. "What's up with you?" she asked.

"Hmm?" he said, suddenly noticing he wasn't alone.

Emily repeated, "What's up with you?"

Daniel replied, "Gotta lot on my mind."

Emily asked, "Like what?"

Daniel answered, "Oh, Gus, the Shimmering, what Gus said about the Shimmering."

"What did Gus say about the Shimmering?" asked Emily.

"How we evidently changed the timeline just by going through it. He said that everything was different from what we left in 2018. Even in 2218. Slavery still existed. It was like the South won the war between the states and slavery never went away."

Emily replied, "Well, what do you plan on doing? I know you aren't just going to let it pass. But, what can you do? The Shimmering only takes you forward two-hundred years or four-hundred years from here. That won't get you to the 1860s."

"No, it won't. But, Colonel Crockett mentioned to me a while back that there are other locations of Ittola Chuka. He knew of at least five or six. Maybe each one has a different amount of time attached to it. He said David would probably be able to tell me where they are."

"So, I guess you'll be going to Sheboss now?" asked Emily.

"No, not right away. I've got too much to do around here right now. We still have a farm to run and I can't leave it all up to Tommy to take care of everything. I would like you to do something for me if you don't mind."

"What's that?" asked Emily.

"Would you mind riding over to the Gordon's and telling Dolly about Gus? I'm sure she would like to know about his death. They were friends for over forty years."

Emily looked over at Susan and noticed the befuddled look on her face. Then she asked, "How do you feel about a ride to keep me company?"

Susan replied, "Sure, I wouldn't mind that at all. I just want to help wherever I can."

Emily said, "I'll ask Amy to join us. I'm sure she would like to see her family again."

After breakfast was over and the kitchen was clean, Emily and Susan walked to Amy's cabin to ask her if she wanted to ride with them to the Gordon plantation. They could have ridden, but Emily walked the half mile instead. They strolled along the bank of the Beaver Branch and enjoyed the morning air. The temperature was already beginning to rise above eighty degrees, but it wasn't unbearable yet.

Jake tagged along as the two of them conversed in light conversation. Jake sloshed through the creek, looking for anything he could catch to play with. A frog leaped from the bank and landed in the water about ten feet away, which sent Jake into a frenzy. He jumped from here to there, trying to catch the amphibian as it swam away from him. Soon, another frog jumped into the water, causing Jake to change directions.

As they walked along the creek bank, Susan finally asked, "Emily, what is Itto, Itto…"

"Ittola Chuka." Emily finished for her. "Ittola Chuka is the Chickasaw name for what we know as the Shimmering."

Then Susan asked, "What is the Shimmering?"

"Well, that's a little hard to believe unless you have experienced it," Emily replied.

"Have you or Daniel ever experienced it?"

Emily answered, "We have. Tommy too. And Gus. Gus more than anyone."

Susan asked, "So, what is it?"

Emily began, "Well, it is a time portal that can send you either back in time or forward in time, evidently depending on which direction you enter it. It is located in a Chickasaw burial ground north and east of here. It is heavily guarded by a band of Chickasaw called the Black Hand. Gus was the first of us to find it. He and his friend Robbie accidentally went through it in the year 1973. Robbie was killed by the Black Hand but Gus got away. The Shimmering took him back to 1773. He had no idea where or when he was, how he got there, or how he could get home. That diary that Daniel is always reading was written by Gus. It tells of all that happened to him after coming through the Shimmering.

Daniel and his friend Jimbo accidentally went through the Shimmering in 2017. Jimmy was also killed by the Black Hand. Daniel was able to discover information about the Shimmering by developing a friendship with David Colbert, the Chickasaw man who owns Sheboss Stand.

I learned about the Shimmering from some old documents I found while trying to discover what had happened to Daniel when he seemingly fell off the face of the earth. I'm the only one who went through it intentionally. Tommy and I were. He came through with me.

Then Gus went through intentionally while attempting to return home to find his family whom he hadn't seen in forty-five years."

Susan was mildly amused when she asked, "So, is that why Daniel seems to know so much about the people around here? Is that how he knew about Charles?"

Emily replied, "Exactly! Daniel was a history teacher at one time. History has always been his passion. He knew about all the people in this area before he came through. Everyone that is except Gus. He and Gus became very close in the short amount of time that they were together."

Susan replied, "And I thought Daniel was a prophet all this time."

Emily said, "Susan, I need you to keep this information to yourself. Don't tell anyone, okay?"

"Sure, Emily. But does Amy know?"

"Amy, Dolly and Sarah and David Colbert all know. And, I think Daniel may have told Colonel Crockett."

Susan smiled as she replied, "Don't worry, Emily. Your secret is safe with me."

After a fifteen-minute walk, Amy's cabin came into view. As they approached the little cottage, they saw Amy outside hanging out the wash to dry.

Emily called out, "Hello!"

Amy turned and saw the ladies as they moved closer.

"Well hello, Emily! Hi, Susan! What brings y'all out here this morning?"

Emily replied, "We've come out to invite you on a little trip with us."

"Oh?" Amy asked. "What kind of trip? Where are you going?"

"We're going to see your family. Daniel asked me to go and let them know about Gus. You want to come along?"

Amy was thrilled to hear of their destination. "Oh, I'd love to come along. When will you be leaving?"

Emily said, "I think we should plan to leave right after lunch."

Amy bit her bottom lip as she thought to herself, then replied, "That sounds good. I just need to go and talk to Tommy about it."

Emily responded, "Alright, why don't you and Tommy have lunch with us today. We can leave from our cabin afterwards."

"Sounds good to me. I'll see you at lunch."

CHAPTER 4

After lunch, the ladies pitched in to clean up the lunch dishes while Tommy and Daniel walked out to the corral and saddled three horses. They saddled one of Susan's Morgan mares, Amy's black mare, and the Sorrel gelding with blue eyes for Emily.

As they led the horses up to the cabin, they met the ladies as they were coming out. Each of them was holding a saddlebag. Amy wore a brace and pistol over her shoulder while wearing a riding outfit resembling a skirt but a pair of big-legged pants. Susan also wore a riding habit that she found among her vast array of clothing from Virginia. Emily appeared to be wearing her typical skirt, which she wore most days around the homestead. However, after further inspection, Daniel realized she was wearing her Wranglers underneath the skirt.

Daniel said, "I'm surprised you were able to get them on."

Emily smirked at him and replied, "Ha, Ha, very funny. I haven't gained that much weight yet. Besides, I just zipped them up as far as I could and left them unbuttoned."

Emily swung herself into the saddle with very little trouble. Then, Daniel said, "Hold on a minute."

He walked back into the cabin and reached just inside the doorway. When he pulled his hand back out, he was holding a brace and pistol as well as a powder horn and shot bag.

"Here.", he said as he handed them to Emily. "You forgot this."

Emily smiled wryly at him and responded, "Have you ever known me not to be prepared?" She patted her saddlebags on the back of the Sorrel, indicating she had already packed her weapon.

"Well, take this one too. Keep it handy."

Emily took the brace, wrapped it over her shoulder, and then bent down and kissed Daniel goodbye.

As the women turned their horses toward the Beaver and began to ride away, Jake looked at them, then at Daniel, and whimpered.

Daniel looked at him and said, "You go too, Jake. Keep them safe."

Emily called out, "Come on, Jake!"

Jake happily bounced toward the small caravan, then leaped into the Beaver to lead them.

Daniel and Tommy stood and watched as the ladies rode away at a slow walk. Then, when their images faded into the darkness of the trees, they turned and went back to work.

They headed up to the hog pen to work for a while. There was a new litter of four-week-old pigs that needed attention. Daniel pulled out his hunting knife and a whetstone to sharpen the blade. As he pulled the knife's edge across the stone back and forth, Tommy scattered some shelled corn into the pen to occupy the attention of the hogs.

Ten pigs were in the litter: six gilts and four boars who would soon be barrows. The pigs and the older hogs were quite used to the men walking among them in the pen, so they gave their full attention to the corn scattered on the ground.

Tommy walked over and eyed one of the young boars with his head down, looking for more corn. Tommy quickly reached down, snatched the pig by the back leg, and lifted him off the ground. The pig initially responded to squeal but then relaxed and only grunted as he hung upside down in Tommy's grip. The pig weighed only about ten pounds, so he wasn't much to handle. Tommy carried the pig over to the fence where Daniel was waiting outside. Tommy swung the pig over the wall and rested the pig's back against the outside of the wall, with his belly facing Daniel. Daniel reached over with his left fore and middle fingers and pushed down on the pig's testicles, bringing them down into its abdominal cavity. Daniel made two quick slits with the newly sharpened knife and watched as the testicles escaped from the pig's body through the two slits. Next, Daniel reached up with his left hand, grabbed each testicle one at a time, and pulled it out of the pig's body. He then dabbed the opened wounds with some iodine to prevent infection. Tommy released the pig into the pen and watched the pig squeal, running back to his sow.

They repeated the procedure thrice until all the male pigs had been castrated.

Then, Daniel asked, "What's next?"

Tommy answered, "Well, that other sow over there just had a litter yesterday. I reckon we ortta clip their teeth."

Daniel said, "Alright! Let's gitter dun!"

Piglets are born with razor-sharp teeth called needle teeth because they are so sharp. They have four sets of two. Uppers and lowers on each side of their mouth. If they are not clipped soon after birth, the sow will become sore and eventually quit nursing because of the pain. If that were to happen, the pigs could starve to death.

Daniel and Tommy climbed into the pen carrying a bushel basket and a pair of wire cutters. Daniel told Tommy, "Whatever you do, don't run."

They placed the basket on the ground, and each man began snatching up pigs one at a time. Once a pig had been captured, they began to squeal, which alerted the sow that something was wrong. The sow grunted, snorted, and barked at them as she walked over quickly to see the matter. Daniel paid little attention to her as he moved the small pig into the grip of his left hand and held the wire cutters in his right hand. He held the pig around the back of the neck, which caused the pig to squeal even louder, but that was okay because the pig's mouth needed to be open for this procedure to work. Daniel showed Tommy how to clip just the tips of the teeth off with the clippers. Snip. Snip. Snip. Snip. It was done. He then dropped the pig into the bushel basket to keep it separate from the other pigs and tell which ones had been clipped.

"Do you think you can handle it?" asked Daniel.

"No problem.", said Tommy.

Daniel handed Tommy the wire cutters so Tommy could clip teeth while Daniel caught up with the pigs and distracted the sow. Daniel would snatch up a pig and hand it off to Tommy while pushing away the sow with his leg to keep her away. A quick poke in the snout would deter her for a moment; then, she would return when she heard her pigs squealing.

Once they had finished, they tumped over the basket, releasing twelve piglets to run back to Momma.

Daniel said to Tommy, "Good job!"

"Thanks!" he replied. "That wasn't as bad as I expected.

———◆○◆———

Emily, Amy, and Susan rode together up the Trail toward Gordon's plantation. They walked their horses at a leisurely pace; there was no need to hurry. The ride typically took them five to six hours, but it might take a little longer at their current pace.

Two hours down the Trail, Emily noticed the Sorrel prick up his ears, and he looked to the right side of the Trail. Jake noticed something, too. Occasionally, he would pause on the Trail, give a low growl, and *"chuff"* under his breath.

Emily looked east to see who or what might catch Jake's and Sorrel's attention. She noticed a slight movement in the trees about seventy-five yards out. Riders. But she couldn't know how many were as thick as the brush. Nevertheless, she said in a low voice, "Ladies, I think we may have some company."

Emily drew her pistol from its brace and checked the load. Susan looked at her with fright. Emily asked, "Do you know how to use one of these?"

Susan nodded, then said, "I never shot at a man, though."

Emily handed her the pistol and said, "Hopefully, this won't be your first time."

Amy readied her pistol while Emily reached back into her saddlebags and retrieved the other gun. She was glad now that Daniel had insisted she carry both pistols.

Emily felt the Sorrel tense underneath her legs as they topped a short hill on the Trail. Jake was more alert now as well. Then Jake let out a *"woof."* Jake was in full alarm mode as two men rode out in front of them onto the Trail about forty yards out. He barked and growled incessantly. He bared his teeth, showing the men that he meant business. The ladies pulled up their horses and stopped about twenty yards from the riders who blocked their path.

The Natchez Trail had been known as the Devil's Backbone because of the notorious scoundrels and bandits that frequented the area, laying traps for travelers that they might rob, pillage, and even kill. In this case, rape was not out of the question as well. Emily had hoped they were far enough off the actual Trail that they wouldn't have to be concerned with such nonsense as this. But, there is always a good chance these men were riding off the main trail, avoiding militia or local law from Nashville, which might be in their pursuit.

The two men were rough and rugged-looking, well-mounted, and well-armed. One of them was older, wearing a long black beard. His face was filthy, and his eyes looked cold and white against the darkness of his tanned skin.

She guessed the other was younger—probably only twenty or twenty-two—yet just as evil-looking and intimidating as his partner.

The older bandit spoke loudly and boisterously when he said, "Well, hello, ladies! Fancy meeting you out here all alone."

Emily didn't reply. Instead, she turned the Sorrel around, hoping to escape to the Water Valley. However, there was no escape. Two more riders came up the Trail from behind them. They were trapped. Emily tried to keep the panic at bay rising from within her. The new bandits walked their horses slowly up the Trail toward the women.

As they slowly approached, Jake continued to bark, snarl, and growl at the riders. The bandits seem unconcerned about the dog's demonstration of ill will toward them. They continued to move forward as the first man announced, "Okay, ladies! You can drop your pistols. They won't do you much good. Besides, we don't want ta hurt cha none. We just want to have a little fun, that's all."

Emily didn't drop her pistol as instructed. Instead, she raised her weapon, pointed it at the old man, and ordered them, "Don't come any closer. You won't be laying a hand on any of us, Mister. So, just turn around and keep on riding."

The men kept slowly riding toward the ladies. Step by step, they moved closer. They were in no hurry and knew they had the advantage over these unaccompanied female riders.

As they came within ten feet of the women, Jake's attention turned to something else in the forest. His ears perked up, and his demeanor changed. Suddenly, both companies of riders were surrounded by twenty

Chickasaw braves. They rode out of the forest on three sides of the Trail. Six men encircled the bandits riding toward the ladies from the north, while six more rode up from the south. Eight more braves came from the east and surrounded the ladies, providing protection around them. Emily recognized one of them. He was Thomas Colbert, David's brother.

"Shobohli Eho, are you safe?"

"We are now. Thank you, Thomas. Thank you for watching over me."

"We always watch. We like the Great Spirit always watch, always protect."

Thomas' braves disarmed the bandits and knocked them from their horses. Then, they tethered their hands and led each back into the forest on foot, dragging them behind their ponies. Other braves gathered up their mounts and led them into the woods back to the east.

Emily asked, "What will you do with them?"

Thomas replied, "They will be punished. Chief William will decide what to do with them." Then he asked, "You ride to John Gordon's camp?"

"We do."

Thomas spoke to four of the braves in his native tongue, then turned and spoke to Shobohli Eho. "My braves will ride with you. No one will cause harm to you while you travel."

Emily responded, "Thank you, Thomas. I appreciate that you are always watching over me."

Thomas nodded to Emily, then turned his pony back into the forest. Emily and the ladies kicked their mounts forward and continued their journey, thankful for their rescuers.

CHAPTER 5

The ladies rode into the Gordon's encampment around seven in the evening. There was still plenty of daylight, so they found their way through the camp and rode up to Dolly's house without effort. The braves left them on the trail just outside the encampment, not wanting to be seen by anyone other than their charges.

Dolly Gordon saw them ride up through one of her brick federal-style house windows. She quickly approached the front door and flung it open to greet the women.

"Amy!" she cried out as she bounded down the steps of the house.

It had only been about three weeks since Amy and Tommy's wedding. But it already had seemed a lifetime since Dolly and Amy had seen one another.

"Momma!" Amy cried out as she slid off her horse and ran to hug her mother.

Dolly embraced her youngest daughter and asked, "How are you?"

"I'm fine."

"How's Tommy? You haven't left him already, have you?" Dolly asked.

"No, ma'am! Tommy's fine. I just came along to keep Emily and Susan company."

"Oh?" said Dolly. "Hello, Emily. Miss Claiborne. Good to see you again."

Susan replied, "Mrs. Gordon, it's good to see you as well, but please, call me Susan."

"Alright." said Dolly. "But you must call me Dolly, then."

Emily broke in, "Dolly, I'm afraid we have some bad news to share with you. May we go inside to talk?"

"Sure," said Dolly. Nathan, come take these horses and look after them, please."

"Yessum, Miss Dolly." replied an older black man.

Emily recognized the man from earlier visits. She smiled as he came to take her reins.

"Thank you, Nathan. It's so good to see you again. How are you doing?"

"Jes fine, Miss Em'ly. Good to see you too."

Susan looked at Emily questioningly. No one in her family back in Richmond would have ever traded such niceties with one of the enslaved people. It was undignified.

Dolly led the ladies into the parlor and had them sit. "Alright, Emily. What's so important you had to ride six hours to come and tell me?"

Emily replied, "It's Gus. He came back."

"Oh?" said Dolly as her stomach tightened, waiting for the bad news.

"Yes," said Emily. "But he was wounded when he came back through. Daniel and Susan found him lying on the trail. He had been shot. By the time they got him back to the Water Valley, he had lost too much blood. His lungs had collapsed too. He didn't make it."

Tears filled Dolly's eyes. Gus had been a dear friend to Dolly for many years. She had been able to lean on him for support whenever her husband was off fighting in some war. So when he told her he planned to return home in his own time, she was disappointed yet happy for him. They were both young when they first met in Nashville. Gus worked for her husband, first as a postal rider, then on their plantation. He had been more like family than an employee. Yet, Gus had been more than a friend or employee. He had been there to comfort her when the captain was away fighting his wars. He had even shared her bed at times. It wasn't uncommon when a man was away from his family for long periods for a woman to seek comfort from others. Many times, they never knew if their husbands would ever return.

No one ever knew it, but Gus was the father of her twins, Luke and Mark. Over the years, people have commented that the twins do not have the same facial features as her other children. If people had seen the twins standing next to Gus, they would have noticed the resemblance. However, Dolly never told Gus that he was their father. He may have suspected it, but he never said anything.

"When?" asked Dolly.

Dolly's eyes began to water, so she wiped the tears away with her handkerchief.

"Yesterday," replied Emily. "We buried him on our place."

Amy changed the subject, "Is Lucy here?"

Dolly sniffled a little, then said, "No, dear. Your sister went back to Nashville after your wedding. She couldn't stand the thought of your finding a husband before her. So she's gone back to find one for herself."

Just then, the women heard the front door open and close. A man's footsteps moved across the floor, entering the parlor. It was Amy's oldest brother, John Jr. As he entered the parlor somewhat preoccupied, he stopped dead in his tracks and realized his mother was not alone.

"Oh, sorry, Mother. I didn't realize . . . Amy? What are you doing back so soon?"

Amy stood and walked over to John and hugged him around his waist.

"Johnny, do you remember Emily Lane?" Amy introduced.

"Why yes. How are you, Mrs. Lane?"

Emily responded, "I'm fine, thank you."

"And Johnny, this is Susan. Susan Claiborne. She's from Richmond."

Susan's beauty took John aback. His mouth was agape as he tried to speak but could only stutter. "How, how, how do you do, Miss Clay Clay Claiborne?"

John Gordon Jr was the eldest son of the Gordon clan at age twenty-two. He ran the trading post for his mother. He stared at Susan as he stood there, forgetting why he had entered.

Dolly finally interrupted his thoughts and asked, "John, you were asking?"

John continued to stare at Susan and said, "Hmm? Oh, Mother, I just wanted to let you know that I finished the inventory. Here are the results along with sales receipts for the year so far."

"Thank you, John," said Dolly as she reached for the ledger. "Is there anything else, son?"

John continued to stare at Susan, "Hmm? Oh! No, ma'am. That's all."

The women stood in silence, waiting for John to leave. But he lingered just a moment longer, keeping his eyes on Susan.

"Well, I guess I'd better go. It was very nice meeting you," he said to Susan as he began to sweat.

Susan responded, "Likewise, I'm sure."

John finally left the parlor and found his way out the door. Just as the door latch clicked shut, the women all giggled.

Amy asked her mother, "When did Johnny develop that awful stutter?"

Dolly replied, "The moment he saw Susan."

Susan said, "He is a handsome man, though."

Dolly replied, "Oh that he is. He takes after his father in that respect. That's the only thing that he got from John, though. Thankfully he never got the itch to go off to war like his father. John Jr is content to work at the trading post."

The following day, after breakfast, Emily decided it might be a good idea to walk down to the trading post and see if there might be something they needed at the homestead. She asked Susan if she wanted to come along, and she replied, "Do you think it's safe? I'm afraid John Gordon Jr might knock something over if I show up unannounced. He might catch the store on fire and burn it down."

The two of them giggled as they leisurely walked to the post. It was a warm and humid summer morning. The crickets hid in the tall grass and sang a tune as the ladies walked nearby. A mockingbird was perched on a tree limb not too high up. She sang her tune, changing the cadence from time to time. Emily thought about a time back at their farm in Hampshire when she tried to count the number of songs she once heard a mockingbird sing. But, unfortunately, they were just too numerous to count.

When they finally reached the post, Emily turned the latch to open the door, which swung open. She and Susan walked in and noticed how dark it was inside. They momentarily paused at the door until their eyes adjusted to the dim light. There were only two windows in the small shed that served as the trading post, and they were small.

A voice behind the shed said, "I'll be right there!"

John soon came from the back to help whoever had entered his little store. He had dressed in his usual dress slacks, a dress shirt with a string bow tie, and a waistcoat. Even though he lived and worked on the frontier, he was always dressed to impress and seldom saw anyone other than the occasional traveler, fur trapper, or local Indian.

"Oh, Mrs. Lane and Susan. How nice to see you again. Is there anything I can help you with?"

Emily replied, "Well, I really just wanted to see the trading post. I've never been here before, and I thought I might find something we might need at home."

John smiled and replied, "Well, please look around. If I can help you find anything, please don't hesitate to ask."

Emily and Susan took their time wandering around the little store. There weren't many unusual items, and there was very little clothing for ladies. They mostly carried dry goods.

After a while, John approached them again and asked, "Have you found anything you might need?"

Emily replied, "Well, I wish I had thought to bring a packhorse along with us. I could have used some things, but I don't think I can get it home on the Sorrel."

John sensed an opportunity here, "I can deliver anything you might need."

Emily said, "Oh, that would be too much trouble. We can wait for another time."

"Oh, it's no problem! I can get Mother or one of the boys to watch the store for me. I'd be happy to oblige."

Emily said, "Well if you're really sure, I could use a large sack of flour, sugar, coffee, and baking powder."

John made a mental list of each item and then said, "When do you plan to go back?"

Emily asked, "Is tomorrow too soon?"

John replied, "No, ma'am. I'll have everything ready to go right after breakfast."

That night, when everyone gathered outside for supper, everyone sat together at the long tables at the campsite. Even though they now had a lovely brick house on the property, it didn't have enough room to seat the army that now lived together.

As the meal was nearing the end, John caught Amy's look and motioned for her to join him for a moment out of earshot of the larger group.

Sunlight was fading as the two of them walked away from the campsite.

"What is it?" Amy asked.

John reluctantly asked, "Is she married?"

"Is who married?"

John rolled his eyes as he answered, "Susan!"

Amy had a little fun with her older brother and responded, "Why do you ask?"

"Amy!"

"Okay, okay! She's a widow."

John thought for a moment, "How long ago did she lose her husband?"

Amy coyly said, "I don't know. Two or three days ago, I think."

John asked, "How did he die?"

"Daniel Lane shot him."

"What?" asked John.

Amy said, "Look, Johnny, you really should be hearing all of this from her if you're really interested in her. But, of course, I don't know all of the details. I just know that her husband was an outlaw."

After a short moment of nothing being said as they walked, Amy suggested, "Why don't you ask her to go for a walk with you? I'm sure she wouldn't mind."

John lit up, "Why? What did she say about me?"

Amy replied, "She said that you're handsome."

The corners of John's mouth curved slightly at the sound of those words. He hadn't been able to get her out of his mind from the moment he first saw her. He knew almost immediately that there was something special about her. He wanted to spend the rest of his life with her.

CHAPTER 6

John and Nathan saddled the ladies' horses and one for John after breakfast. Then he loaded a pack containing Emily's dry goods onto another horse, and he and Nathan led them all up to the brick house where the ladies had been sleeping.

As Amy, Emily, and Susan came out the door and walked down the steps, John's heart flipped inside his chest when he saw Susan coming out. She looked at John and smiled as she gracefully walked down the steps. She walked in front of John toward her horse, glanced at him, and said, "Good morning."

Amy hugged and kissed her mother before mounting her horse. Emily shook Dolly's hand and said, "Thanks for your hospitality."

Dolly replied, "Thank you for bringing me the news about Gus. Tell Daniel thanks, too."

"I will."

They all walked their horses back onto the trail that led to the Water Valley with Jake in the lead. Emily and Amy followed, with Susan behind. John and the packhorse brought up the rear.

This morning, there was a mild breeze, and clouds were rolling in from the west. The sun was above the horizon in the east, creating a painting of washed reds, oranges, and yellows.

Emily looked to the east and said, "I don't like the look of that."

Amy replied, "Me neither. Do you think we can make it home before it starts?"

Emily replied, "If we hurry, we might."

Emily turned to look at John and announced, "We're going to pick up the pace and see if we can't outrun the storm."

Riding about fifteen yards behind, John raised his hand to acknowledge her. They rode at a steady canter down the trail for about an hour. Finally, Emily decided to give the horses a break, so she pulled up and let the Sorrel lead the pace at a walk. The Sorrel's nostrils flared as he inhaled and exhaled heavily, trying to catch his breath. Over the past hour, he and the other horses had worked up a pretty good lather. The sweat had foamed around the reins as they lay across the horses' necks.

Without stopping, Emily swung her leg off the horse, jumped to the ground, and walked alongside her horse. The other travelers followed her cue. Emily felt alive walking along the trail beside her horse. She had now lived in this frontier for a year and loved it. Emily loved the people. She didn't miss the hustle and bustle of her life in the twenty-first century. She knew she had made the right decision to come here rather than her and Daniel returning to their lives in the future.

As they walked down the trail, Susan slowed her pace so that John could catch up. They walked side by side for a while until Susan decided she would need to start the conversation if they would have one.

"I understand your father was a captain?"

"Yes.", replied John. "He fought with Andy Jackson."

Susan asked, "Was he killed in the war?"

John answered, "No. But the war killed him."

"How do you mean?" she asked.

John replied, "He fought in many wars. The Revolution. The French and Indian war. The war in 1812. He fought down in Florida against the Seminoles. That one ended up being what did him in. Father caught malaria and had to come home to rest. Emily did what she could for him but, after a few months, he passed."

Susan said, "Oh, I'm sorry to hear that."

Then John asked, "Do you mind if I ask . . . I mean . . . Amy said you were married?"

"Yes, I was. But for only a short time."

John asked, "Did he die recently?"

Susan answered, "Only a few days ago."

John replied, "I'm sorry for your loss."

"I'm not!" exclaimed Susan. "I'm glad he's gone! He was a crook, a thief, and a confidence-man! But, from what Daniel told me, he was also a murderer! He tried to kill me! If it hadn't been for Daniel, I'd be dead."

Then John asked, "Forgive me but, why did you marry him?"

Susan answered, "It was my father's decision. Charles conned him into thinking that he owned a large shipping company in New Orleans and several other interests. My father's business ventures were wavering a bit. Business wasn't as good as it should be. He was led to believe that a merger with Charles would save his assets. So, he offered my hand in marriage to seal the deal."

John said," How awful for you. How long had you been married to him?"

"Only about a month. We were on our way to New Orleans. Your mother had told us about Emily being a doctor. I required some attention, so we drove down to find Emily. While we were there, Daniel came up as we were about to leave. He recognized Charles's name when he was introduced. Daniel drew his gun and held Charles and his men captive until he could get the local militia to come and pick them up. About a week later, I was asked to ride to New Orleans with some U. S. Marshals to testify against Charles and his men. Daniel escorted me. The marshals turned out not to be what they said they were. They were more of Charles' men. They had come to help Charles escape, which they did. But Charles decided he wanted more than his freedom. He wanted me dead since I was a witness to his latest crimes. That's when Daniel shot and killed him."

They walked in silence for a moment, then John said, "I'm glad you weren't killed."

Susan smiled as she looked at him and replied, "Me too."

After resting the horses for about an hour, Emily decided to speed things up again. Everyone else followed suit and mounted their horses as she mounted the Sorrel. Again, they cantered down the trail together. This time, John and Susan rode side by side.

Two hours later, they topped the ridge just above Emily's valley. They slowed the horses to give them easier footing going down the hill. When Jake saw the cabin in the distance, he bounded down the hill until he reached Beaver Branch. He barked across the creek, looking for Daniel. He turned his head to make sure Emily was coming.

Emily said, "It's okay, Jake. Go ahead."

Jake leaped into the clear waters of the Beaver and swam across to find his master. He reached the other side and shook himself off, water spraying in all directions from his golden coat.

After noon, the caravan pulled into the valley and settled in front of Emily's cabin. The skies were much darker than they should have been at this time of day. A storm was moving in quickly. Emily told the others, "Let's unpack these horses and get everything inside before it starts raining."

John unloaded the packhorse, carried the dry goods into the cabin, and laid them on the table for Emily to put away later. Daniel and Tommy walked in from the cornfield as the others moved indoors. Daniel said, "We'll get these horses corralled, then meet you back here for lunch."

Thunder rumbled in the distance. Lightning flashed about the ridge overlooking the Duck River. Then the skies opened up, and the rain began to pour down on them by the buckets full. Tommy and Daniel would not be able to dodge the rain. They were soaked to the skin in a matter of minutes. Even Daniel's buckskin britches couldn't repel the water away. Finally, they managed to unsaddle the horses and put them in the corral with the other horses. Then, they ran back to the cabin, uselessly dodging the heavy raindrops along the way.

Thunder rolled, and lightning lit up the cabin as six humans and one dog sat inside out of the rain. Daniel and Tommy stood next to the fire, stripped down to as little clothing as possible without being considered indecent.

Everyone ate bread and cheese for their lunch. Jake lay on the floor next to the fireplace, whimpering every time a clap of thunder shook the cabin. The storm seemed to last forever, but it let up and subsided to light rain just before suppertime.

Daniel went back out to check the livestock while Tommy and Amy walked back to their cabin. Emily prepared a supper of bacon, beans, and cornbread. She also sliced tomatoes and cucumbers.

When what was left of the evening sun finally disappeared, Susan decided to excuse herself for the night. She would go back to her wagon and bed down. As she approached the door, she looked at John and asked, "Would you mind walking me out?"

John replied, "It would be my pleasure."

John turned to the Lanes, bid them "goodnight," and then escorted Susan to the wagon.

As they reached the wagon, Susan asked him, "Where will you sleep tonight?"

"I'll find a dry spot out here on the ground somewhere," he said.

"Why don't you bed down in the wagon? There's plenty room for two."

John replied, "I don't think that would be proper. People might get the wrong idea about us."

Susan said, "There's nothing improper about your staying dry rather than sleeping on the wet ground. Besides, when Daniel escorted me to New Orleans, he slept right next to me under my carriage. There was nothing improper about that now, was there?"

"I guess not," replied John.

"Well then," she said. "Let's get inside and bed down for the night."

Susan climbed into the wagon, and John followed her. She spread out a blanket to lay on and then pulled out her grandmother's old quilt to cover them. They lay still in the dark of the night, talking to each other in low voices.

After much small talk, Susan finally asked, "John, do you like me?"

The question caught John off guard, but he answered, "Susan, I think it's more like I love you."

"Really?" she asked. "How do you know it's love?"

"Well," said John. "From the moment I saw you for the first time, I knew you were special. You're the most beautiful girl I've ever seen. I haven't thought of anything or anyone else since I met you."

Susan smiled in the darkness and asked, "John, would you like to marry me?"

John sat halfway up on one arm and looked at her silhouette as he said, "I would love to marry you. It would be a dream come true for me."

Susan said, "I think I'd like that. Let's get married then. I don't feel like I was married before. To Charles, I mean. I only felt violated. I don't think he loved me, and I know I didn't love him. I was just his prisoner. But, John, there's something you should know before we get married."

"What is it?"

"Well, I don't know for sure, but I might be with child. There's that chance anyway."

John said, "I don't care, Susan. There's nothing that you've done in the past or could do in the future that would stop me from loving you."

CHAPTER 7

Susan slowly began to wake when the morning sun rose over the eastern horizon. The rain had persisted throughout the night but was now gone. When Susan finally opened her eyes, she realized that John's arm was wrapped around her. He was still sleeping when she slowly and carefully tried to extricate herself without waking him. It was no use. As soon as she stirred, he awoke. John retracted his arm from the grip he had on Susan as she said, "Good morning."

John mumbled his own "Morning" as he stretched and yawned.

They both climbed down from the wagon and surveyed the amount of damage the storms had caused yesterday and last night. The ground was quite muddy in places where the grass no longer grew. They carefully walked down to the Beaver and found that its banks were overflowing. The Duck River, too, had expanded its banks. The water was deep and swift. It would be too dangerous for John to cross to go home until the water subsided.

Emily opened the cabin door and called them into breakfast. John took Susan's hand as they walked together toward the cabin. Emily noticed this gesture immediately. She smiled a very slight smile to herself as they approached. "Are you two hungry?"

John replied, "I sure am."

Emily said, "Well, you better get in here before Daniel eats it all."

Jake greeted them both as they walked into the cabin. Susan reached down and rubbed his head as she walked past him. She sat down at the table, and John sat next to her. Emily and Daniel swapped telling glances. Mostly, everyone sat silently as they dined on biscuits, fried eggs, fried apples, and bacon.

Susan helped Emily clear the table and clean up after breakfast, while Daniel and John made small talk.

John asked, "How long will it take for the creek to go down enough for me to cross it safely?"

Daniel replied, "I'd say it should be passable by nightfall. I'd count on spending the night again if I were you."

Then John asked, "Well, is there anything I can do to help out today?"

Daniel answered, "I don't think you're dressed for farm work today. I'd hate for you to mess up your nice clothes. Besides, you should just relax. Maybe Susan would like to show you around. It's been a while since you've been here."

Susan added, "I'd love to show you around."

John said, "Alright. That sounds good."

The two of them spent the rest of the morning and most of the after-noon walking through the valley, talking and getting to know each other more. Eventually, Susan and John reached the valley's far end, where the Beaver meets Leiper's Creek. They could go no farther, so they turned and headed back to Emily and Daniel's cabin.

John stopped suddenly and asked Susan, "Were you serious when you said you wanted to marry me?"

Susan replied, "Absolutely!"

"When do you want to get married?" he asked.

"As soon as we can find someone to marry us. Do you know of a preacher or a Justice of the Peace close by?"

John replied, "No. The nearest preacher is in Nashville, and the only Justice I know of is Colonel Crockett. Either way you go, it would be about a fifty-mile ride. Maybe I could send word to Mother somehow and let her know we're going to Nashville, and we'll be back in a couple of days."

Susan asked, "You mean, elope?"

"Sure!" said John. "Why not?"

Susan suggested, "Well, won't your mother be upset that she didn't get to see you get married?"

John answered, "She might. But she'll understand when I explain that we just didn't want to wait. Then, after that, she'll be okay."

Susan replied, "Alright! Let's do it. When can we leave?"

"Well, Daniel said the creek should be down enough for us to cross by nightfall. Can we leave in the morning?"

Susan said, "Yes. I can wait 'til then. The morning will be fine."

When they came within a hundred yards of the cabin, they saw riders approaching the south ridge into the valley. John counted six men on horseback. The riders moved to the front of the house and tied their horses to the hitching rail. John and Susan saw from a distance that one of the men walked up to the cabin door and knocked. When Emily answered the door, she saw the man and hugged him. John thought to himself, "*Well, at least they're friendly, whoever they are.*"

Daniel and Tommy walked in from the cornfield and joined the reunion. Each man shook hands with all the others in attendance. John began to think, as they got closer, that the leader seemed somewhat familiar.

Then John's face lit up when he realized who it was. "Davy!" he called out.

Colonel Crockett turned to see who was calling his name.

"John Gordon! What are you doing here?"

John reached out to shake Davy's hand and said, "I delivered some dry goods for Emily yesterday and got rained in. Had to spend the night."

Crockett asked, "How's the family?"

John replied, "Oh, they're all doing well. Oh Davy, do you know Miss Claiborne?"

Crockett replied, "Well, I certainly do. How are you, Miss Claiborne?"

"Fine, Colonel. It's nice to see you again."

Then Davy said, "I would have expected that you would be halfway back to Richmond by now."

"No, sir. I've decided to stay in this area. I'm not going back to Virginia."

One of the other militia walked over to Susan and said, "Miss Claiborne? Do you remember me?"

"Sergeant Clark! How could I ever forget one of the men who saved my life? It's so good to see you again!" she exclaimed.

Colonel Crockett announced, "We got trapped by the rain too trying to get back to Lawrenceburg. If y'all don't mind, we'll set up camp here. Young Sikes there shot a deer today, so why don't we get it to cookin' and have us a little party."

Emily said, "That sounds good. Tommy, why don't you go and get Amy?"

Tommy nodded in approval and trotted off to fetch his bride.

Susan then pulled John off to the side and asked, "Didn't you say that Colonel Crockett is a Justice of the Peace?"

John answered, "Yeah, why?"

"Well, ask him to marry us tonight. Then we won't have to drive all the way to Nashville", she suggested.

John's eyes widened with the realization of what she said. Then he smiled as he called out, "Davy? Can we have a moment with you, please?"

The three of them walked away from the crowd, and John began to speak, "Davy, do you still have the authority to marry folks?"

Crockett answered, "I do."

John continued, "Well, Susan and I were going to drive to Nashville tomorrow to find a preacher. But, you could save us the time and trouble if you would marry us tonight."

Davy smiled at the young couple and asked, "Really? Well, congratulations!"

He then turned to all the others and announced, "Folks! Looks like we got ourselves something to celebrate tonight. These two young people want to get married, so we're gonna have a wedding tonight!"

Everyone cheered with delight and then moved toward John and Susan to congratulate them.

When Amy and Tommy eventually returned and saw everyone celebrating, Amy asked, "What's going on? Why is everyone so happy?"

Emily walked over to her and said, "John and Susan are going to get married tonight."

Amy was delighted. She turned to Susan and hugged her and said, "Congratulations! I'm gonna have a new sister!"

Then she moved over to John and hugged him, "Johnny! I'm so happy for you. I just knew you two would hit it off."

Then Colonel Crockett announced, "Well, I'll get with the couple and fill out a marriage license, then when they're ready, we'll have the ceremony."

Susan excused herself from the men. Emily and Amy went with her to pick out a proper gown for the ceremony. They climbed into the wagon, and she pulled dress after dress from her trunk, looking for just the right garment for the occasion. Finally, she settled on a long light blue satin gown with white lace cuffs and white trim around the bodice.

The women gathered all she would need and retreated to the cabin for privacy. When Emily opened the door to the cabin, Jake tried to sneak in with the women. "Oh, no, you don't. Jake, you stay out here with the rest of the men."

The sun was beginning to sink below the horizon, so two of Crockett's men lit torches and placed them around the camp for more visibility. Sergeant Clark pulled out a fiddle from his pack and began to play to help pass the time as they waited for the ladies to rejoin the party.

When Susan and the other ladies came back outside to join the others, Colonel Crockett took her and John aside to fill out the marriage license. He had the Lanes sign as witnesses. Once the couple had exchanged their vows before the party gathered, everyone cheered, and the celebration began.

Marriage License

I, David Crockett, Justice of the Peace for the State of

Tennessee, do affirm and certify that on this date:

June 25, 1819 John Gordon Jr and Susan Elizabeth Claiborne have exchanged vows in the presence of witnesses to cling to each other in holy matrimony.

David CrockettJohn Gordon Jr

Justice of the PeaceGroom

Daniel LaneSusan Elizabeth Claiborne

WitnessBride

Emily C. Lane

Witness

Later in the evening, John and Susan retired to the wagon. They both disrobed and got ready for bed. As they lay next to each other on the floor of the wagon, Susan asked, "What now? Do we have a place to live? Or, will we just stay here in the wagon?"

John thought for a moment, then responded, "Well, I've been living in the back of the trading post. But it's pretty cramped in there. We could make do there for the time being if you're willing, then my brothers and I could build us a cabin suitable for raising a family. I mean, should the need arise. Did you have something else in mind?"

Susan thought before responding, "Well, that sounds good to me. I only wonder, will there be a place where I can raise horses?"

John said, "Sure, we've got about fifteen hundred acres. What kind of horses do you want to raise?"

"I have three Morgan horses that my father gave me when I left home. My stallion and two mares."

John asked, "What are Morgans? I've never heard of them."

Susan replied, "They are a fairly new breed developed by a man named Morgan. They can be used as saddle horses or for pulling a wagon. They have an unbelievably even trot. They have a beautiful gait."

John said, "They sound great. I can't wait to see them. Tomorrow."

He pulled Susan close to him and stroked her soft, smooth skin. He had never felt anything so smooth. His hands were rough from hard work. He kissed her mouth and held her even tighter. They made love to each other until they were exhausted and finally fell asleep in each other's arms.

The following day, they woke up still wrapped in each other's arms. They heard stirring outside, noting that Crockett's men were probably making breakfast and preparing to pack up to leave.

Susan and John washed and dressed before exiting the wagon to join the others for breakfast. The sky was clear. While the birds were singing, a slight breeze was whisking through the valley.

As the new couple approached the men, one of them handed John and Susan a plate of eggs, bacon, and biscuits.

"Mornin'," said Crockett.

Both of them replied a polite and quiet, "Mornin'."

Then Crockett remarked, "The creek is back down. Do you plan on returning home today, John?"

"Yessir. I speck Mother will be wonderin' bout me. We'll be leavin' as soon as we can get everything packed." Crockett said, "Well, tell Dolly I said, 'Hi!'"

"Sure will," replied John.

Jake hung around the breakfast area, sitting, waiting for someone to toss him a morsel. Emily held out half a biscuit to him, and he quickly accepted it. Jake held the half-eaten biscuit in his mouth and wandered from person to person within the camp, seeing who might try to take it from him. He always turned his head away whenever someone reached out to him to try to take his biscuit. Finally, after a while of playing this game, Jake turned and walked away to enjoy his biscuit in peace.

After breakfast, John and Daniel walked to the corral to retrieve Susan's Surrey and the five horses John and Susan would would take with them. Daniel hitched the Morgan stallion to the Surrey, then tied the two Morgan mares to the back, one behind the other. John saddled his horse and tied the packhorse behind the first horse. Daniel drove the Surrey up to the cabin while John brought his horses following behind.

When they arrived back at the cabin, John and Daniel lifted Susan's trunk with all of her belongings from the back of the wagon and placed it into the back of the Surrey. John tied his horses behind Susan's mares so he could ride in the Surrey with Susan.

Susan walked over to Emily and hugged her, and then said, "I don't know what I would have done without your help. You've been a good friend to me."

Emily replied, "Don't be a stranger. Come back and see us when you can."

Then Susan moved over to Daniel and hugged him as well.

"I owe you my life. I can't thank you enough for what you have done for me."

Daniel replied, "I'm just glad you're safe and can now start a new life with a new husband. Let me know should you need anything else."

John and Susan climbed into the Surrey and waved to everyone as they drove away. They crossed the Beaver Branch and followed the trail to take them to the Gordon encampment. They rode along at a leisurely pace. Neither was in much of a hurry to get anywhere. Instead, they enjoyed just riding side by side in the Surrey, talking to each other, making plans for their future together.

Six hours later, they arrived home. John drove the Surrey up to the brick house where his mother and sister lived. Lucy bounded out of the house first and raced toward them with excitement. Dolly followed behind at a much slower pace while Lucy ran toward the wagon and cried out, "John! We thought you were dead! Where have you been?"

John replied to Lucy and his mother, "The rain flooded the creeks and rivers, so I couldn't get out of the Water Valley until today. Lucy, when did you get back?"

Lucy replied, "I arrived two days ago, a few hours after you left."

It suddenly occurred to both women that John wasn't alone.

"Hello, Susan." said Dolly. "I didn't expect to see you again so soon."

John helped Susan down from the Surrey to stand in front of his mother and sister as they broke the news to them.

"Mother, Lucy, I'd like you to meet my wife, Susan Gordon."

They both stood and looked at John and Susan, dumbfounded. They stumbled over their words but were clearly excited to hear John had married.

Susan was nervous as to how Dolly would react to the news. She had been afraid Dolly would think it too soon for such a union to occur. Finally, Susan asked, "You're not angry, are you?"

Dolly chuckled as she replied, "Wuh, angry? No. I'm not angry. I'm shocked, but I think it's wonderful news. I was afraid my boys would never find brides living out here in the wilderness like we do. I couldn't be happier for you two. When did this happen?"

Susan replied, "Colonel Crockett was at the Lane's last night. He and his men rode in because they, too, had been flooded in. We asked him to marry us."

Dolly instructed, "Well, John, grab her things, and we'll get you two set up in one of the upstairs rooms."

"Mother, that won't be necessary. Susan and I will just sleep in the back room of the store like I've been doing."

"Nonsense!" said Dolly. "There's barely room in there for one of you. You can move your things back down here."

John replied, "Well, okay. Thanks! But, it will only be temporary. I promised Susan we would build a cabin somewhere close by that would be suitable for raising a family."

Dolly grabbed Susan by the arm and said, "Come along, dear. Let's get you settled in."

CHAPTER 8

After John and Susan left the valley, Crockett and his men packed up their gear and prepared to go as well. Daniel asked Davy, "Are you headed to Lawrenceburg?"

Davy replied, "Yeah, we're going toward Columbia first, then turn south for Lawrenceburg." He paused and asked, "Did you ever talk to David Colbert about Ittola Chuka?"

Daniel answered, "No, not yet."

Crockett said, "You might not want to wait too long. I hear there's talk about a big pow-wow or celebration coming in the fall at one of those locations. It might be something that could be of help to you."

"Thanks!" said Daniel. "I've got a lot to do around here right now, but maybe I can get away before all that happens so I can ask about it. Thanks for the tip!"

"Anytime!" said Crockett as he mounted his horse. He tipped his hat to Emily and rode out of the valley to the eastern ridge.

Emily commented, "Every time I see that man, I think of Grandpa Bill."

"Really?" asked Daniel. "Wild Bill?"

"Yeah, I guess it's because Grandpa was always talking about us being descendants of the great Davy Crockett. I never believed him, though. At least not until you went missing."

Daniel asked, "You miss him a lot, don't you?"

Emily replied, "Yes, I do. Especially on his birthday."

"Would you like to go back and see him again?" asked Daniel.

Emily answered, "I would be too scared to travel through that time warp again. Especially after what Gus discovered."

Daniel said, "Yeah, that is disconcerting. I was so careful about us keeping the timeline in order. I wish we could do something to correct it. I hate to think that because we traveled through the Shimmering, we caused slavery to continue for centuries after it was supposed to end. I hate that it existed at all."

Emily replied, "Well, there's nothing we can do about it."

Daniel said, "I'm not so sure."

Emily looked at him sternly and said, "You are not going back through that thing. You saw what happened to Gus. I didn't travel back in time to see you run off into another time zone and get yourself killed."

Daniel put his hands up as if to stave off an attack from Emily. "Hold on there, Missy. I'm not going to run off and do something stupid. I promise. I just want to talk to David about it."

Emily asked, "Why? What does David Colbert have to do with this?"

"Crockett once told me that David knows the locations of other Ittola Chukas. They might have different times that they would travel to. But, I promise, I will never go through another time warp without discussing it with you first."

Emily asked, "So, when are you planning on talking to David?"

Daniel replied, "Not until after the crops have been harvested."

Over the next few weeks, Tommy and Daniel worked tirelessly on improvements to their homestead. They built a new corn crib large enough to hold the seventy-five acres of corn that grew in the valley. They also cut and stored hay for the winter.

By late August, they began to harvest the corn that had dried in the field. Emily drove the mules, Rusty and Pepper, while hitched to the wagon

Daniel and Tommy had converted. Daniel and Tommy raised the sides on the back of the wagon to hold more corn. The men broke away the ears of corn from their stalks and threw them into the back of the wagon while Emily slowly moved it forward, keeping pace with the men. Amy tried to help the men but found she could not do much. She was weak from not being able to keep her meals down. Tommy was worried about her and expressed his concerns to Emily occasionally.

On the second day of harvest, Emily decided to examine Amy to see if anything could be done. So, while the men began hitching up the mules to the wagon, Emily took Amy inside the cabin.

Tommy tried not to show his worry, but Daniel could tell Tommy was worried for his bride. Tommy knew Emily was an excellent doctor, but he also knew that resources were limited in the early 1800s.

After a while, Emily and Amy came to meet the men out in the field. To Tommy and Daniel's surprise, both women were smiling.

Tommy asked Amy, "Are you alright?"

Amy replied, "Couldn't be better."

"So, you're not sick?" Tommy asked.

Amy said, "Oh, I feel like vomiting all the time. But at least now I know why."

"Huh?" questioned Tommy.

Amy couldn't hold her delight in any longer. "You're going to be a papa."

"A what?"

"A papa," said Amy. "We're going to have a baby."

Tommy, stunned, replied, "Well, I be! When will it be born?"

Amy replied, "Emily says probably sometime in March."

Daniel shook Tommy's hand and said, "Congratulations!"

The couples took a moment to enjoy the news that two babies would soon arrive at their homestead, and then they returned to harvesting the corn and putting it into the crib. Picking seventy-five acres of corn by hand was hard work and time-consuming, but they managed to finish the job within the week.

Two days after the harvest was completed, Daniel and Tommy began constructing a new barn and stables for the horses. They intended to store hay in the barn's loft instead of leaving it exposed to the elements of the winter weather as they had done in the past.

As they were marking a spot to build the barn, a rider came from the south, over the ridge, and into the valley. Daniel could tell the rider was Indian even from a distance. As the rider entered the valley and rode toward Daniel and Tommy, Daniel realized the familiar figure.

Daniel raised his hand in a greeting and said, "Hallito, Mahli chukwa ilap immi ee-pahn-she," which translates to *"Hello, Wind-in-His-Hair!"*

Wind-in-His-Hair greeted Daniel likewise, "Hallito, Daniel!"

Daniel asked in the Chickasaw language, "What brings you to our valley?"

Wind-in-His-Hair replied, "David Colbert has asked that I come to you. He needs to speak with you about important things. He has asked that you come right away."

Daniel turned to Tommy and translated what he had said, then looked back at Wind-in-His-Hair and said, "Come, I will prepare to ride with you. But, I must first speak to Shobohli Eho."

Wind-in-His-Hair slid down from his pony and walked Daniel and Tommy back to the cabin. Jake ran ahead of the men and greeted Emily as she walked out of the cabin.

Emily wasn't expecting company as she exited the cabin but recognized the brave as soon as she had seen him. Wind-in-His-Hair was the friend that David Colbert had sent to retrieve Emily when his wife Sarah was in labor. He had escorted the Lanes from their valley to Sheboss Place eleven months ago. He was a quiet man who had little to say. His long black hair was shiny, and the slightest breeze caused it to wave above his shoulders.

Emily looked at Daniel and asked, "What's going on?"

Daniel replied, "I don't know exactly. He says David needs me to come."

Emily asked, "Did he need me as well?"

"He didn't mention you. But, if you'd like to come along, I'm sure that would be fine. You can check in on Sarah and little Danny."

Emily asked, "When do we leave?"

"Right now!"

Daniel looked at Tommy and asked, "Would you mind saddling our horses? I hate to leave you with so much still to do, but it sounds urgent."

Tommy replied, "Naw, I don't mind none. We'll be jest fine. I'll let Amy know where y'all are."

Emily said, "Thanks, Tommy! Hopefully, we won't be more than a couple of days."

Emily turned and went back into the cabin, where she began packing. First, she gathered medical supplies and placed them into one of her saddlebags in case she needed them. Next, Emily packed an extra set of clothing and food for the trip. Finally, she changed into something more suitable for riding, then grabbed her pistol and brace as she exited the cabin.

Daniel, too, had packed his saddlebags with food, extra powder, and ammunition. He grabbed another brace and pistol as well as a tomahawk and two rifles as he met Emily outside.

Tommy came back from the corral leading the two bays, Emily's mare and Daniel's big stallion, Hoss. When Hoss saw the Indian pony at the front of the cabin, he reared up on his hind legs and whinnied. Tommy nearly lost his grip on the reins but recovered before the horse got away. Daniel walked over to Hoss and quietly spoke to him, trying to settle him down.

"Easy, boy. Easy."

Daniel and Emily loaded their horses, then mounted them and followed Wind-in-His-Hair to the south side of the valley with Jake following behind. They climbed their horses up to the valley's ridge and disappeared from Tommy's view.

The trail they traveled down was less known than the one they typically traveled that led to the Gordon Plantation. It was narrower, less traveled, and unknown except by the Chickasaw. Wind-in-His-Hair led the caravan through a winding trail that weaved through limestone outcroppings. Cedars protruding from cracks in the earth's large flat rocks seemed as if they were being expelled from its bowels. Once in a while, prickly pears could be seen growing from the rocks as well. Daniel noticed as they rode that Wind-in-His-Hair led them away from the large flat stones. They rode their horses through areas of soft green moss as much as possible to hide their tracks and to muffle the sound of their horses' hooves. They rode their mounts in silence, never speaking to Wind-in-His-Hair nor each other. Even Jake seemed to recognize the need for silence on the trail. Occasionally he would lift his head to the wind and sniff the air, but he never barked, he never growled, and he never whimpered.

Eventually, they reached a spot at the Duck River where the banks narrowed, and the water was shallow. Wind-in-His-Hair paused at the bank, allowing his horse to drink. Daniel and Emily followed suit. Wind-in-His-Hair remained quiet, listening for other riders' sounds or any other danger that might be lurking nearby.

Jake lapped water from the bank's edge, and the horses sipped. Suddenly, Jake froze. He looked upriver and let out a muffled *"woof!"* Wind-in-His-Hair looked upriver and listened. He slid off of his pony on the left side. He looked at Daniel as if telepathically telling him to do the same. Daniel and Emily dismounted and followed the brave as he led his pony back into the cover of the forest. Daniel looked back and noticed that Jake was not following. "Jake!" he whispered a call. Jake looked toward Daniel and followed his master out of sight from whoever might come their way.

They waited in silence for those who were coming down the river. Minutes later, six dugout canoes floated past them on the shallow waters of the Duck. Daniel peeked out of his hiding place to see who they were evading. Twelve braves with faces painted bright red, and their arms and hands painted black up to their elbows floated their canoes downriver. Daniel turned to Emily and whispered, "Ilbuk Losa."

Emily recognized the name right away and shivered with fear. Ilbuk Losa was a band of unfriendly Chickasaw men known as the Black Hand. They were keepers of the sacred lands or burial grounds of the Chickasaw Nation. They would kill anyone who trespassed upon their lands. They were the ones who killed Daniel's best friend, Jimbo, when Jimbo and Daniel came through the Shimmering. They also killed Henry Slater, who had followed Emily and Tommy through the Shimmering six months later.

Jake gave a quiet whimper. Daniel cupped his hand around Jake's muzzle to keep him quiet. One of the braves raised his hand as a signal to the others. They all stopped paddling momentarily. They listened and looked toward the banks. First to their left, then to their right. Daniel and his fellow travelers remained still. Even Jake must have realized he needed to stay still and not make a sound. He sat as still and quiet as a statue. Emily suddenly realized she was holding her breath.

The leader of Ilbuk Losa decided it was safe to continue down the river. So they all dipped their paddles back into the water and drew the water toward them to propel themselves forward.

Emily finally let out her breath. "Are they looking for us?"

Wind-in-His-Hair shook his head, "They go to prepare for Hush-to-lah um-mol nah."

Emily looked at Daniel for translation.

"Autumn."

Then Daniel asked as he looked to Wind-in-His-Hair, "Does something special happen on the day on which the day and the night are equal?"

Wind-in-His-Hair nodded, "This is the time of choosing."

Daniel asked, "Choosing what?"

The brave answered, "Nuk-neh nohn-wah hush-ekun-ut-le ulh-pe-sah."

Daniel thought for a moment as he translated the words in his mind.

Emily asked, "What did he say?"

With a look of realization on his face, Daniel answered, "I think he said they will be choosing someone who travels through time."

Chapter 9

Sometime in the mid-afternoon, Wind-in-His-Hair led Daniel, Emily, and Jake into the clearing where Sheboss lay. Sheboss was a stand along the Natchez Trail owned and operated by a Chickasaw man, David Colbert, his white wife, Sarah, and their newborn son, Danny.

David was at the corral as the riders came in. When Sarah heard horses riding into the stand, she came out of the cabin to greet whomever it might be. Her face lit up with delight when she realized it was Daniel and Emily.

The riders rode up to the corral to drop off their mounts and saw David exiting a pen where six other horses were corralled.

"Hallito, Nafkl!" David said as he approached Daniel.

Daniel and David approached one another and embraced. David looked up to Wind-in-His-Hair, still mounted, and nodded to him. The two seemed to be able to communicate without words. Wind-in-His-Hair understood David's nod of thanks as he turned his horse back into the forest and rode away.

Daniel and David unsaddled the horses and penned them with the others while Emily waited in silence. Then, finally, she looked to her left and saw Sarah walking quickly to join them all at the corral.

"Emily?"

Emily turned and saw Sarah. "Sarah! It's so good to see you again. How is the baby?"

Sarah turned slightly to show Emily the young boy strapped to her back. "He's not much of a baby anymore. He weighs a ton."

Emily reached up to hold the toddler's hand in greeting, "Hello, Danny! How are you?"

Danny smiled and giggled at Emily's question.

Emily asked, "Is he walking yet?"

"No, but he is pulling up and standing. It won't be long, now."

Daniel walked over to greet Sarah and hugged her. "Hello, Sarah."

"Daniel, it is so good to see you and Emily again. Y'all come on into the cabin and get settled."

After Daniel and Emily had placed their saddlebags in their room, they joined David and Sarah in the dogtrot for coffee. As they sat around the table and caught up on the news, Daniel finally asked, "Well, David. Wind-in-His-Hair said something was very important. What is it?"

David glanced at Sarah, then began, "Chief William has asked me to find you and ask you a very important thing. He knows that you and Emily are very strong with medicine."

Daniel interrupted and said, "Well, Emily is the one with medicine skills. I just . . ."

David held his hand up to quiet Daniel. "Not that kind of medicine, Nafkl. You are friendly to our ways. You have learned the ways of my people and have helped us. Chief William says the Spirits of our people walk with you and Emily. The one true creator protects you and leads you."

Daniel and Emily were both honored by these words and a little embarrassed by the praise they were being given.

David continued, "Hush tola ummona is soon approaching."

Daniel interrupted again, "Yeah, we saw Ilbuk Losa traveling down the river on our way here. Wind-in-His-Hair said something about Hush tola ummona. What is it?"

David replied, "This is a special season. You call it autumn. It is a time of choosing."

Daniel asked, "A time for choosing what?"

Solemnly, David said, "A time of choosing Hoh-pah-e. Then David closed his eyes as if he had spoken something most reverent.

This time, Daniel didn't interrupt. He waited.

Finally, David spoke again. "Hoh-pah-e is very special to our people. We have been without Hoh-pah-e for a long time. Every year my people meet at Tobi Okla for the choosing of Hoh-pah-e. Three men will be brought before the one true creator. Only he will choose who will be Hoh-pah-e for the people. These three men represent the three clans of our people. Chief Levi, Chief George, and Chief William make the selections from their clans. But, they cannot choose who will be Hoh-pah-e. Only the one true creator can choose. Hoh-pah-e."

Daniel translated, "Prophet. I've never heard of this before. Who is Hoh-pah-e now?"

David replied, "Hoh-pah-e has not existed for many years. Not since I was very young. Every year three men are presented, but none have been found worthy by the one true creator."

Daniel asked, What happens to the men who are presented but not chosen?"

David answered, "It is a very difficult thing to be presented. Some are not strong enough to withstand the ceremony of the choosing. Some die, some go out of their head. No one knows where any of the presented are now. They are no more."

The women sat in silence as their men spoke to one another. Emily felt sick in the pit of her stomach. She knew where this conversation was leading.

Daniel asked, "David, why have you asked us to come? What does this have to do with us?"

David replied, "My uncle, Chief William, has chosen you to represent his clan. He believes that the Spirit is strong with you. He believes that you will be the next Hoh-pah-e."

Both women gasped at the news. Daniel sat at the table stunned, unable to move or speak. Questions tumbled around his head so quickly he couldn't express them verbally. Finally, after several minutes of silence, Daniel was able to speak. "What exactly does Hoh-pah-e do?"

"Hoh-pah-e judges the people. If you are chosen, you will travel between the clans. You will lead the council of leaders. People will listen to you and hear you. Even the chiefs of our clans will listen to and abide by your words because you are the chosen of the one true creator. And you will be the keeper of Ittola Chuka."

Daniel was stunned again. "What does that mean?"

"You will control Ittola Chuka. You will be Nohn-wah Hush-ekun-ut-le ugh-pe-sah."

Daniel looked at Emily and translated, "Time Traveler?"

Chapter 10

Emily and Daniel stared at each other with their mouths agape. Neither knew what to say or ask next. Finally, Sarah, seeing the two dumbfounded, asked David what was an obvious question to her.

"David, what happens during the time of choosing?"

David looked at his wife, then at Emily and Daniel.

"I do not know what happens during the ceremony of choosing. Only the chiefs of our people and the medicine men of the tribes know what happens. It is secret. It is an act of faith when a man submits to the choosing."

Thoughts and questions tumbled inside Daniel's brain like sneakers in a tumble dryer. Time travel appealed to him, but he knew it could be dangerous, too. Not just to himself. He had already heard through Gus's experience how time travel could alter the course of history. He wasn't sure he wanted to be responsible for disrupting the narrative again. However, he also saw it as an opportunity to right the wrong they had already caused. Convincing Emily to go along with it was not going to be easy. He had already promised her he wouldn't go near the Shimmering again without consulting her first.

Finally, Daniel spoke. "I think Emily and I should take a walk together and discuss this."

As the couple walked together in the meadow, they both hesitated to begin the conversation. Finally, Emily began. "What do you know about these types of Native American rituals?"

Daniel answered, "Nothing! At least not as far as this ritual is concerned. The Chickasaw have kept this one secret for hundreds of years. I mean, we never even heard of Ittola Chuka until I stumbled upon it by accident."

Emily asked, "Well, how about other rituals or ceremonies?"

Daniel replied, "I've read about many of them. Most of them incur some form of hallucinogen. The Western tribes typically used peyote. But as far as I know, peyote doesn't grow this far east. The ceremonies sometimes include a certain amount of pain as well. I just don't know what to expect."

Emily added, "Therein lies the problem. If we knew what to expect, I could at least prepare some combatant to ensure you wouldn't go crazy or even die."

After a moment of silence, Daniel looked into Emily's eyes and stated, "I feel responsible for what has happened to the timeline. However, if this will allow me in some way to correct the problem, I think I should take the risk."

Emily closed her eyes as she turned away from Daniel. She folded her arms in front of her as a gesture of trying to protect herself. "Alright," she said. "I'll try to come up with some way to alleviate the pain at least that you could potentially endure."

Daniel reached out and pulled Emily to him, hugged her, and then kissed her. "We can do this," he said. "We'll find a way to fix it."

They walked back to the cabin where David and Sarah were waiting. Daniel stood before David and asked, "When do we leave?"

David responded, "Soon. We must wait for Chief William. He comes soon. You will travel with him."

For the rest of the day, the two couples tried to busy themselves around the stand, trying not to think about the events that would soon come. Sarah and Emily started preparing the evening meal while Daniel helped David down at the corral, caring for the stock.

Sheboss stand was a quiet little place nestled at the edge of the Natchez Trail. Travelers on the trail stopped quite often here for shelter. It was about a half-day ride from the Gordon ferry that crossed the Duck River. A dogtrot joined together two small cabins. One of the cabins was the living quarters for David and Sarah. The other served as an inn for travelers who sought shelter during their journey along the trail. Many who journeyed along the route preferred to camp outdoors. But occasionally, people would stay at the stand to escape rain, snow, or frigid temperatures.

Daniel and Emily always opted to stay in the extra cabin whenever they visited. Sarah never charged them, however. They were like family to David and Sarah. Sarah and Daniel discovered they might be relatives by marriage.

When Daniel and Sarah first met, she told him she had been married to a Lane, who was killed by Indians while crossing through into Tennessee from North Carolina. David was riding with a band of braves led by Chief William, who came to her rescue during the deadly encounter.

Chief William offered Sarah the sanctuary of living and operating a stand if she would marry one of his braves. That brave was now her husband, David.

⸻◈⸻

The following day brought a misty rain into the meadow of Sheboss. The rain made the air chillier than the actual temperature. Nevertheless, autumn was crawling into sight. Trees that outlined the field were slowly transforming their green hues, opting for reds, oranges, or golden yellows.

Emily helped Sarah prepare breakfast inside the tiny cabin. Baby Danny crawled along the plank floor of the cabin, babbling to himself as he did. Danny was nearing nine months of age. He was not yet walking, but he got around wherever he wanted just the same.

With Jake in tow, Daniel met David at the corral to feed the horses. They reminisced about their first days together and how David had taught Daniel how to survive on the frontier. He taught him to hunt, trap, and track. They talked about their first turkey hunt together and how David had not wanted Jake to tag along for fear he would scare away their prey.

Once satisfied that the horses were well-fed and in good health, the men walked back to the cabin to join the ladies for breakfast. The women had prepared a feast of biscuits, bacon, fried apples, and scrambled eggs. As they all sat at the table eating and talking together, Sarah spoon-fed corn mush to baby Danny, who seemed more interested in the yellow dog who sat beneath him on the floor.

No sooner had they all finished breakfast and the ladies had cleared the table than the horses at the corral erupted in nays and grunts, signaling that riders were approaching. Jake, too, heard the riders and let out a short "*woof*," then began to bark loudly and furiously.

Twenty riders appeared from the forest, riding into the meadow at a canter. Daniel recognized two of them immediately. Chief William led the parade of braves that rode astride various colors of horses. Just behind the Chief and to his right was Wind-in-His-Hair.

They pulled their horses up about 20 feet from the cabin, and the Chief saluted his nephew, saying, "Hallito!"

David approached his uncle and clasped his hand, bowing his head in reverence. He then looked to Wind-in-His-Hair and nodded to him.

David looked back to his uncle as Chief William asked in his native language, "Has he agreed?"

David replied, "Yes, uncle. He will travel with you and accept the honor you place upon him."

Chief William looked at Daniel and said in English, "It is good you have accepted my invitation. We must leave now."

Then he looked at Emily and asked, "Will Shobahli Eho go too?"

Emily answered, "Yes, I would like to if it is permitted."

Chief William nodded and said, "You may ride with us, but you cannot enter Tobi Okla. You may camp nearby."

Emily replied, "I understand. And, thank you."

Daniel and David trotted off to the corral to saddle the horses while Emily went into the cabin to pack their things. They all joined back up with the caravan five minutes later, ready to ride with them. Daniel and Emily said their goodbyes, and Emily kissed baby Danny on the top of his head. Then, they mounted their horses and rode alongside Chief William and Wind-in-His-Hair, heading east.

Mostly, they cantered their horses, making good time down the trail. Daniel figured they must be trying to make it to Tobi Okla before sundown. Daniel was taken aback a little when they arrived at the Gordon ferry. The Chief led the band across the river on horseback rather than waiting for the ferry to come. At first, Daniel thought it odd. He knew it wasn't a matter of paying the fee to cross. There wouldn't be a fee for the Chief because he had allowed the Gordons to set up the ferry here. In reality, he was part-owner of the ferry. It must have been a decision based on time.

Emily and Daniel followed suit, moving their horses into the muddy Duck with the other riders. The water wasn't that deep—only about three and a half feet at its deepest point. But the water was cold. Icy cold. Emily lifted her feet from her stirrups above her saddle, trying to avoid the cold water as she rode through. Then, after forging the waters, they steered their horses up the bank of the river and continued for another mile toward the Gordon farm.

Dolly wasn't surprised to see the Chief and his braves ride onto her farm. They did it every year at this time of year. She was, however, surprised to see Daniel and Emily Lane riding along with the clan of Chickasaw.

Dolly greeted them as they rode up and said, "Hello, William! Daniel, Emily! Won't you all get down and rest a while?"

Chief William raised his hand and said, "No time. We must go."

The Chief kicked his horse forward away from Dolly, and the others followed. As they rode away, Emily called out to Dolly, "Sorry, Dolly! We'll catch you next time!"

Dolly Gordon looked puzzled and concerned as the band of riders quickly rode away. She knew something was amiss. It wasn't so much that Chief William and his braves rode through without stopping. They did this every year. She knew it had something to do with one of their customs but didn't know more than that. What puzzled her was Daniel and Emily riding with the Chickasaw band.

The caravan turned slightly north into a wooded area about an hour down the trail. Then slowed down, dodging trees and outcroppings of limestone. William led them down an almost invisible path. He seemed to know exactly which way to go, but there didn't seem to be any method of their travel to Daniel. Instead, they now traveled in a single-file formation because the trail was extremely narrow.

Thirty minutes later, the Chief pulled up his mount and raised his arm to signal everyone else to stop. Daniel looked over the Chief's shoulder and saw a familiar site. An open meadow spread out in front of them. Off in the distance, about fifty yards out, Daniel could see a grassy knoll. But it wasn't a knoll. It was a mound. A burial mound. Daniel had been here before but had not noticed the mound. He had been too afraid for his life. It was here that his lifelong friend, Jimbo, was killed. Daniel's stomach churned as he realized he was resting at the edge of Tobi Okla.

Chief William looked back at Emily and said, "Shobohli Eho must go no more."

Daniel looked back at Emily and asked, "Why don't you go on back home? I'll be fine."

Emily replied, "I'm going to stay here for now. I'll rest here and wait for you."

Daniel said, "We don't know how long I might be. I think it best if you go on home."

Emily said, "I think I'll stay here for a while. This baby has been jostled around inside me enough. We both need to rest. If I'm not here when you get back, look for me at home."

Daniel pulled back on his reins to encourage Hoss to back up next to Emily. Then, Daniel leaned over to Emily, kissed her, and said, "Take care of yourself."

"You, too!"

Daniel looked down at the yellow dog standing next to him and said, "Jake! Stay!"

Jake whimpered but obeyed his master.

Chief William turned back toward the meadow and led his band of braves into the clearing known as Tobi Okla.

CHAPTER II

The caravan moved slowly into the meadow of Tobi Okla. At first, no one seemed to notice them as they approached the camps of the other two tribes. Then, as they neared the camps, someone called out to everyone else, "Keyu! Keyu!" meaning "Forbidden."

Everyone turned to look when William and his band approached. When they saw Daniel riding alongside Chief William and his braves, they all began to chant, "Keyu, Keyu!".

From the crowd, two older men approached the chief. One of them looked especially angry. Daniel didn't recognize the man, but he did identify the markings on his hands. They were painted black. There was hate in his eyes and anger in his voice as he turned to William and said, "Why do you mock Hoh-pah-e?"

The man who spoke was George Colbert, William's younger brother. He was chief of the Chickasaw tribe, which protected the sacred grounds called Tobi Okla. The warriors who protected the lands and traditions of the Chickasaw were known as Ilbuk Losa or Black Hand.

George lived along the banks of the Tennessee River in Alabama. He ran a stand and a ferry from his home while farming thousands of acres with the more than fifteen hundred enslaved people he owned. Some of the slaves were white, some were Native Americans from other tribes like the Creek or Choctaw, but most were black.

William responded, "I do not mock Hoh-pah-e."

"Then why do you bring this white man into Tobi Okla?" questioned George.

Chief William replied, "Daniel Lane is brother to the Chickasaw. He is brother to your son, David. He has been taught our ways, and he respects them. But, most of all, he is the only man among us who has traveled Ittola Chuka."

The crowd of braves heard this and erupted in angry cries and jeers. "We must kill this man!" many of them shouted. "He does not belong here!"

Finally, a third man raised his hand to silence the crowd. Levi Colbert was the younger brother to William and George. He, too, lived in Alabama, where he ran a stand and a farm but was less successful than his older brother George. Levi wasn't interested in commerce as he lived a quiet life away from wars and tribal disputes.

As the crowd quieted, Levi began to speak. "For many years, our people have gathered here at Tobi Okla to select the next Hoh-pah-e. Even before I was born, the people of our mothers would gather here for this purpose. Yet, no one has been found worthy of being called Hoh-pah-e. It is not up to us to say who the one true creator will choose for this honor. If this white man is found worthy, he will survive the test and become Hoh-pah-e. If the one true creator says he is not worthy, then he like so many before him will die."

Daniel thought about the words that Levi had just spoken. He didn't say "might die." Instead, he said, "will die." What is it about this ceremony that causes death? What could he do to ensure his safety?

Preparations had been made for the ceremony, and a temporary lodge had been constructed to hold it. A large fire was lit at the center of the encampment. Darkness approached quickly. Everyone gathered around the fire and sat down as the three candidates were presented.

Chief George presented his candidate first. His name was Hatuk app ala which translated washing bear or raccoon. Daniel understood this man's name because of how he chose to paint his face. A band of black paint covered his eyes from the right side of his head to the left. Daniel wasn't sure whether this was to cover a deformity or scar on his face; he could not tell.

Hatuk app ala was not a large man. He only stood about five foot nine inches, by Daniel's estimation. His build was slight, and he walked with a limp. His hands were painted black as well, but not like the brothers of his tribe. His were black only up to his wrists. The warriors of Ilbuk Losa wore their paint up to their elbows. Daniel guessed that Hatuk app ala had not yet reached the other braves' status.

Next was Chief Levi's candidate. His name was Iss-kun-oh-se soh bah or Little Horse. This young man was slightly taller than the first man. However, he was quite chubby, especially around the middle. Daniel was beginning to see that these men were presented not because they were great warriors of their respective tribes but because they were considered cast-offs.

When Chief William presented Daniel to the people, Daniel walked over and stood next to the other two men. Daniel's six-foot frame towered over the other men. He was a prime specimen of a man.

The candidates were told to have a seat around the fire. They were evenly spaced from each other, with the different tribes sitting behind their prospective candidate. Daniel sat cross-legged on the ground about ten feet away from the fire. An older man came to each of the presented ones and handed them a pipe to smoke. Daniel was glad to see that each man took his turn in the order they were presented because it allowed him to see what the others were doing so he could follow suit without looking like a fool.

Daniel took two puffs and then a long draw of smoke and held it in his mouth. He finally let it out without inhaling the smoke, then swiped his hands through the air, gathering the smoke back to him. Daniel had never been a smoker, so he knew that he would most likely go into a choking fit if he inhaled the smoke.

Next, a gourd of liquid was given to the men to drink. Daniel was a little nervous to drink whatever he would have to drink. For all he knew, he'd be drinking fermented yak urine. That's what it smelled like, anyway. But he had seen each of the others take a big swig of the drink, so he did as well. He managed to hold the liquid down with great difficulty even though his stomach had other ideas about it.

They continued to sit around the fire as elders from each tribe droned on about what a great honor it was for each man to enter into this ceremony. Daniel thought it felt a little like being back home as a kid with his mom and dad in church. Listening to a long-winded preacher go on and on about how sinful they all were.

Daniel's eyelids began to droop. He fought the urge to lie down and take a nap. Instead, he looked at his counterparts and saw they, too, were struggling. He rubbed his eyes with the back of his hands, trying to stay awake.

Finally, the last elder had finished his speech. Two men took Daniel by the arms and lifted him to a standing position. Daniel was grateful for the assistance. He knew he wouldn't be able to walk on his own.

He and the other two men were escorted into the lodge for the next part of the initiation. Daniel was stripped of his shirt and instructed to lie on his back on a mat. The other two were already bare-chested, so they were placed on mats inside the lodge. Each man lay on his back and waited for what was next.

Lying down made it even more difficult for Daniel to stay awake. Finally, someone grabbed each of Daniel's hands and his feet and began tethering him to the ground so he couldn't move. Daniel struggled to keep his eyes open, but what he saw next awakened him. A man came to him holding what looked like a chicken foot. But, no, it was too large to be a chicken. An eagle talon?

The man took the talon and pierced Daniel's pectoral muscle on his right side. The talon passed through the skin and then muscle until it looped through and came out of his skin again. Daniel's whole body tensed in pain, but he tried with all of his might not to cry out. Instead, he gritted his teeth as the man pulled out the talon and replaced it with a six-inch length of bone that was pointed on both ends.

Daniel felt somewhat relieved when the man had finished until the man began doing the same thing on his left pectoral. Then, the pain started all over again. Daniel couldn't believe what was happening to him. He heard Washing Bear cry out in pain. Daniel wanted to do the same but was determined to make as little sound as possible.

Something told Daniel that this was just the beginning of his pain and struggle. He was right. Two men lifted him to his feet once again and held him there. Then, another man reached up and grabbed two leather ropes hanging from the lodge ceiling. Daniel saw that each of the ropes had a loop on one end. "Oh, this can't be good," he thought. The bone pins implanted into Daniel's chest were threaded through the loops. Then, two men began to lift Daniel toward the lodge ceiling by pulling on the leather ropes. Daniel agonized as he was raised. Still, he wouldn't allow himself to cry out. Finally, the ropes were tied off, and Daniel and the others were left hanging as everyone exited the lodge. They were to be left there overnight.

Daniel awoke. He was no longer in the lodge. Instead, he was high atop a mountain. How had he gotten here? He looked around and felt he could see the whole world from here. He stood upon a bluff that reached miles above a river. He could see a herd of buffalo grazing near the river. An eagle floated among the treetops that stood below Daniel. Had he died? Was he in heaven?

Suddenly, he heard a low rumble behind him. He slowly turned and saw a large black bear moving toward him. This bear was much larger than the one that had attacked him last year—as large as a grizzly. When the bear stood on its hind legs, it was at least a foot taller than Daniel. The bear snarled as it moved closer to Daniel.

Daniel looked around for anything he could use as a weapon. There was nothing there. He slowly backed away until he found himself at the edge of his mountain bluff. Daniel saw no way out. It was mauled and chewed up by this monstrous animal or fell to its death from a height he couldn't even fathom.

All at once, he slipped. His feet had failed him. His eyes widened in terror of his impending doom. Then, he realized that gravity was not his enemy. He was moving through the air but not falling. He was flying. He felt a wave of satisfaction as he swooped above the trees. He saw the eagle just below him and decided to move closer to get a better look.

Daniel and the eagle flew circles around each other. They moved through the treetops like brothers. Daniel moved closer to the ground to look at the buffalo munching on the grassy meadow below. He thought maybe they would run away at the sight of him swooping down upon them. But, instead, they seemed to be oblivious to his movement.

It was the most exhilarating feeling he had experienced in his life. He saw the eagle dive toward the river and capture a trout with its talons. Daniel thought he might like to try that, so he began to move closer to the river. Suddenly, he fell with a thud to the ground.

Chapter 12

The sun had not yet reached the treetops as Daniel and Washing Bear were escorted from the lodge. Streaks of orange, yellow, and red mixed with azure lined the morning sky. The two candidates were taken to a familiar place at the northwest corner of the meadow. Daniel wasn't sure what to expect next. He had an uneasy feeling standing at this part of the meadow. This was where his friend, Jimbo, had been killed by the Black Hand after accidentally discovering the Shimmering.

The congregation of men gathered together, forming a horseshoe. Chief William's clan stood behind Daniel on the right side of the horseshoe, while Chief George's clan stood opposite and faced them on the left side. Finally, Levi's clan looped around, joining the two ends of the shoe.

Three elders, one from each clan, walked together, each carrying a deer-skin case that looked much like a quiver. Each elder stood in front of their respective clan. When the sun finally peeked over the treetops, the elders reached into their quivers and removed what appeared to be a war club. Each one was spherical at one end and connected to a shaft about three feet long. Each one was decorated in the colors and designs of the different clans. George's clan's scepter was painted red, black, and white, with two eagle feathers dangling from the head of the staff. Levi's was painted red, yellow, and white with one feather. William's was painted yellow, green, and white with three feathers. Daniel and Washing Bear were each handed a scepter from the clan they were representing.

Suddenly, a shimmering light appeared at the edge of the meadow. Its light waved in a circular motion in a clockwise direction. Daniel had seen this before but had never noticed the direction of the wave. Ittola Chuka had opened. Daniel's scepter began to vibrate slightly in his hands. It was as if the staff was communicating with the Shimmering.

Daniel was under the impression that it only opened twice a year. He had passed through it during the winter solstice, while Emily had come through during the summer solstice. He wondered, "Could it be that it also opens during the autumn equinox?"

One of the elders began to speak in his native tongue. Daniel was able to understand most of what was said. "If the one true creator chooses you to be Hoh-pah-e, you will also be Nohn-wah hush-ekun-ut-le ulh-pe-sah and command Ittola Chuka. You will travel with the spirits through time. You will be able to speak with our ancestors from the past. Our grandfathers and grandmothers. Their grandfathers and grandmothers. You will speak to our grandchildren and their grandchildren. These staffs you hold give you the power to call upon Ittola Chuka. You can call upon that power whenever and wherever you need it. How to control this power can only be revealed to you by the spirits of the one true creator. You will travel through Ittola Chuka now and discover the secrets of its power. Ittola Chuka will close once you have entered. If the one true creator selects you to be Nohn-wah hush-ekun-ut-le ulh-pe-sah, you will return before the sunsets. If you are not selected, you will be lost forever. If you are still willing to take on this honor to represent our people, stand before me."

Both Daniel and Washing Bear walked over to the elder and stood before him.

"You will now pass through Ittola Chuka."

They passed through the Shimmering together. Daniel felt a cold sensation enter his body as he passed through. The same feeling he had felt nearly two years ago. Once they had traveled to the other side, Daniel looked back and saw the Shimmering fade away. His staff stopped vibrating. He turned to look at Washing Bear, and just as he did, Washing Bear lifted his club above his head and swung it down toward Daniel's head. Daniel stepped aside just in time to dodge the blow from the staff. Washing Bear was quick even though his bad leg limited his movement.

With his scepter, Daniel blocked attack after attack from the little man. Washing Bear was relentless in his attack. Finally, Daniel decided he needed to go on the offensive. He had no desire to kill this man, but he didn't want to die either. As Washing Bear lifted his club high above his head to strike a killing blow to Daniel's head, Daniel thrust the head of his club into Washing Bear's midsection. Washing Bear doubled over in pain for only a moment, then pursued Daniel again. Daniel wasted no time, however. He swung his club with a backhanded swing, nailing Washing Bear in the right side of his head, causing him to drop to the ground unconscious.

Daniel felt the side of Washing Bear's neck to see if he had a pulse. He did. Daniel took Washing Bear's scepter and tossed it as far as he could into the brush. He turned back to the area where the Shimmering had disappeared and lifted his scepter. The scepter began to tremble, but the Shimmering didn't reappear. He lowered his scepter and decided to think things through.

When Gus had traveled through the Shimmering in the summer of 2018, He had moved forward to the year 2218. Gus had told him when he came back that walking through the portal on one side sent you ahead in time, while from the other direction, you would go back in time. Was that true? Or was it something else?

Both David Colbert and the Chickasaw elder had said that whoever would become Hoh-pah-e would be able to control Ittola Chuka. Was it just a matter of thinking about the day to which he wished to travel?

He decided to give it a try. Daniel once again raised his scepter and concentrated on the date. The fall equinox would be on September 22nd. Once again, the scepter began to vibrate as he repeated the date to himself, "September 22, 1819".

Still no portal. Daniel lowered the scepter once again and searched his mind for the answer. Negative thoughts began to creep into his mind that he might never make it back home to Emily. He quickly brushed those thoughts away. There had to be something he was missing. What was it?

Then, it came to him. When he and Washing Bear had stood before the Shimmering, the portal was swirling in a clockwise direction like the hands of a clock. Time moves forward with the hands of the clock's movement. So, if Gus had gone forward in time while the portal was moving in a clockwise motion, then someone on the opposite side of the portal would see it moving in a counterclockwise motion. But Gus could go back in time because, from his perspective, the clock was going backward.

Daniel tried again. This time, as he raised the scepter, he made a circular motion with his arm counterclockwise. He concentrated once more on the date, "September 22, 1819." Slowly, the Shimmering began to appear before him as the scepter vibrated in his hand. He continued to recite the date within his mind and swirled his scepter until the power of the portal was at its full strength.

Daniel was excited to see that it worked. Or had it? He wouldn't be sure until he passed through and found his Chickasaw brothers waiting for him on the other side. He turned back to Washing Bear, who lay lifeless on the ground. Daniel picked him up and draped him over his left shoulder. As he walked through the portal, he once again felt the cold sensation of its power.

Daniel exited the portal and found the three clans of the Chickasaw waiting, anticipating his return. Suddenly, everyone burst out into yelps and hoots of high-pitched cheering, honoring Hoh-pah-e, who once again had come back to them. He would help to lead the people. He would serve as a judge for the people. He was the one the true creator had selected to make the people whole again. They were no longer three clans but one nation.

A celebration began. Food was prepared and served around the big fire they had sat around the night before. They drank, danced, and sang in celebration of Hoh-pah-e. Then, as darkness fell on the meadow and the celebration began to die, William, George, and Levi approached Daniel to make a request.

William spoke for the others as he said, "We would like you to travel to our villages so that all people of the Chickasaw will know that you are the chosen one."

Daniel replied, "I would be honored great chiefs to meet all the people. I will travel to your villages so they may see Hoh-pah-e. I only ask that you allow me to take Shobohli Eho back to my valley first. She is with child and will soon deliver. Please allow me to delay my visit to your villages until the spring."

The chiefs looked at each other and nodded, agreeing that they would allow Daniel to come in the spring. "Go, Hoh-pah-e. We will send someone in the spring to bring you to our villages. You will meet the people then.

"Thank you, my brothers. I look forward to seeing you all in the spring."

Daniel bowed to the chiefs, then walked away from them to find Hoss, who was tied up with all the Indian ponies in the back of the camp. He saddled his horse, placed the scepter now stored inside the deerskin quiver into his saddlebags, and rode out of the meadow to find Emily.

Rain began to fall as Daniel rode out of the meadow into the wooded area where Emily had left. He now wore his buckskin shirt that had been removed during the ceremony. His chest muscles were sore from the piercings he had endured. He had removed the bones that were used to hang him from the ceiling of the lodge during the ceremony. The holes in his chest would eventually heal, but the scars would always be prevalent.

He found Emily's camp after a ten-minute search. Jake ran out to meet him as he approached. Emily had started a campfire, but the rain quickly extinguished it. Black smoke thickly rose above the camp with every drop of rain.

Emily sat inside her little tent, waiting for her husband's arrival. When she saw Jake leave the camp, she suspected Daniel was near. If anyone else had entered her camp, Jake would have surely barked out an alarm. But, instead, the wagging of his tail indicated that Jake's master was close at hand.

Daniel dismounted and tied Hoss next to Emily's mare before entering the tent.

"Well?" asked Emily. "What happened?"

Daniel lay down next to where she sat inside the tent and began to tell of the ceremony. "Well, there were three of us. A man named Washing Bear, who represented Chief George's clan, another named Little Horse that represented Chief Levi's clan, and me. Last night, everyone sat around a fire and listened to the elders make their speeches about the ceremony's importance. Then we smoked a pipe. No, I didn't inhale." Emily smiled at his remark. "We were then given a terrible tasting drink that caused hallucinations. After that, we were taken into a lodge for the second part of the ceremony. First, they pierced our chest and threaded bone through the piercings." he opened up his shirt and showed her his wounds. "Then they strung us up like hanging meat and left us there."

Emily reached for her medical bag and mixed oils to make a salve for Daniel's wounds while he continued his account.

"While I was hanging, I had a dream or some kind of vision. I was being chased and attacked by a bear. A huge bear. It knocked me off the edge of a cliff, but instead of falling to my death, I began to fly. An eagle was flying nearby, and I flew alongside him. The eagle soared down to the river and caught a fish. I thought I would try to do the same, but when I moved closer to the river, I suddenly fell out of the sky and hit the ground. I awoke and was escorted out of the lodge along with Washing Bear."

Emily asked, "What about Little Horse?"

Daniel continued, "He was dead when I woke up. Evidently, being hung by your chest piercings was just too much for him. So they took us to the edge of the meadow where the Shimmering opens up, and there it was. Only, it was different."

"How's that?" asked Emily.

"Instead of looking like heat waves from the desert floor, it had a swirling motion. It was swirling clockwise. They handed each of us scepters and instructed us to go through and navigate the Shimmering. As soon as we got through, the Shimmering disappeared. Then, Washing Bear decided to try to bean me with his scepter. We got into a fight, and I was able to knock him out with my scepter. I then used all the knowledge I had been given from Gus when he came back through the Shimmering, and I was able to figure out how to create the portal for myself and determine where or, more precisely, when I would end up. The scepter helps me create the portal. If I rotate it clockwise, it will create a portal to take me into the future. If I rotate it counterclockwise, It will take me back in time. Then, it's just a matter of thinking about the date that I want to travel to."

Emily asked, "How long did it take for you to figure that out?"

"Maybe fifteen minutes. You see, Gus had said that one side of the portal would take you back in time, and the other would take you into the future. But, it wasn't just the side of the portal. It was the direction of the spin. Clockwise takes you ahead in time just as a clock moves forward as time does. So, reversing to counterclockwise should take you back in time. After a couple of tries, I was able to open up the Shimmering. I picked up Washing Bear and carried him through. Then, they threw me a big party. You're looking at the newest Time Traveler of the Chickasaw nation."

Emily smiled and asked, "Well, are you hungry? I can fix you something."

Daniel replied, "No thanks. I ate at the party. I just want to rest, lying on the ground instead of being hung from the rafters."

Emily chuckled and asked, "What's next?"

"Well," said Daniel. "They want me to take a tour of the villages so everyone can be introduced to Hoh-pah-e. But not right away. I asked if we could put it off until the spring. We're going to stay home until that baby you've been lugging around arrives."

Chapter 13

Four men lifted Morgan into the back of an ambulance once it arrived at their location. Soldiers continued to march and sing along the trail while glancing into the ambulance to see who had been loaded into it.

Sergeant Sikes commanded, "Alright, boys, let's get back into formation. The Captain will be fine."

Henry and Hawlsey followed the sergeant back to their unit, where they fell back into formation.

Morgan was afraid to fall asleep. He was worried he might have a concussion. So he asked the ambulance driver, "Hey, driver! Do you happen to have a mirror on you?"

The driver responded, "Beggin' your pardon, Captain. What do you need a mirror for?"

"Morgan replied, "I want to check my pupils to see if I have a concussion."

"No, Sir! I don't have a mirror."

Then the driver turned to some men marching with the ambulance and said, "Hey! Any of you have a mirror you can let the Captain borrow for a bit?"

A young corporal wearing a smartly trimmed handlebar mustache said, "I got my shaving mirror. Will that do?"

Morgan looked over the wagon's side and spoke to the Corporal, "That would be perfect, Corporal. Thanks!"

Morgan accepted the corporal's mirror and grabbed a blanket that lay in the bottom of the wagon next to him.

He searched through his haversack and found a box of matches. Morgan spread the blanket and covered his head to keep out as much light as possible. Next, he struck a match and looked into the mirror he held in front of his face. Moving the lit match from side to side, Morgan watched to see if his pupil would contract against the match's flame. First, he checked his left pupil. The pupil constricted and shrunk to avoid the light presented by the flame.

"*Good*!" thought Morgan to himself.

Then he checked his right eye. It was the same. He had not suffered any significant head trauma despite traveling headfirst through the window of his old Chevy.

Morgan "puffed" out the match and removed the blanket from over his head. He returned the mirror to its owner and said, "Thanks!".

Morgan was satisfied that he could safely close his eyes and sleep. Rest would be the best treatment he could receive for now.

—◆—

Rain was falling at an unbelievable rate. The soldiers no longer sang as they marched along the trail, which quickly turned into muck. The farther down the line, the harder it was for soldiers to hold their footing. Many slipped and fell into muddy puddles along the way. They would march all afternoon and into the night to reach their destination.

The Army of Tennessee, led by General Ulysses S. Grant, was roughly 50,000 in strength. It marched from Fort Donelson along the Cumberland and Tennessee Rivers. Its mission was to take all ground up to and including the Mississippi River. Access to the Mississippi would allow the Union to freely supply its troops and split the Confederate Army.

Grant's Army of the Tennessee would meet up with the Army of the Ohio at Pittsburg Landing on the 6th, where the Union would set up their base of operations. The Army of the Ohio floated in on steamboats that would disembark its soldiers at the landing and provide long-range cannon fire against the Confederate troops in the area.

A tent hospital was erected on the southern end of what would soon become one of the bloodiest battlefields in the Civil War. The hospital was staged just northwest of Lick Creek, a tributary to the Tennessee River. Shiloh Church stood about a mile and a half to the hospital's west.

Three roads created a delta or triangle between Shiloh Church, Pittsburg Landing, and the Union Tent Hospital. First, the Hamburg-Purdy Road ran west to east, more or less between the church and the hospital. Second, Corinth-Pittsburg Landing Road ran from the west to the northeast, ending at Pittsburg Landing. Finally, Pittsburg-Savannah Road made the third side of the triangle, running from the hospital north to Pittsburg landing. The area inside the triangle is referred to as the Hornet's Nest.

When the Army of the Tennessee arrived on April 5th, the medical corp split off and began to set up tents to use as hospitals to care for the wounded. Doctors holding the ranks of Major and Captain spouted off orders to the enlisted men who served as orderlies. Tents measuring about twelve feet by twelve were erected, and make-shift tables were set up inside the tents to serve as the surgery. Other smaller tents were set up throughout the camp for sleeping quarters.

Young boys who usually played in the fife and drum corps were assigned to haul water from the nearby creek. They carried the water in rope-handled buckets from the stream and emptied them into fifty-gallon barrels that stood at the corners of each surgery.

Everyone knew their jobs and rushed to prepare for the inevitable battle that would soon bring dying and wounded their way.

Morgan was impressed. He couldn't believe how many men and boys had shown up for this re-enactment. He collected his haversack from the ambulance and headed toward the camp. He soon found a Major who seemed to be in charge and asked,

"Major?"

The Major replied, "Yes." as he turned and saw Morgan with a look of puzzlement.

"Major, I'm Morgan Turner. Where would you like me to set up?"

The Major answered, "Captain Turner. You must be one of the new surgeons. Glad to meet you. Uh...You are a surgeon?"

"Yes, sir!"

"I'm Major Timothy Tremble. Where did you study, Captain?"

"Vanderbilt, Sir."

"Vanderbilt? Why aren't you fighting for the south?"

Morgan replied, "Well, Sir, I wanted to be on the winning side."

Tremble replied, "I see. Captain, you look like you've been in a fight. Are you alright?"

"Yes, Sir. I had an accident early yesterday morning. I'm feeling fine, though, Sir."

"Good." said the Major. "Well, why don't you set up with the rest of the surgeons on the north side of the surgeries. When you're settled, come and help us set up the surgeries."

"Yes, Sir!" Morgan said, saluting and going to find the other surgeon's tents.

Morgan was impressed by how in-character everyone seemed to be. He had never been to a re-enactment that was so formal. Usually, all involved were content with being regular people, hanging out until the show began. However, these men acted like they were really in the military and preparing for an actual battle.

Around midnight, the hospital was completed. All the men retired to their tents to rest before the morning's barrage of wounded would swarm upon them. The rain continued to fall, making it difficult for Morgan to get more than short cat naps. His mind wandered throughout the early morning hours. His anticipation for the re-enactment battle kept him from reaching any similarity of restful sleep. Instead, his mind ping-ponged from the battle of Shiloh back to Maggie. He looked forward to finishing his residency at Vanderbilt so that he and Maggie could begin their life together as husband and wife.

Then his mind turned back to his wreck. He remembered crashing through the windshield, flying through the air. A tree was in his path of flight. A collision with the large conifer was inevitable. He would certainly not survive such a violent impact. Yet, he did. He couldn't remember colliding with the tree at all. It was as if the tree had just disappeared.

CHAPTER 14

Daniel and Emily walked their horses slowly down the trail. The air was cool, but the morning sun warmed their bodies as they rode side by side. Jake trotted ahead of them quicker, sometimes stopping to sniff a tree or a patch of grass. The horses would catch up and pass him until he finished with his inspection, and then he would run ahead, looking for the next thing to discover.

Emily broke the silence and asked, "Are you ready to serve your role as the 'Prophet'?"

Daniel smiled and replied, "I don't know. I guess. I don't know what to expect."

Emily then asked, "Don't you think it's funny that Susan had you pegged as a prophet when the two of you came back from Lawrenceburg?"

Daniel paused as he looked at Emily and said, "Yeah! It's kind of prophetic, isn't it."

They rode through Beaver Branch into the Water Valley they called home three hours later. They rode their mounts up to the corral, dismounted, and unsaddled their horses. Tommy Brown, their partner, came over from the far end of the corral where he had been trimming the hooves of one of the Indian ponies that Emily had won from a Cherokee man named Young Dragging Canoe.

Tommy welcomed the couple, "You're back! How'd it go?"

Daniel replied, "Oh, it's a long story. We'll tell you all about it at lunch. Can you and Amy join us?"

Tommy said, "Why, sure. I'll jest run up to the cabin and let her know y'all are back."

Emily was in no hurry to return to the daily chores that awaited her. She decided to hang around the corral for a while. She let out a shrill whistle and shouted, "Rusty, Pepper!"

Her two giant mules meandered over to her from the far end of the corral. Emily climbed through the rails of the fence to get closer to them. They towered above her as she reached up and scratched each of them around the face and ears. She spoke gently to them as she caressed them. Emily found a curry comb and a brush, combed their manes and tails, and then brushed them from head to toe.

Daniel released their two horses into the corral and watched as Hoss kicked up his heels and ran through the herd of equine scattered throughout the pen. He snorted, bucked, and tossed his head, letting the herd know he was back.

Sometime around noon, Emily and Daniel walked back to their cabin. They saw Tommy and Amy walking toward them from their cabin as they reached the cottage. Tommy carried a basket in one arm while Amy grasped his other as they walked together.

Amy's face lit up when she saw Emily and Daniel. Amy exclaimed, "Hey, y'all! I'm so glad you're back. We missed you!"

Emily gave Amy a hug, their bellies colliding. Both women were quite pregnant—Emily was starting her third trimester, while Amy was four months pregnant. They went into the cabin arm in arm as the men straggled behind. Amy had prepared bacon and tomato sandwiches for them and served them with fresh vegetables from the garden. They all sat around the table, catching up on the events of last week.

Tommy talked about what he had accomplished on the farm while Daniel had been gone. Next, Daniel and Emily told of their trip to Sheboss and how they had encountered the Black Hand while on the trail. Next, they talked about Sarah and David Colbert and their new son, Danny. Then, finally, Emily said, "Daniel has some news."

Everyone paused to hear the news, but Daniel said nothing.

Finally, Tommy asked, "Well, what is it?"

Daniel remained quiet.

Emily decided she would have to tell them herself. "Daniel has just been given a position as a leader for the Chickasaw nation."

Tommy and Amy both gasped and began assaulting Daniel with questions.

Daniel remained quiet.

Emily asked, "What's wrong, Daniel?"

Daniel looked sheepishly at his wife and explained, "Emily, I told you more than the Chickasaw would be happy with my sharing with you. It is a secret position, especially the ceremony. I told you about it because I would never try to withhold anything from you. But, I must ask everyone at this table to keep my secret. Tommy. Amy. I won't give you any particulars about where we have been or what I have been through. And I hope that the information I tell you now will remain a secret between us four."

Tommy and Amy both replied, "Sure, Daniel!"

Daniel began again, "I have been selected to serve as Hoh-pah-e for the Chickasaw. That translates as Prophet in our language, but it is more like a judge or justice of the peace for them. I had to go through a ceremony along with two other men who were candidates. We endured some, well, some painful trials to go through the process. When it was all over with, I was deemed their chosen one. I will be expected to travel from time to time to the villages of the Chickasaw to handle matters for them. I apologize that it may place a burden on you, Tommy, from time to time. But, I promise I will pick up the slack when I am present to make this farm successful for us all."

Tommy spoke up and said, "Don't worry, Daniel. We'll support you with whatever needs to be done. Shoot, I don't know what Amy and I would be doin' if you hadn't offered me a partnership here. We'll make it work. Don't you worry none."

Daniel replied, "Thanks, Tommy. I appreciate it. Well, we might as well get busy. We've got a lot to do before the spring."

⸺◦⸺

November

Nearly two months had passed since Daniel and Emily returned. Much had to be done to prepare for the quickly approaching winter months. Tommy and Daniel worked on finishing the enlargement of their horse pens; they cut and stacked enough firewood for both households to make it through the winter. They even managed to build an addition to Daniel and Emily's cabin.

Emily had hoped for such an edition so that she could set up a hospital of sorts. She would no longer have to use her kitchen to store her oils and remedies. The edition was twelve feet wide and ten feet long. They fashioned two small beds for Emily's would-be patients and an examination table in the middle of the room. Two window openings were cut into the cabin walls to allow natural light to enter. Unfortunately, there would be no glass, at least not yet. Window glass was expensive and hard to come by. Shutters would be built to cover the window openings in the case of bad weather.

About a week after the cabin work had been completed, Emily awoke just before dawn with labor pains.

She groaned and moaned with each contraction. "Daniel, you need to go and get Amy for me."

Daniel asked, "Why? What's wrong?"

"This baby is coming, and I don't think it's waiting for long. So you need to get Amy, now!"

Daniel stammered as he tried to say, "I can . . ."

"NOW, Daniel!"

Daniel quickly dressed and ran to Amy and Tommy's cabin, a quarter of a mile away, down by Beaver Branch. He banged on the door of the cabin and yelled, "Amy! Amy, come quick! Emily needs you!"

Amy came to the door wrapped in a blanket around her bedclothes and asked, "What is it, Daniel?"

"Emily says you've gotta come quick. She's having the baby!"

Amy replied, "Oh! Alright! Let me get dressed, and I'll be right there."

Daniel didn't wait for her. Instead, he sprinted back to his cabin to check on Emily. Daniel burst into the cabin to find Emily panting and cringing against the contractions. He stood before his wife, not knowing what to do next.

"Daniel, stoke up the fire and boil some water."

Daniel was puzzled when he asked, "I thought that was just in the movies that they said that."

Emily impatiently replied, "Just do it!"

Daniel obliged his wife's orders.

After the long walk from her cabin, Amy entered Emily's cabin to give what help she could. "What do you need me to do, Emily?"

"Amy, get those towels over there and put a couple underneath me, just like we talked about. Remember?"

Amy replied, "Sure. I remember."

Emily reached down to feel her belly. She checked to see where the baby's head was located. "That's good.", she said. "The baby's head is turned in the right direction so we can do this the natural way. Amy, reach down like I taught you and measure the dilation."

Amy flattened out her hand with her fingers side by side to measure the length of Emily's dilation.

"Emily, I get three fingers right now."

Emily replied, "Okay. That's about six centimeters. We've still got time. My contractions are about twenty minutes apart right now."

About an hour later, Emily's contractions had grown in intensity and frequency. She told Amy, "Check the dilation again."

As instructed, Amy replied, "Emily, I have about six fingers now. Oh! I think I see the baby's head trying to come out!"

Emily said, "Good! Daniel, come over here and help me."

Daniel complied.

"When I say go, I want you to lift me so I can push. Don't push me forward; just support what I'm doing."

Daniel said, "Okay."

Emily felt the next contraction and said, "Okay, Go!"

Daniel pushed Emily up from the bed, supporting her back as she moved forward and began to push.

"Augh!" she screamed out.

Amy screamed, "I see it! I see it! Its head is out now."

Emily let out another "Augh!" and pushed.

Amy cried out, "It's out! It's out!"

Emily lay back down on the bed and breathed heavily. Once she caught her breath, she asked, "Is it a boy or girl?"

Amy smiled at Emily and said, "You have a little girl."

Emily smiled back and asked, "How many fingers and toes?"

Amy checked and replied, "Ten of each."

Emily laughed, still heavily breathing as tears began to form in her eyes. Daniel knelt and kissed his wife as he began to weep through laughter.

Amy asked, "What are you going to name her?"

Emily and Daniel looked at each other and smiled. Then, Daniel said, "It's up to you."

Emily replied, "Alyson. Alyson Catherine Lane. Alyson Catherine was my mother's name."

Emily had lost her mother nearly twenty years ago. She died of cancer when Emily was sixteen. She never knew her father. Emily had never met him. She didn't even know his name. Her mother had never told her about him. Grandpa Bill was the only father figure she had had in her life. That was enough.

Amy cleaned baby Alyson and handed her to her mother. Next, she bathed Emily and moved her from the bed to a chair so that clean bedding could be placed on the bed. Emily looked at Amy and said, "You did great, Amy. Thanks for helping me."

Amy smiled brightly at Emily and said, "I hope I can do as good as you did. You made it look so easy."

⸻◆⸻

The following day, around ten, Jake began to bark as a wagon pulled into the valley crossing the Beaver. Daniel walked out of the cabin to see who it was and found Micah Gordon driving up to the cabin.

"Howdy, Micah!"

"How do, Daniel?"

Daniel asked, "What you got there in the wagon?"

Micah Gordon was the youngest of the Gordon brothers, two years older than Amy, the youngest of the Gordon Clan.

"Oh, Ma told me to bring these for Amy and Emily. She knew it was time for the babies to be born, so she ordered some rockers from Nashville. They came in yesterday, so she had me bring them early this morning."

"Wow!" said Daniel. "That's mighty nice of her and you. Can I help you unload?"

Micah untied one of the rockers and handed it down to Daniel. It was made of oak and had hand-turned legs and spindles. Daniel admired its craftsmanship. He carried it to the cabin and asked, "Won't you come in and say hello? This rocker came just in time. Our baby was born yesterday."

Micah replied, "Let me go on down and deliver this other one to Amy. Then, I'll stop back by on the way home to see Emily and the baby."

Micah turned the wagon toward Tommy and Amy's cabin to deliver the second rocker to his little sister.

Chapter 15

Daniel awoke before dawn to the whistling sound of a strong north wind. The cabin was bitterly cold. He tried to extricate himself from the bed without disturbing Emily or baby Alyson, who was nestled between them. Daniel wasn't sure it was a good idea for the baby to sleep between her parents because of his sleeping habits. He was prone to dreams, which often included fights of some sort. Daniel was either fighting off a predator of some kind or throwing punches at a would-be attacker. Emily was always the recipient of the kicks or punches that Daniel released in his sleep. Daniel felt that if Alyson slept between them, she might accidentally incur injuries from his dreams. However, between her parents, it was the warmest place to sleep.

Daniel checked the fire. It was nearly out. He stoked up the coals remaining in the fireplace, then added more wood to fuel the fire. Turning back into bed, he noticed something at the cabin door. Tiny white pellets had crawled under the door and onto the cabin floor. Daniel opened the cabin door against a strong breeze to discover what he had dreaded might be the case. Snow. Not just a little snow. It was a blizzard.

Middle Tennessee was not known for extreme winter weather. Not like this. He stepped onto the porch and closed the door behind him to keep as much cold air out of the cabin as possible. Large flakes of snow were falling rapidly before his eyes. The porch was built two feet above the ground. The depths of the snow had already reached that height and were still falling at a tremendous rate.

Daniel thought of the livestock. He knew they would have difficulty surviving this frigid weather without his help. Daniel went back into the cabin to get dressed. He was thankful that Emily had brought long johns for him when she came to meet him through the Shimmering. He had worn them to bed last night. Daniel pulled his buckskin trousers on, then his linen shirt. Then he donned the buckskin coat Sarah Colbert gave him for Christmas two years ago. Then he pulled on his boots and grabbed his beaver skin cap that David Colbert had made him. He also had a pair of beaver skin mittens that David had shown him how to make. He hoped it would be enough.

Jake followed Daniel out of the cabin. At first, he looked confused when he saw the white fluff that had invaded his yard. Jake took a couple of tentative steps into the icy cold whiteness. Then, he excitedly pounced into the high drifts of snow, bouncing here and there. He ran in quick circles, swiping his backside around like a fishtail. He barked with delight and ran at Daniel as if to play, almost knocking Daniel down as he sped past him.

The snow continued to fall rapidly, and the wind relentlessly blew as Daniel trudged his way through the snow that was up to his knees. Daniel thought it would be much easier if Emily brought snowshoes. However, snowshoes weren't readily available in Tennessee. You couldn't just run down to Walmart and pick up a pair. At least not down south. He knew the first thing he needed to do was clear a path through the snow to allow them to get to the livestock. He had just the equipment for the job, too.

After much struggle, he finally reached the corral. Finally, he found what he needed. One of the sleds they had built to haul rocks in while building the cabin. He needed to modify it, though. He decided to fashion a plow of sorts to the front of the sled to move the snow from its path.

The sun was beginning to rise, but it could barely be seen because of the dark cloud cover the winter storm had brought. Finally, Daniel found the tools he needed in the small shed next to the corral. He took boards and made a panel to mount to the front of the sled. He attached the panel at a forty-five-degree angle so that snow would be shifted away from the sled, clearing a path he and others could eventually walk on without getting bogged down in the snow. It took him nearly an hour to finish the project.

He went back to the corral and called Rusty and Pepper. The two gentle giants came willingly but slowly to Daniel. They stood by, waiting as Daniel put on their harnesses. They knew they would work, but they always seemed to enjoy it. These were strong animals bred for this kind of duty. Once harnessed, Daniel led them out of the corral and hitched them to the front of the sled.

Daniel gathered the four reins and trailed them back to the sled. He climbed on and balanced himself to stand while the sled moved forward.

"Gitup! Yah!" Daniel called out to the mules. They moved forward slowly at first, trying to gain their footing. The snowplow creaked as it slowly moved forward. The plow blade dug into the snow depths and began rolling it out of the sled's path. It worked.

Daniel called out, "Haw!" The mules turned to the left, clearing a path away from the corral.

"Gee!" They turned to the right, making a path toward the hog and goat pens. They made their way around the chicken coop and corn crib. Then, down toward the cabin and up to the bank of the Beaver.

"Gee!" he said, turning them along the banks of the Beaver and heading to Tommy and Amy's cabin.

Snow still fell heavily to the ground, but the mules didn't seem to mind. Instead, they plowed through like it was melted butter.

As they neared Tommy's cabin, Tommy heard the commotion and exited to see what was happening. Daniel pulled the mules up at the cabin as Tommy said, "I've never seen so much snow before. Have you?"

Daniel replied, "No, and I hope to never see it again."

Tommy asked, "How are all the animals?"

"As best I can tell," responded Daniel, "they seem to be okay. I haven't had a chance to feed them yet. I'm just trying to clear a path so we can get to them."

Tommy replied, "Well, I'll get dressed and be right out. Mind if I catch a ride with you?"

Daniel said, "No, I'll wait."

Five minutes later, Tommy came out of the cabin bundled up and ready to ride. As he climbed onto the sled, he handed Daniel a bacon and biscuit sandwich. "Here! I thought you might be hungry."

"Thanks!" said Daniel as he moved the mules ahead.

They plowed their way back to the corral, and Daniel pulled the mules up to the gate.

"Can you get the gate? I'm going to plow around the edge of the corral."

Tommy nodded and dismounted to open the gate for the mules. All the horses stood at the far end of the pen with their ears pricked forward, curious about what monstrous thing was entering their territory. Tommy struggled to open the gate against the snow piled in front of it. He finally swung it open with much effort, allowing Daniel to drive the mules forward.

While Daniel and the mules plowed the snow away from the edges of the horse pen, Tommy began forking hay into the hay racks hanging from the corral fence's top rail. The horses immediately ran through the deep snow toward him with anticipation. Once Daniel had finished plowing the corral, Tommy opened the gate again, allowing the mules to pull the sled to the outside. Next, Tommy and Daniel unhitched the mules and led them back to the pen to release them so they could nibble on the hay set before them.

Tommy and Daniel left the corral and moved to the hog pen and the goat pen. Tommy fed the pigs while Daniel fed and milked the goats. While Daniel finished the milking, Tommy moved to the chicken coop and gathered the eggs. Then, they met back at Daniel's cabin, where they divided the milk and eggs. Finally, Tommy took his supply of eggs and milk and trudged back to his cabin.

As Daniel and Jake entered the cabin, they found Emily preparing to bake loaves of bread in the kitchen. Daniel asked, "Have you looked outside?"

Emily replied, "No, not yet. Why?"

Daniel said, "Come here."

Emily walked over to him as he opened the door to show her the boundless drifts of snow that had piled up overnight.

She stood momentarily agape, then said, "Close the door. It's too cold."

Daniel shut the door as Emily asked, "How deep is it?"

"So far, about two feet."

Emily replied, "Two feet! I don't remember ever having more than six inches back home. How are you going to take care of the stock?"

Daniel replied, "They're already taken care of. I made a snow plow out of one of the sleds and Rusty and Pepper helped me clear a path all the way to Tommy and Amy's cabin."

Emily was impressed by her husband's ingenuity.

They spent the rest of the day puttering around the cabin. Emily was baking bread, and Daniel was keeping the fire going. They took turns holding the baby, keeping her entertained. Jake was always ready to help, sticking his nose as close as possible to the tiny human while sniffing her.

The snow continued to fall all that day and into the night, bringing eleven inches more to the valley. The following day, Daniel went out and hitched up the mules to the sled and re-plowed the paths he had made the previous day. Although the snow was no longer falling, it wasn't melting either. The snow lingered on the ground for the next three days because of the uncommonly cold temperatures and the lack of sunshine. As a result, farm work was at a standstill. Daniel and Tommy could only go outside these days to feed, milk, and gather eggs.

The snow slowly melted when the sun finally came out, causing a soggy, mucky mess. Everything was dirty, muddy, and wet. Daniel and Tommy spent most of the time replenishing their firewood stacks at each cabin. They also spent time setting traps along the riverbank of the Duck and the creek bank of the Beaver. Daily, they checked their traps to see what they might have caught. Daniel had learned how to trap, skin, and tan wildlife pelts from David Colbert. David had taught Daniel everything he needed to know about living off the land and surviving on the frontier. Finally, Daniel realized he was doing what he had always talked to Emily about doing. He was living a simpler life and living it to the fullest.

CHAPTER 16

Daniel woke before dawn. The cabin was cold, so he got up and added wood to the fireplace. Once he was satisfied that the blaze of the flames was sufficient to warm up the cabin, he got back into bed. Sleep evaded him. His thoughts were on other things. Mostly, he thought about the Shimmering. Would he be able to control it? Could he choose a destination as well as a time to travel? Could he control the time of day? After much contemplation, he decided he would need to experiment. That meant he would need to talk to Emily about it. He had already promised Emily he wouldn't go through the Shimmering without talking to her first.

The sun finally peeked through a crack in the chinking of their cabin, letting Daniel know that morning had arrived. He stirred from his bed as Emily awoke to greet him. "Morning."

"Morning," said Daniel.

Emily asked, "Did you have trouble sleeping? I heard you tossing and turning."

Daniel replied, "Yeah, a little."

"What's the problem?" she asked.

Daniel responded, "I've just been thinking about the Shimmering. I wonder if it is strictly for time travel or if you can also travel to a location."

Emily said, "Hmm. That's a good question. Maybe you should try it out."

Daniel was shocked by her statement. He thought she would challenge anything to do with the Shimmering. Instead, Emily saw the look on his face and said, "What? You thought I was going to fight you on this, didn't you?"

Daniel replied, "Well, yeah."

Emily said, "Daniel, I know how important this is for you and for the Chickasaw people. I think you should try to understand what this thing is all about. I know you're going to have to go through again, so maybe you should do it in a controlled situation."

"Like how?" asked Daniel

"Start with something simple and work your way up. Why don't we try it out this morning after breakfast?"

"We?" asked Daniel.

Emily smirked at him, saying, "You're not going through that thing without me until I'm sure you know what you're doing. We'll figure it out together; then you can fly solo."

Daniel smiled, then reached over and kissed his wife. "Thanks!" he said.

Daniel got dressed and left the cabin with Jake in tow. Emily got out of bed carefully, trying not to wake the baby. Finally, she dressed and began preparing breakfast.

Daniel walked to the corral, where Tommy was already feeding the horses and mules. The morning was chilly but not as cold as a typical January morning. The sun shone through a clear sky, and the air was still. The two men greeted one another and began tossing hay into the racks on the corral fence together. The horses snorted as the dust from the hay entered their nostrils.

They finished their feeding and milking chores and met at the coop to divide the milk and eggs. Daniel told Tommy just as they were about to part ways, "We're going to be gone for a while today. Do you mind taking care of things while we're gone?"

Tommy replied, "Naw, I don't mind none. Whar' ya goin'?

Daniel explained, "I need to experiment with my new found power. Emily and I will be going through the Shimmering trying to figure out just when and where we can go."

Tommy asked, "Well, do ya thank that's safe?"

Daniel replied, "I don't know for sure. But, I need to try to figure it out and until I do Emily says I'm not going alone. If we don't come back, the farm is yours."

Tommy nodded and said, "I jest as soon y'all come back."

Daniel smiled at Tommy, and the two parted.

Daniel entered the cabin just as Emily was setting breakfast on the table. Alyson was still asleep, so the couple let her alone, allowing them to eat their meal without disruption. After they finished, Emily changed and fed the baby while Daniel got ready to travel. First, he gathered up his rifle, two pistols, braces, and tomahawk. Then, he reached into his saddlebags and retrieved the deerskin quiver that held the scepter.

When Emily finished feeding Alyson, she bundled the baby in a warm blanket and stepped out of the cabin with Daniel and Jake. The family walked out to a clearing in the yard. Then Daniel removed the scepter from the quiver.

"Where should we go first?" he asked.

Emily thought momentarily, then said, "Let's try something simple first. Why don't you try taking us to Tommy and Amy's cabin?"

Daniel said, "Okay. So, rather than traveling through time why don't we just try the transporting theory to see if that works?"

Daniel stretched out the scepter in his right hand and closed his eyes. He tried to picture the area in front of Tommy and Amy's cabin. The scepter began to vibrate within his hand. A wave of energy opened up before the couple. Daniel opened his eyes and saw the Shimmering standing before him. He placed the scepter back in its sheath and grabbed Emily's hand to lead her through the portal. Even though the Shimmering had opened, they couldn't be sure whether it would take them to their desired destination and time without traveling through it.

A blast of cold air seemed to travel through their bodies as they walked. As they stepped out of the portal, they stood in front of Tommy and Amy's cabin. Amy was stepping out of the cabin when they exited the portal. When she saw them appear seemingly out of thin air, Amy dropped the dishpan and spilled water everywhere as she let go of a yelp.

"Where did y'all come from?" Amy squealed.

Tommy ran out of the cabin to see who was talking to Amy.

"Sorry, Amy!" said Daniel. "We were just trying out the scepter to see if it would transport us to a location without sending us back or forward in time."

"Did it work?" asked Tommy.

Daniel replied, "Well, it depends. Is today January third?"

Tommy answered, "Yep!"

Then Daniel asked, "And, did you and I just talk to each other about an hour ago over by our cabin?"

"Yep, we shore did."

"Then I guess it worked!" Daniel exclaimed.

Amy asked, "What are y'all talking about?"

Daniel explained, "Amy, you know I've been given the gift of time travel, right? Well, we were just testing to see if that also included teleportation."

"What's that?" she asked.

"It's the ability to travel from one place to another just by stepping through a portal like the Shimmering. Emily and I came from our cabin just now, to here without walking."

Amy asked, "And you can go anywhere with this teleporting thing?"

"Anywhere that I can see in my mind." replied Daniel.

Amy said, "Well maybe you could use that thing to let me visit my family sometime."

Daniel replied, "We could probably arrange that. But Amy, you can't tell anyone about this. The Chickasaw have entrusted me with this gift. It is a secret among their people and I can't let anyone know about it. If I take you to see your family we will have to be secretive about it."

"I understand.", replied Amy.

Daniel looked at Emily and asked, "Well, where should we go next?"

Emily replied, "Why don't we go and visit Sarah and David? They haven't met Alyson yet."

Daniel replied, "Alright! Let's go."

Daniel stretched out the scepter with his right hand and thought about an area in the woods behind Sarah's cabin where he and Jake had hidden when the four strangers raided Sheboss Stand two years ago. Then, the scepter vibrated, and the Shimmering appeared before him. Daniel looked at Tommy and Amy, then said, "See you later."

Then, Emily, Daniel, and Jake passed through the portal. They immediately found themselves standing behind Sarah's cabin at Sheboss. They peered through the dogtrot and saw Sarah and Danny in the front of the cabin. Sarah held one of Danny's hands, leading him around as they practiced his walking.

Daniel said, "Follow me."

He led Emily around the cabin to the trail that led to the Duck River. They turned left onto the trail and entered the tiny meadow of Sheboss Stand.

Jake saw Sarah as they approached her and let out a "*woof*." Sarah turned around and saw Jake loping toward her with his tail furiously wagging. She was shocked to see her friends coming into the stand. It had only been a couple of months since she had seen them, and she was thrilled to see them back so soon.

"Hey! What are y'all doing back here so soon?"

Emily replied, "We wanted you to see the newest addition to our family."

Emily opened the bundle she was carrying and revealed Baby Alyson to Sarah. She said, "Sarah, I want you to meet Alyson Catherine Lane."

"Oh, she's so beautiful!" exclaimed Sarah. "Can I hold her?"

Emily handed over the bundle to Sarah. Sarah's face lit up at the tiny being she held in her arms. She knelt beside Danny and said, "Danny, this is your cousin, Alyson."

Danny looked at the baby, intrigued. Sarah looked at Danny and began playing a game that they often played together whenever he discovered something new. She opened her mouth, widened her eyes, and gasped a great "Ooh!". Danny mimicked his mother. He pointed to the tiny baby in her arms and said, "Ooh!" They all chuckled at the little game.

Then Sarah said, "Can you give the baby a kiss?"

Danny clumsily bent over and gave the baby a smooch on her head.

"Awe! That's a good boy!" exclaimed Sarah.

David noticed the Lanes from his post at the corral and wandered over to see them. Just as he arrived, Sarah started to say, "David, can you take their horses?" She glanced around to see the horses, but none were there.

"Where are your horses?" she asked.

Daniel sheepishly looked down at his feet, then cocked an eye toward David, who was watching.

With a tiny glimpse of a smile, David said to Daniel, "You learn fast, Nafkl."

"What?" asked Sarah.

Daniel said, "We didn't bring the horses, Sarah. We traveled here through Ittola Chuka."

"You can do that?" she asked.

"I can now," he replied. "Emily and I were just experimenting. I wanted to see how I can use this gift to help the Chickasaw and us. I now know that I can travel from place to place as well as from time to time. I will be meeting with all the Chickasaw clans in the spring. I want to make sure I know what I'm doing before I meet them."

The two families spent the day together. David and Daniel talked about the Chickasaw clans and what Daniel should expect. Emily and Sarah tended to the children and got to know each other more deeply.

As dusk approached, Daniel decided it was time to go home. Daniel opened Ittola Chuka while rotating the scepter counterclockwise and concentrating on their destination. They walked through the portal and found themselves immediately back home, standing in front of their cabin. Only, it wasn't near dusk. The sun was still hanging high above them.

Emily asked, "Did we travel back in time?"

Daniel replied, "About four hours. I wanted to extend our experiment to see if we could time travel and teleport at the same time."

"Daniel, what about the space-time continuum? Won't we have a problem if we see ourselves in a different time?"

Daniel replied, "I don't think that will happen. We're not traveling to another dimension. We're traveling through time. If you go to a different time, then you're gone from this time. You won't see yourself in another time because there is only one you."

Emily asked, "So, we've got an extra four hours today?"

Daniel answered, "Yes. Unless, you want to go back through the portal and move on to dusk."

"No thanks!" she replied. "I think we've done enough traveling today.

CHAPTER 17

Daniel woke to the sunlight entering their cabin window shutters. The air was cold, moving through the cracks in the shutters. Daniel got out of bed and stoked the coals still glowing in the fireplace. He blew against them to reignite the coals into tiny dancing flames. He added more tender and wood to help the fire grow.

Emily awoke as the baby began to stir. She dressed, changed Alyson, and fed her before starting the morning meal. Daniel went outside to begin the morning chores and met Tommy as he walked from his cabin to help with the morning duties. As they met at the corral to feed the horses and mules, Daniel noticed that Rusty and Pepper seemed unusually energetic. They were kicking up their heels at one another and the horses. Daniel thought they seemed restless, like they needed to work off some energy.

Once Tommy and Daniel had finished the morning chores, they headed back to their respective cabins. As Daniel entered the cabin, he found Emily setting the table for his breakfast. She laid out a spread of biscuits, fried apples, bacon, and eggs. Daniel started the morning conversation, "Looks like the mules need to work off some energy. They're kicking up their heels out there like they've got too much energy."

Emily replied, "I don't blame them. I'm feeling a little cooped up myself. I'm ready for winter to be done."

Jake sat at the end of the table near Emily's feet, whimpering and drooling in anticipation of a morsel of food to drop near him. Instead, Emily ignored him and said, "Is there anything that needs to be done around here that we could use the mules so they can work off some energy?"

Daniel replied, "I've been thinking about that. You know, we've got a huge crib full of corn from last year's harvest. If we could build a mill we could grind our own corn or wheat or whatever. We can use the mules to power the mill. We can get the word out and even grind meal for others around here. What do you think?"

Emily replied, "Yeah, I like that idea, but what do we know about building a mill?"

Daniel answered, "I think I've seen enough Youtube videos on the subject that I can figure it out. I've just got to get someone to build the right tools for the job. I may have to go to Nashville to find a good blacksmith."

"When do you want to start building the mill?" asked

Emily.

Daniel said, "Well, there's no time like the present. I'll check with Tommy this morning and see if there's anything they might need from Nashville. In fact, we could all make a day of it. We'll all go together and do some shopping."

Emily replied, "That's sounds great! Let's take the wagon and the mules so we can load up on supplies."

"I'll go down and tell Amy and Tommy so they can get ready. Then, I'll hitch up the team and saddle the horses."

Once Daniel had finished his breakfast, he left the cabin and began the walk to Amy and Tommy's cabin. Jake walked alongside him. Daniel contemplated using the scepter to travel to the young couple's cabin but decided to walk instead. He didn't want to overuse his ability to travel through time and space. Besides, it only took about ten minutes to walk.

As Daniel stepped onto the porch of the tiny cabin, the door opened just as he reached up to knock. Amy stood in the doorway with a dishpan in her hands. "Hi, Daniel! What brings you down here this morning?" She dodged Daniel and pitched the water from the dishpan into the front yard.

"Amy, how ya feeling this morning?" asked Daniel.

Amy replied, "I'm doing pretty well considering all this extra weight I've been carrying around."

Tommy, hearing Daniel's voice, walked up to join the conversation.

Daniel said, "Well you two, Emily and I are thinking about going to Nashville today to pick up some supplies. We've got a project in mind for the farm. We thought maybe you would like to come along and make a day of it."

Tommy replied, "That sounds real nice. How long do y'all plan on us being gone?"

Daniel answered, "We'll only be gone for the day. We can take the Shimmering so we don't waste so much time traveling. It will be easier on Amy too."

Amy asked, "When do you plan to leave?"

"Just come on down to our place when you're ready. I'll be hitching up the team and saddling a couple of horses."

Daniel and Jake walked back to the corral and began hitching the mules to the wagon. He tied the team to the hitching rail outside the cabin while he went back to saddle two of the horses. Daniel decided to leave Hoss behind for a change. His trusty barrel-chested Bay stud was always dependable. But Daniel thought this would be an easy trip, so he saddled the Sorrel gelding and the Black mare instead. He tied them up behind the wagon, then went inside to check on Emily.

Walking into the cabin, he found Emily bundling up Alyson in preparation for the trip. Daniel collected his rifle, brace and pistol, tomahawk, and powder horn. Emily picked up a brace and pistol for herself and then dropped them into the floorboard of the wagon. Daniel grabbed the quiver holding the scepter and draped it over his shoulder on the way out the door.

Emily handed Alyson to Daniel so she could climb up onto the wagon. Daniel handed Alyson to Emily to hold onto her during the journey. Daniel looked back toward Tommy's cabin and saw the young couple walking toward them about halfway down the trail. Daniel climbed onto the wagon and took the reins, urging the team toward Tommy and Amy.

They reached Amy and Tommy in less than a minute.

Daniel climbed back down from the wagon and helped Amy climb up next to Emily. As Amy sat down, Emily handed Alyson over to her to hold so Emily could drive the mules. Daniel mounted the Sorrel while Tommy climbed onto the Black.

Daniel kicked the Sorrel up and situated him in front of the mule team. Tommy rode up to Daniel's left side and waited. Daniel took the scepter out of the quiver and held it in front of himself. He closed his eyes and concentrated on a location in Nashville, just behind the post office. He hoped it would be inconspicuous enough to hide their entry. The scepter began to vibrate in Daniel's hand as the Shimmering gateway opened up before them all.

Tommy and Daniel rode through the portal while

Emily drove the wagon, following behind. Almost immediately, the travelers found themselves standing in a vacant lot behind a row of buildings. They moved their rides toward a street at the end of one of the buildings as the Shimmering disappeared behind them.

They drove their animals down the street, looking for a place to park the wagon. Within minutes, they discovered a dry goods store on the left. Emily pulled the team up just in front of the store and hopped down to tie the mules to a hitching rail. Amy handed little Alyson down to her mother and climbed down with Tommy's help.

They all four entered the store together. Jake also tried to come in but stopped when Daniel commanded, "Wait, Jake! We'll be back soon. Stay!"

The store was spacious, especially in the eyes of Amy, who had never seen such a large store before. Of course, it was nothing to compare to Walmart for Tommy, Emily, and Daniel, but Amy thought it was four times as large as her brother's trading post back home.

The store was divided up into sections. First, an area was set up for canned foods, spices, and the like. Another was set up for housewares like pots, pans, and dishes. Then, there was an area for clothing. Amy's eyes lit up when she saw all the lovely dresses and undergarments displayed on racks. Bolts of colorful fabric were piled up on tables. Spools of thread and lace were hung on the wall.

An older lady approached them as they entered the store. "May I help you find something, ladies?"

Emily said, "We'd like to look at some fabrics, please."

"Why certainly," replied the lady.

She was short and plump, wearing a homemade tan cotton dress. She fought through the store, her hips bumping the display tables as she waddled through the aisles.

A short, balding man approached Daniel and Tommy and asked if he could help them find something.

Daniel replied, "Do you know anyone in town who sells windows?"

The clerk replied, "Yes, there's a store just on the left as you travel east of here. Morris' Doors and Windows."

Daniel then asked, "How about a blacksmith?"

"Yessir! Farther down and on the right you'll find Jake Brown's Smithy."

Daniel replied, "Great! Thanks for your help. Do you sell grain?"

"No sir, I can help you with flour and sugar and other dry goods, but you should check with the livery stable at the end of the street for grain. It's not too far past Brown's Smithy."

Daniel thanked the man again, then said the ladies would order any dry goods they needed. I'll be back to pay after a while."

"Very good, sir!" the clerk responded as Tommy and Daniel headed for the door.

Jake was happy to see them as they exited the store. He panted a happy greeting and wagged his tail. Tommy and Daniel turned east as they walked through town, leaving their horses tied near the wagon. Just a short walk down the street, they found the window shop. The two men entered the store, once again leaving Jake outside.

Daniel guessed that a young woman about twenty-six years old greeted them as they entered. "Hello, gentlemen! How may I help you?"

Daniel asked, "Do you have any ready made windows or do you only build to order?"

The lady answered, "Yes, we have windows already made. What size do you need?"

Daniel replied, "Well, I'd say about twenty-four inches squared."

"And how many will you be needing?"

Daniel looked at Tommy and asked, "How many windows do you want for your cabin?"

Tommy thought momentarily and replied, "Well, I guess maybe two? Would that be too many?"

Daniel smiled at Tommy and said, "Not at all!"

Daniel looked back to the young lady and remarked, "He'll need two and I'm going to need four."

Young Mrs. Morris smiled and said, "That will be fine. Let me show you what we have."

She took them to the back of the showroom, where many windows were displayed. Some were ornate and shaped decoratively, while others were built more for functionality.

"These windows are probably suitable for your needs," she said. "They are just the size you requested."

Daniel asked, "How much are they?

She replied, "These windows are only seven dollars each."

The young clerk half expected Daniel to balk at the extravagant price. She saw these two men dressed in buckskin frontier clothing and assumed they could not afford her windows.

Instead, Daniel smiled as he heard the price of the windows. He looked at Tommy, who returned his smile. They both were thinking the same thing. Windows back home in their time would have cost them at least one hundred dollars apiece.

Daniel looked back to Mrs. Morris and said, "That will be fine."

He noticed the look on her face as he agreed to her price. He then reached into a pouch tied to his belt and counted forty-two dollars in gold coins.

"We'll be back later to collect the windows." Daniel replied. He tipped his hat to her and exited the store.

Their next stop was the smithy. Jake Brown was hammering something against an anvil, shaping it into whatever form he desired. Daniel and Tommy watched for a while without speaking as the smithy swung his hammer repeatedly, shaping the piece of hot metal.

Daniel couldn't help but think of the poem by Henry Wadsworth Longfellow. *"Under the spreading chestnut tree, the village smithy stands; The smith a mighty man is he, with large and sinewy hands..."*

Brown then plunged the metal into a bucket of water to cool the metal. Steam rose from the bucket as the water cooled the hot metal. He then looked up at his visitors and said, "Howdy! What can I do fer you gents?"

Daniel replied, "I'm planning on building a mill back at my farm and I need some millstone dressing tools. Do you have any already made?"

Brown replied, "You mean small picks and shaping tools to carve your millstones?"

"Exactly!" replied Daniel.

"No, sir. I can't rightly say I do. But, I can make you some. When do ya need um?"

Daniel answered, "Well, I'd like to get them today. Can you make them right away?"

Brown said, "Well, I've got this other job I'm working on right now so . . ."

"I'll pay extra if you can get it done today!"

Brown thought for a moment, then said, "Alright. I'll get you a set made today. It'll take me about four hours, though. And, it'll cost you fifteen dollars for the set."

Daniel smiled and replied, "Thanks, Mr. Brown. I'll be back later on today."

Tommy and Daniel left the smithy and walked down to the livery. An older man of about sixty-five met them as they entered the stables. He had a long grey beard stained from tobacco juice that had dripped from his mouth while chewing.

"Howdy, gents! The name's Baxter. Isaiah Baxter. What can I do fer ya?"

Daniel replied, "I'm Daniel Lane and this is my partner Tommy Brown. We need to buy some grain and were told you might have some for sale."

Baxter replied, "Well sir, that depends. What kind of grain and how much do you want?"

Daniel said, "I'd like to get about four hundred pounds of oats and six hundred pounds of wheat if you've go it?"

"Yeah, I can sell you that much. So, a thousand pounds of grain at five cents a pound will run you fifty dollars. Can you pay that?"

"Yes sir, Mr. Baxter. We can."

Baxter then asked, "How ya gonna haul it?"

Daniel said, "We've got a wagon waiting down the street a ways. We'll drive it down here to pick up the grain after a while.

"Alrighty then. I'll be here when you're ready."

Baxter shook their hands, and the two of them walked back up the street to meet the women. When they arrived at the dry goods store, they found Emily and Amy had loaded up on fabric for dresses, skirts, and curtains for the cabins. They had also stocked up on canned goods, flour, sugar, and coffee. When Daniel went to the counter to pay, he asked the clerk, "Do you happen to have any nails?"

"Yes, sir," replied the clerk. How many ya need?"

Daniel said, "How about a small keg?"

"No problem. I'll fix you right up."

He added the price of the nails to the total he had already figured for all the other items the ladies had bought. Then he looked to Daniel and said, "That brings your total to twenty-five dollars and forty-two cents."

Daniel paid the man in gold and asked, "Is there a decent restaurant nearby where we can get some lunch?"

"Why don't you try Burke's. They have real good food and they're real clean too. A little pricey for my taste, but they say the food's the best in town. You'll find them about a block over from the courthouse. Just head west till you see the courthouse, then turn left."

"Thanks!" Daniel said. "Can you get our items loaded into the wagon out front while we have lunch?"

"Absolutely!" said the clerk. "We'll get you all loaded up."

The four friends walked to the restaurant and opened the door to find a beautifully decorated establishment with crystal chandeliers hanging from the ceilings and red carpets on the floors. Half the tables were empty of customers, so they had no trouble finding a place to sit. They enjoyed a delicious meal of roasted chicken, sweet potatoes, steamed vegetables, and yeast rolls that nearly melted in their mouths. For dessert, they had the most decadent chocolate cake any of them had ever eaten.

When they finished their meal, they returned to the dry goods store and collected the wagon already loaded with all its contents. They drove the wagon up the street to pick up the windows from Morris', then down to the livery to load up the grain.

Finally, they stopped at the smithy's on the way back through to see if he had finished the millstone carving tools. As Daniel walked into the shop, Mr. Brown finished the last pick. Brown showed Daniel the tools he had shaped for him. Four small picks of various sizes and shapes would be ideal for carving the tiny trenches needed to grind the grain at his new mill. Daniel's face lit up when he saw the tools. He was excited to see the excellent craftsmanship Mr. Brown had displayed.

The sun was beginning to lower itself behind the tall hills on the western side of Nashville. The group started their little caravan back to the vacant lot behind the post office. Daniel again took out the scepter and presented it in front of them. The scepter began to vibrate once more as the Shimmering opened up again, allowing them to travel instantly back home to the Water Valley.

They arrived in front of Amy and Tommy's cabin, where they dismounted and said goodbye to the Lanes. Emily drove the wagon back to their cabin while Daniel held Alyson in his arms, riding atop the Sorrel.

When they reached their cabin, Emily stepped down from the wagon and took Alyson inside while Daniel tended to the horses and the mules.

They then settled in for the evening for a light supper while warming themselves by the fireplace.

Daniel heard a cry from outside the cabin about an hour after supper. Jake let out a "*woof*" in response.

"Daniel! Emily! Come quick!"

Daniel opened the cabin door and found Amy crying as she stepped onto the porch.

"It's Tommy! He's awful sick! Emily, you've got to come help him."

Emily stepped onto the porch and asked Amy, "What's wrong with him?"

Amy responded through tears, "He's sweatin' somethin' fierce and his belly hurts so bad that he's moanin'. He says he feels like he's gonna throw up his guts."

CHAPTER 18

Emily grabbed her medical bag and darted through the cabin door. Amy followed behind as best she could while the two moved quickly down the trail to Amy's cabin. Daniel bundled up Alyson, grabbed the quiver with the scepter, and followed behind when he could.

Ten minutes later, Emily and Amy entered the cabin and found Tommy lying on the bed, writhing in pain. Emily asked him, "Tommy, tell me what's wrong."

Through his pain, Tommy managed to utter, "My belly. It hurts something awful. I think I might have got food poisoning from that fancy restaurant."

Emily replied, "That's not likely. It takes more than a few hours for food poisoning to show up. Have you ever had any surgery?"

Tommy replied, "I had my tonsils out when I was a kid. But, that's all."

Emily had him lie back on the bed as she began pressing around his abdomen. "Where exactly is the pain located?"

Tommy said, "Right around my belly button."

Daniel entered the cabin carrying Alyson. When Alyson saw Tommy in so much pain, she began to cry. Daniel bounced her up and down slightly, trying to soothe her. Emily turned around and saw them enter the cabin. With widened eyes, she looked at Daniel and said, "I think it's his appendix."

Daniel asked, "Can you do anything for him?"

Emily replied, "It will need to be removed if it hasn't already ruptured. But, unfortunately, I can't do that kind of surgery. It's too dangerous. We've got to get him to a hospital."

Daniel pondered and asked, "Nashville?"

Emily shook her head and said, "No, we've got to get him to my old hospital, in Columbia."

Daniel realized what she meant. He would need to take Tommy through the Shimmering and get him to a hospital in the 21st Century. "I'll take him." he responded. "We'll need a few things though. Get Tommy's old clothes on him and make sure he has his wallet with his identification. I'll be right back."

Daniel stepped outside, pulled the scepter from the quiver, and opened the Shimmering. He walked through the portal and found himself back at his cabin. He raced into the cabin and quickly changed his clothes, wearing his old blue jeans and T-shirt. Next, Daniel looked through his saddlebags, found his wallet and cell phone, and took them. Finally, he put on his old windbreaker and headed out the door.

Moments later, Daniel entered Tommy's cabin and found that Tommy was also dressed in his old clothing. Daniel helped Tommy out of the cabin into the front yard, where he used the scepter to open up the Shimmering again. Daniel looked back at Emily and Amy and said, "We'll be back soon."

Amy anxiously asked, "Can I come, too?"

When Daniel was interrupted by Emily, who said, "Yes. Take Amy with you. She needs to be there."

Daniel nodded his acceptance and waited for Amy to join them before entering the portal.

A familiar blast of cold air entered their bodies as they traveled through time. Daniel took them into the future to 2020. They walked through and found themselves standing in the back parking lot of Maury General Hospital in Columbia. The same hospital where Emily had worked as a nurse for many years. With Tommy leaning against him for support, Daniel led Tommy and Amy through the parking lot to the emergency department entrance. Amy looked around at everything as she was led to the entrance. She wondered at the large wagon-like things lined up side by side in the blackened hard field behind the hospital. Amy watched more wagons quickly travel down a blackened trail in the distance. She had never seen anything move so fast. It was nighttime, but the whole area around them was lit with lanterns, making it look like daytime.

As they entered the automatic doors, Amy timidly walked through, half expecting the doors to close upon her before she could make it through. But instead, Daniel walked up to the receptionist's desk and said, "Excuse me. I think my friend here might be having trouble with his appendix."

The receptionist looked up and handed Daniel a clipboard with several sheets of paper. "Have a seat and fill these out. Someone will be with you as soon as possible."

Daniel knew what that meant. They could sit in the waiting room for hours before anyone calls them back. So Daniel took the clipboard and found a place for them all to sit. He lay the clipboard on a chair next to Tommy and said, "Hang on a minute. I'll be right back."

Daniel walked outside again and found a deserted place in the back of the building. He stretched out the scepter and opened up the Shimmering again. Daniel found himself standing at the back of Walmart when he walked through. He walked into the store and back to the electronics department. There, Daniel looked for a charging cable for his cell phone. He purchased the cable and then hooked it up to his phone. He found an outlet where he could charge the phone and waited until he could get about fifty percent charge on his phone. He knew that the phone probably would no longer have service, but he also knew it would still dial 911.

Daniel left the store and used the Shimmering again to return to the hospital. He went back inside and found Tommy and Amy still waiting. "Come on," he said.

They followed him back outside into the parking lot. Daniel opened the Shimmering again and returned them to the Walmart parking lot. Daniel took out the cell phone and dialed 911.

"911 dispatch, what is your emergency?" a voice said.

Daniel replied, "Yes, I'm at Walmart just outside in the parking lot. My friend is in pain and needs an ambulance."

"Can you give me your name, please?"

Daniel replied, "Daniel. Look, I talked to my wife. She's a nurse and she said it sounds like he may have a ruptured appendix. We need an ambulance right away."

The voice on the other end stated, "Yes, Sir. I've got an ambulance heading your way. Can you tell me your friend's name?"

"Tommy. It's Tommy Brown."

"And, how old is Mr. Brown?"

Daniel answered, "He's in his thirties. I don't know exactly."

Suddenly, Daniel heard the siren of the ambulance calling in the distance. Amy began to look around, searching for the source of the strange screaming she was hearing.

Daniel said into the phone, "The ambulance is here. Thanks!" He hung up the phone without waiting for a reply.

Daniel waved down the ambulance as it approached the store entrance. The vehicle stopped in front of them, and two EMTs got out of the van. One of them opened the back of the van and began collecting gear. The other approached Tommy and began triage to discover Tommy's symptoms. Daniel interrupted, saying, "I spoke with my wife, who is a nurse. She said it sounded like his appendix."

After taking Tommy's vital signs, the EMTs loaded him into the ambulance to take him to the hospital.

Daniel said, "This is his wife. Can she ride with him?"

"Sure." said the driver. "Hop in."

Amy climbed into the back of the ambulance and sat next to Tommy.

The EMT riding with her in the back asked, "How far along are you?"

Amy, confused, asked, "Pardon?"

"Your baby. When are you due?"

Amy replied, "Oh! In about a month."

"Well, try to relax. We don't want that baby coming too early. We'll take good care of your husband."

Ten minutes later, the ambulance pulled into the emergency loading area. The attendants unloaded Tommy from the back of the van and began wheeling him into the hospital, with Amy following. One of the EMTs noticed Daniel standing at the entrance door. While doing a double-take, he asked, "How'd you get here so fast?"

Daniel responded, "I know a short cut."

They wheeled Tommy into one of the examining rooms while Daniel and Amy followed. First, a nurse took Tommy's vital signs and had Amy fill out paperwork. Daniel helped her with the paperwork, using information from Tommy's wallet. Next, a physician's assistant came in to examine Tommy, poking his belly and asking him questions. The young P.A. said, "I think it's your appendix. But, I want to get an X-ray and a C.T. Scan to make sure. Someone will be down from radiology to get you in just a moment."

Amy noticed a panel high on the wall in Tommy's examination room. There were pictures of people moving on a screen. She looked at Daniel and asked, "What's that?"

Daniel replied, "It's a television."

Then Amy asked, "What's if for?"

Daniel said, "Mostly for entertainment. Have you ever seen a stage play or musicians performing in a theater?"

Amy replied, "I've heard about it. I've never seen it though."

"Well, it's the same thing, except you can watch it right from your home. You can also get the news instead of reading a newspaper."

Amy asked, "Does everybody have one?"

Daniel smiled and replied, "Most people have two or three."

"Why so many?" Amy asked.

"Well, they have one in their parlor and most people have one in their bedroom. Some even have one in the bathroom." Daniel replied.

"What's a bathroom?" asked Amy.

"It's an indoor privy. It has a toilet like an outhouse, a sink to wash your hands, and a bathtub."

Amy's head was spinning over the thought of such indulgence. "How convenient! But doesn't it kind of smell having the privy inside your house?"

"Not at all." said Daniel. "There is a special plumbing system that eliminates that. Come on. I'll show you."

Daniel took Amy by the hand and led her into the hallway. He asked a nurse at the desk, "Excuse me. Could you please tell us where the ladies' room is?"

The nurse pointed down the hallway and said, "Down there and to your right."

"Thanks!" said Daniel as he led Amy down the hallway.

They turned the corner and found a door on the right, with a placard reading "Women."

Daniel said, "Go on in there and check it out. When you are finished come back down to Tommy's room. I'll be waiting for you there."

Amy timidly pushed the door open and peeked inside. She was amazed at how clean everything seemed to be. She softly walked around the room, looking at the fixtures. Four compartments looked like horse stalls. She went up to one and pushed on the door. She couldn't believe what she saw. There was a big white ceramic pot standing on the floor. On top of the pot was a big horseshoe-looking thing. She gently lifted the horseshoe and then set it back down. When she turned to leave the stall, a loud noise made her jump and scream as the toilet automatically flushed.

When Amy left the stall, she saw a woman coming out of one of the other stalls. The woman walked over to the washbasin. She pumped a handle mounted on the wall, and a foamy substance came out into her hand. Amy watched as the woman twirled the foam in her hands repeatedly, then stuck her hand under a silver nozzle. Water came out of the nozzle. As the woman continued to rinse the soap from her hands, Amy decided to try it. She stuck her hand under the pump handle, but nothing happened. Finally, she bent down and looked under the pump but couldn't figure out how to make it work. The woman noticed Amy having trouble and also noticed Amy's garb.

"Haven't you ever seen one of these?" the woman asked.

Amy replied, "No ma'am. We have an outhouse where I live."

Curiously, the woman asked, "Are you Amish?"

Amy said, "No ma'am. I'm Baptist."

The woman chuckled and then showed Amy how to wash her hands in the modern sink. She then showed her how to dry her hands by holding them under a machine that hung on the wall and made an awful racket.

The warm air blown onto Amy's wet hands felt good. She lingered a little longer than she needed to. When the woman left, Amy followed her out of the restroom and went back to Tommy's room.

When she got to the room, she found Tommy was missing. "Where's Tommy?" Amy questioned Daniel.

Daniel replied, "They've taken him up to X-ray. He'll be back in a moment."

"Whats's X-ray?" she asked.

Daniel instructed, "They take a picture of the inside of your body. They can tell from the pictures if something is wrong with you like a broken bone or in Tommy's case, if there's something else wrong."

"Does it hurt?"

"No. Not at all." Daniel replied.

An orderly pushed Tommy's bed back into the room and said, "Someone will be down to tell you the results soon."

Thirty minutes later, a doctor came into the room. He said, "Mr. Brown, I'm Doctor Williams. I'm the surgeon who will be performing your surgery. You do have a problem with your appendix but, luckily you got here before it ruptured. We'll set you up for surgery tomorrow morning. In the meantime, We'll get you into a room and get you on an I. V. with some pain medication to help you feel better. Do you have any questions?"

"No, Sir. I recon that sounds purdy good."

"Alright then," said the doctor. "I'll see you in the morning."

Chapter 19

Early the following day, a nurse came in and prepared Tommy for his surgery. When she had finished hooking him up to new wires and tubes, she told Amy and Daniel, "The surgery shouldn't take more than an hour or two plus time in recovery. This would be a good time for you to go get some breakfast."

Daniel said, "That sounds good."

Luckily, Daniel still had money in his wallet from when he initially got lost on the Trace. It would be enough for them to eat for a few days if they were careful. Daniel and Amy took the elevator downstairs and left the hospital's front entrance. Things were bustling outside. Traffic was high as people traveled to work, and others entered the hospital for various procedures. It was too congested for them to open up a portal in plain sight for traveling. The weather was chilly, but Daniel felt there was no other way to travel than to walk.

They set out together, heading east to a strip of highway where several restaurants were operating. Amy asked, "Where are we going?"

Daniel replied, "I thought we might have breakfast at Waffle House."

Amy asked, "What is a Waffle House?"

"It's a restaurant that serves breakfast. I think you'll like it."

They walked for a mile. The air was cold as it gathered in their lungs, but the sun was out, so the walk wasn't so bad. When they reached the restaurant's parking lot, Daniel saw it was about half full of cars and trucks.

There was only one booth available when they walked in, so they quickly sat down before someone else came in and grabbed it away from them. The jukebox was playing some hip-hop tune that Daniel had never heard of.

An older lady approached them from behind the counter and greeted them. "What can I get you to drink?"

Daniel said, "Black coffee."

Amy looked at Daniel and questioningly replied, "Coffee?"

Daniel nodded his head approvingly.

"You folks know what you want to eat?"

Daniel asked Amy, "How hungry are you?"

Amy replied, "I'm pretty hungry."

Daniel looked at the server and said, "We'll have two Allstar breakfasts. Cook the waffles well done. Hash browns. Eggs over medium."

The server asked, "You want anything on your hash browns?"

Daniel told Amy, "You can get toppings added to your hash browns like onions, tomatoes, mushrooms . . ."

"Tomatoes!" Amy exclaimed. "And mushrooms!"

The server asked, "You want bacon, sausage or ham?"

Daniel responded, "Bacon, crispy."

"Alright, we'll have that right out for you," the server replied. Then she turned to the cooks and yelled, "Ordering, drop two bacon crispy, two dark waffles, two over medium plates, one scattered, diced, and capped."

It seemed only minutes before the server presented their coffee, with their breakfast plates following closely behind.

"Oh, my word!" exclaimed Amy. "All this is for me?"

Daniel smiled and said, "Well, you are eating for two. And, I don't know when we'll get another chance to eat."

"What is this thing?" Amy asked.

"That is a waffle. Its taste a lot like a flap jack, but it's crispy. Put a little syrup on it. It's good."

The two enjoyed their breakfast without saying much other than Amy's occasional "Mmm" as she savored the newly discovered cuisine.

A familiar face looked over at Daniel from the bar. Daniel had worked at the post office with Roger Gentry, a rural carrier. Daniel nodded his head to Roger in recognition but continued eating breakfast. They all managed to finish their breakfast at the same time. When Daniel went to the cash register to pay for their meal, Roger got up to do the same.

"Long time no see!" Roger said as he stuck out his hand to shake Daniel's.

Daniel shook his hand and replied, "How's it going, Roger?"

"Oh, not bad. I'm retired now."

Daniel replied, "Really? That's great! I bet you're glad to be away from that place."

Roger said, "Yeah, I'm really enjoying myself. Who's this?"

"Oh, Roger this is Amy Brown. Her husband and I are business partners. He's having surgery this morning so we came down here to grab some breakfast."

"Nice to meet you, Mrs. Brown."

Amy nodded without saying anything.

Roger then asked, "What kind of business?"

Daniel replied, "We've got a heritage farm over in Water Valley."

"Heritage, huh? You mean you finally did it? What was it you were always saying 'bout a simpler life?"

Daniel proudly replied, "I'm living a simpler life and living it to the fullest."

Roger said, "So you went and did it. No car? No tractor? Living off the grid?"

Daniel replied, "That's right."

After Roger paid his bill, he asked, "Well, can I drop you off somewhere? Or, are you against riding in a car?"

"No." replied Daniel. "We're not against it. We would appreciate a ride to the hospital if you don't mind."

"Sure thing."

They all piled into Roger's car. Daniel sat in front while Amy rode in the backseat. Amy was nervously excited to be inside one of the machines she had seen traveling so fast down the black hardtop road. Roger's radio was playing music from a classic rock station in Nashville. Amy recognized the song immediately.

"I know this song!" she exclaimed. "Gus use to sing it all the time!"

Amy sang along as "No More Mr. Nice Guy" by Alice Cooper played across the airwaves.

They pulled up in front of the hospital. Before they exited the car, Roger asked Daniel, "Do you have a phone?"

Daniel replied, "Yeah, right here."

Roger said, "Here take my number and give me a call if you need anything. I live right here in town so it's no trouble for me to come if you need a ride or anything."

"Thanks, Roger," said Daniel. "I may just do that."

Amy and Daniel got out of the car and entered the hospital. They took the elevator to the fifth floor back to Tommy's room. Unfortunately, Tommy had not arrived yet, so they waited in his room for his return.

It was nearly an hour before they returned Tommy to his room. Then, finally, a nurse came in with him and gave them a report of all that had happened.

"Everything went well. There wasn't any rupture so there's a low chance for infection. The surgery was done laparoscopically so it won't take too long for him to heal. He should be able to return to work in about six weeks. No heavy lifting or overexertion until then. He'll need to come back to see Dr. Williams for a follow up visit. We want to keep him overnight just to make sure he's alright before he goes home."

After the nurse left the room, Daniel asked Tommy, "How are you feeling?"

Tommy replied, "I'm real tired right now."

Daniel said, "Well get as much sleep as you can. Once you've rested we'll get you out of here and back home."

Tommy said, "You mean without them discharging me?"

"Yep!" said Daniel. "They can't keep you here if they can't find you."

When lunchtime rolled around, Tommy was still sleeping. Daniel asked Amy, "Are you hungry?"

She replied, "I could eat."

Daniel pulled out his cell phone and made a call. "I need one with everything delivered to the front entrance of the hospital. The name is Lane. Thanks!"

Thirty minutes later, Daniel went down to the entrance and met a driver delivering Daniel's order. Daniel paid and tipped the driver, then went back upstairs. When he entered the room, Amy's eyes lit up. "Mmm, what's that smell?"

Daniel replied, "This is what's known as pizza."

Daniel opened the flat box containing the pie and showed Amy how it had been cut into slices. Amy took a piece and bit into it. "Mmm! That's the best-tasting thing I've ever had."

A few minutes later, Tommy awoke to the smell of hot pizza.

"Hey, can I get a piece of that?" he asked.

Daniel said, "I'm not so sure you should. How about we take off some of the toppings? Peppers and onions and pepperoni might not be a good idea for you right now."

Tommy took a bite from the slice of naked pizza and savored it slowly in his mouth.

"Oh, I've missed that," he said. "All I need now is a nice cold beer."

They all three sat and enjoyed their pizza while reruns of NCIS played on the television. Tommy fell back to sleep after eating his one slice. Daniel and Amy had no trouble finishing up the rest of the pizza.

Tommy awoke a little after 4:00 pm when the nurse checked on him. She checked his blood pressure and oxygen level and seemed satisfied that Tommy was doing well. "You're looking good. You should be out of here sometime tomorrow morning."

Tommy, Amy, and Daniel looked at her and smiled without saying anything. As soon as she walked out, Daniel asked, "Are you ready?"

Both Amy and Tommy nodded as Tommy began trying to extricate himself from the bed. Amy helped him put on his jeans and shirt while Daniel kept a lookout at the door. The hallway outside the room was empty, so Daniel motioned for them to follow. Daniel wasn't sure how or if the Shimmering would work inside, but he was willing to try it. He took the scepter from its sheath and held it out, rotating it counterclockwise. The gateway opened up inside the hallway just as it had any time they were outside. The three of them walked through, and the portal closed just as a janitor came walking into the hallway. The janitor began rubbing his eyes, unsure of what he had just witnessed.

With the help of Amy and Daniel, Tommy walked out of the portal into the front yard of his cabin. "What time is it?" he asked.

"I took us back to 9:00 this morning." said Daniel. "I didn't want Emily to worry about us too long."

Amy said, "Let's get you inside and into bed."

Once they got Tommy into bed, Daniel left the young couple and headed home. Emily and Alyson were sitting on the cabin's front porch while Jake lay in the front yard under the warm sunlight. Emily asked, "How did it go?" when Daniel reached the house.

Daniel replied, "He's fine. It was his appendix."

Emily asked, "Did they take it out?"

Daniel replied, "Well, technically he's still in surgery. I cheated on the time a little. But, he's at home resting. We snuck out when no one was looking."

Emily asked, "Are you hungry?"

"No. We had pizza just a little while ago."

"Ooh! That's sounds so good," Emily said. "Did you bring me any?"

"Sorry, but no. I can go back and get you some if you like."

Emily responded, "No, I'm just glad you're all back home."

CHAPTER 20

The sun rose early in the eastern sky of the Water Valley. Daniel awoke as its beams showed through the newly installed windows of their cabin. For the past two weeks, he worked installing the windows in both their and Tommy's cabins. Tommy tried to help as much as possible, although his recent surgery didn't allow him to participate much more than holding a window in place while Daniel nailed it down.

Today would be different. Emily had cleared Tommy for full duty as long as he didn't overexert himself. Tommy and Daniel planned to begin plowing the seventy-five-acre field to plant corn by the middle of April. Emily would help, too. She was as good at driving the mules as anyone. Two mules and two plows would make the work go twice as fast. Emily and Tommy would take turns driving Rusty through the intended planting site, while Daniel would drive Pepper.

Daniel led the way, plowing the first row. The turning plow easily moved the dirt aside, creating a trench. The soil moved easier this year, having been plowed once before the previous year. Tommy drove Rusty alongside the row that Daniel and Pepper had just plowed. Once they reached the end of the field, they turned the mules back to return, cutting a new trench beside the ones they had just made. When they reached the original end of the field, Emily switched places with Tommy. She drove Rusty through the field effortlessly while carrying Alyson on her back in a sling Daniel had made for her with leather from a deer hide.

Tommy and Emily continued taking turns at the plow until just before noon. Then, Emily returned to the cabin and began preparing lunch for them all. She found Amy had already started slicing bread for sandwiches. They fried bacon and cooked beans to go along with the bacon sandwiches.

Tommy and Daniel unhitched the mules after making another round trip in the plowing. They released the mules back into the corral to eat with the horses. When the men reached the cabin, they found that lunch had already been set out for them.

While they ate, Daniel began to talk. "You know, I've been thinking about how we might make our corn field better this year."

"How's that!" asked Tommy.

Daniel answered, "What we need is a harrow."

Amy asked, "What's a harrow?"

Daniel explained, "It's a piece of equipment we could hook up behind the mules that will continue to cut the earth that the plows have already churned up. We won't have to deal with such large clods of dirt when we start planting. It won't take us anytime to row up the field for planting."

Tommy asked, "Do they have such a thing yet?"

"No, but we can get the blacksmith to make us up a bunch of tines that we can attach to some cross beams. We'll join the beams together so that they lay one behind the other. And, we'll stagger the tines so that they cut about eight inches apart from each other."

Emily asked, "How long will it take to make a harrow?"

Daniel replied, "Time isn't really an issue, is it? I'll draw up something after we finish plowing the field, then take it to the blacksmith. He won't know what it's for so we won't have to worry about infringing on someone's invention in history."

After lunch, Daniel, Emily, and Tommy returned to the field to finish plowing. Once again, Emily and Tommy took turns driving Rusty through the rows of turned dirt. The mules made quick work of it and plowed the whole field before dusk the next day.

The threesome returned to the cabin for supper and found that Amy had everything prepared: deer stew made with carrots and potatoes served with cornbread. The stew was delicious and filled their bellies, so they could barely move away from the table.

Emily and Amy began clearing the table while Tommy sat with Daniel and discussed the design of the new harrow they planned to build. Daniel took a piece of scrap leather, about six inches wide by eight inches long, and used a piece of charcoal from the fireplace to draw out the shape of one of the tines. He drew a figure that looked like a large "question mark." It would be shaped from a flat piece of steel about two inches wide. The curved end of the question mark would be shaped to a point like an arrowhead, and the flat end would have two holes cut in it so that it could be bolted to a beam.

Daniel asked, "What do you think? We can space them about eight inches apart on a beam, then the next beam the tines will fill in the gaps of the previous beam. We'll have four beams in all tied together so the beams won't roll when pulled through the dirt."

Tommy replied, "Sounds like you got it all figured out. I think it'll work jest fine."

"Great!" said Daniel. "I'll take it to Nashville tomorrow and get the smithy started on it."

Once Emily and Amy finished cleaning up the supper dishes, Tommy and Amy decided to return to their cabin. They said goodbye to the Lanes and proceeded out the cabin door. Emily stood on the porch holding Alyson as she watched the Browns leave when suddenly Amy cried out.

"Ooh! Emily! I think my water just broke!"

"Emily turned to Daniel and instructed him, "Go light the lanterns in the hospital. Start a fire and boil some water."

Then she called out to Tommy and said, "Tommy, take Amy into the hospital."

Tommy and Daniel did as Emily instructed them. First, Tommy got Amy into the hospital, then Emily pushed him out of the room, handing him Alyson as he left.

Emily told Amy, "Get that skirt and your bloomers off and get under that blanket."

Amy quickly undressed before Daniel came back into the room.

Emily said, "Now, lets have a look."

She raised the blanket to examine Amy and said, "You haven't dilated much. Are you having any contractions?"

Amy replied, "No, I don't think so . . . ooh! That hurt! Awe!"

Emily said, "It's okay! Just breathe! In through your nose and out through your mouth. Breathe!"

Amy continued to breathe as Emily had instructed until the pain finally subsided. Then, when Emily turned to check on the men, she found both Tommy and Daniel dumbfounded behind her.

"Alright, you two. This may take a while. There's no sense in you just standing there. Tommy, you look like you're about to fall over. Take that bed over there and get some rest. I'll let you know when it's time. Daniel, take Alyson into the cabin and rock her to sleep. Then you go to bed too. If I need either one of you, I'll come and get you."

Again, the men did as they had been instructed. Fortunately, they were both dead tired anyway, and there wasn't anything either one could do to help.

Tommy awoke to the sound of a baby crying. He lazily sat up in bed, wiping his eyes. It took him a minute to get his bearings. Then, he finally remembered that Amy was having their baby. Tommy suddenly jumped out of bed to check on his wife. He found her sitting up in the other bed across from his. She was holding their new baby. Amy smiled at him and said, "Good morning, Papa. Come and meet your new son."

Tommy's head began to spin. He could hardly believe he had a new son. He was a father. He had never thought that he would become a father. He had resigned himself to being a bachelor his entire life, until he met Amy. If Amy hadn't been so forward with her intentions with him, he probably would still be a bachelor.

Tommy asked, "What are we gonna name him?"

Amy replied, "Well, all of my brothers have Bible names. We could name him Jeremiah, Matthew, Mark . . ."

"How 'bout Noah?" replied Tommy. "Noah was good with animals and he was good at building stuff."

Amy smiled at Tommy's suggestion. "Noah. I like that! Noah Brown!"

Tommy corrected Amy, "Noah Gordon Brown."

Amy's face lit up, and tears came to her eyes when she heard her husband name their son in honor of her family. Emily's eyes began to water as well. It was like watching her little brother grow up right before her eyes. Although they weren't related, Tommy and Emily had made a special connection with one another when they first met.

Emily met Tommy when she went looking for Daniel. Tommy, along with Ranger Matthew Douglas, was a park ranger for the Natchez Trace Parkway who helped Emily search for Daniel when he went missing. Emily made a special connection almost immediately with Tommy. Tommy insisted on accompanying her when she decided to come through the Shimmering to find Daniel.

Daniel softly knocked on the door to the hospital and slowly opened it, waiting for permission to enter.

"Come on in!" Emily called out.

Daniel entered the hospital, holding Alyson in his arms. "I take it everything went well?"

Emily said, "Amy did great! It was the easiest delivery I've ever seen. I didn't even need to be here. She could have done it all by herself."

Amy retorted, "Don't let her fool you Daniel. It hurt like hel . . . heck! Pardon my French."

They all laughed at Amy's apology.

Daniel broke up the party when he said, "Well, I need to get busy. There's lots to do around here."

Emily asked, "Whatcha got planned for today?"

"I'm going to get started on building a harrow so we can break up the corn field a little better. So, I think I'll make a trip to Nashville and get my tines built. Then I want to scout around and see if I can find some rocks big enough to carve out a couple of millstones. But first, I've got to get the chores done."

Emily said, "I'll make breakfast for us all while you're doing the chores."

⸺◆⸺

After breakfast, Daniel saddled Hoss and prepared for the quick trip to Nashville. He took Jake with him but told Tommy to stay behind and rest. Daniel took the scepter from its quiver and held it out in front of him. The scepter began to vibrate as a portal opened up. Daniel rode his horse through, with Jake following behind.

They instantly arrived in Nashville, just behind the post office, as they had before. Daniel turned Hoss toward the street that led down to the Brown's Blacksmith Shop. When Daniel arrived at the smithy, he found Mr. Brown banging out horseshoes.

"Good Morning, Mr. Brown!"

The smithy looked up and saw a familiar face. "Well, Mr. Lane isn't it? Good to see you again. What can I do for you today?"

Daniel replied, "I've got a special project I need help with."

Daniel pulled the drawing from the inside of his buckskin shirt and handed it to Brown.

"What is it?" asked the smithy.

Daniel replied, "It's called a tine. I'm making a contraption to help me break up the soil in my corn field better. I'm going to mount them onto the underside of some heavy beams and pull them behind my mules to break up the ground and make it easier to hoe the rows."

Brown studied the drawing and said, "Hmm. I've never heard of such, but it might work. How big do you want them?"

Daniel said, "I think the straight part should be about six inches long. The rounded part should be about eight inches long before you make it into a semi-circle. The straight part needs to have two holes so I can attach them to a beam with lag bolts."

Brown thought for a minute, then said, "Do you need me to make the lag bolts too?"

Daniel replied, "Yessir, that would be great."

"When do you need them and how many of each?" asked Mr. Brown.

Daniel answered, "Two weeks? And I'll need thirty of the tines and sixty lag bolts."

Brown did some figuring in his head, then stated, "How does thirty dollars sound?"

Daniel said, "Sounds fine. Pay you half now?"

"Yessir, that works for me."

Daniel paid the smithy and then left, walking Hoss behind him with Jake following behind. When they got to the open field behind the post office, Daniel once again stretched out the scepter and made the Shimmering appear. They walked through and instantly found themselves back home in front of the cabin.

CHAPTER 21

Daniel was on a mission. He needed to find two large stones that he could carve into millstones. Daniel didn't think it would be that difficult. The Water Valley was full of limestone outcroppings, so it shouldn't have taken long to find what he needed. However, finding the right size wasn't as easy as he initially thought. Finding two of the right size was twice as difficult.

He and Tommy searched throughout the valley, combing the ridges high above the valley. They rode as far away as Leiper's Creek before finding what they had been searching for. Two large slates of limestone lay at the creek's bank, where they had been pushed out of the ground by years of erosion. One was reasonably rectangular, about four feet wide and six feet long. The other was closer to the shape Daniel had hoped for, being neither quite a circle nor a square. Both rocks were pretty thick, about twelve inches at their deepest point. They would be ideal for what Daniel had in mind.

Daniel and Tommy rode their horses back through the valley for about two miles until they were back at the corral. They harnessed the mules and brought extra ropes back to where their chosen stones rested. They wrapped the stones in rope and then attached them to each mule's harness.

Daniel had concerns that the rocks might be more than either mule could handle alone. He feared they might have to make two trips, hooking both mules up to one stone at a time. However, Rusty and Pepper proved even stronger than Daniel had realized. They hitched Rusty to the larger of the two stones while Pepper dragged the smaller one. Neither mule showed signs of difficulty moving the heavy boulders across the ground.

Daniel drove Rusty while Tommy drove Pepper. They guided the mules along the bank of Beaver Branch down through the Water Valley. The mules pulled the stones for two miles without showing any signs of struggle. They pulled past Tommy's cabin, continuing down the branch's bank, eventually passing Daniel's cabin. They pulled to the Duck River that intersected Beaver Branch. Daniel shifted their direction left as they reached the Duck, following its banks until they nearly reached the valley's edge.

They unhitched the mules and led them back to the corral, loosing them to join the horses. Daniel and Tommy gathered the tools they needed to shape the huge rocks into millstones and headed back to the site Daniel had selected for the mill to stand.

They began by laying out the size they wanted each stone to be. After measuring both stones using a length of rawhide, Daniel decided on a diameter of about three and a half feet. Many mills used millstones twice that size, but three and a half feet would suffice for their needs.

They drew an outline on each of the stones as a guide for where they would cut away the unwanted rock to form the desired circles. Next, Daniel attached a stick to one end of the rawhide and had Tommy hold it at the center of a stone, while Daniel attached a piece of charcoal to the other end and drew a circle around the edge of the boulder, outlining a near-perfect circle. Once their outlines were drawn on both stones, they worked together, chipping away at the edge of the rocks, moving slowly to the shape they had drawn on each one. It was tedious work. Their hands began to ache from holding a stone chisel in one hand and swinging a heavy hammer in the other, constantly striking the

chisel and occasionally the hand that held it.

After four days of chipping away at the edge of the stones, Daniel and Tommy were satisfied with the results of their labor. However, they were nowhere near being done. First, the tops of the stones would need flattening. A hole was also required to be drilled in the middle of each stone. Finally, the top stone also required an additional opening to act as a hopper for grain to be poured into to be ground between the two millstones.

They asked Emily to help with this phase of the wheel construction. Her job would be to pour water onto the stones as Tommy and Daniel drilled the needed holes into the middle of each stone. The water would hopefully help to keep the rocks from cracking and splitting apart while the drilling occurred. Drilling the holes was a two-man job. They took turns holding the star drill while the other hit the drill with a heavy hammer. Each time the hammer hit the star bit, it was twisted and turned on the stone, eventually creating a hole. After the hole was driven through, Daniel and Tommy used their stone chisels to square up the holes so that a large wooden peg could be driven through. This would secure the stones into place.

Once Tommy and Daniel had finished the center holes in both stones, an additional hole had to be cut into the top stone. This hole would be much larger and act as a hopper for the grain to fall between the two millstones for grinding. After three weeks, they had shaped the stones and built a structure around them to house the mill while in operation. However, they weren't finished. The stones were still not flat on the surface, and grooves would need to be cut to channel the grain away from the middle of the stones to collect the meal.

While pondering how they might get the stones to have the desired smooth surface, Tommy commented, "What we need is a bunch of sandpaper."

That gave Daniel an idea: "*We don't have sandpaper, but we have plenty of sand. We can haul up sand from the edge of the river, dry it out, and then pour it into the hopper while the stones are turning. It will take a while, but the sand will eventually grind the millstones down to the flat surfaces we need.*"

They spent the rest of the day hauling buckets full of sand up to the site from the river's edge so it could dry out. The next day, they brought the mules up to the mill site and hooked Rusty up to the arm that extended away from the top millstone. Daniel pushed Rusty forward, driving him around the mill, causing the topstone to turn while the bottom millstone remained stationary. Tommy poured small amounts of sand into the hopper at the top stone's top, allowing it to fall between the two large stone wheels. When the sand fell through the hopper and emptied it, Tommy poured in more.

After an hour, Daniel switched out the mules, hitching up Pepper so Rusty could rest a spell. They continued this routine for three days until Daniel was satisfied that the stones were smooth enough to lay face to face without bumps or ripples. However, they still weren't finished. They dismantled the millstones and drew out a pattern on each. This pattern would be carved using the newly made mill tools Daniel purchased from Nashville. They were precision carving tools used to cut small trenches on the surface of each stone. These trenches would fit together on each millstone, so the ground corn or wheat would move away from the stones and into a collection vessel to be scooped out and stored in sacks.

Daniel and Tommy used various tools to carve out the needed trenches on the stones. Some tools made very narrow trenches, while others made larger grooves. However, none of the channels was more than a quarter of an inch wide. The channels made wavy lines like snakes on the surfaces of the stones. They radiated from the center of the stones to the outer edges, so the ground meal was moved away from the center.

Two more days of carving stone brought them to an end. After a month of continuous work on their project, they were ready to try it. They hauled corn from the crib using the wagon. They had to shell the corn before running it through the mill. Since they didn't have a corn sheller, they had to remove the kernels of dried corn from the cobs by hand. The chickens immensely enjoyed this. They stood nearby, snatching up every seed that missed the bucket and fell to the ground while the men twisted the ears of dried corn between their hands.

Once they had shelled what they thought to be ten pounds of corn, they started the mill, pushing Rusty forward in circles, moving the millstone just as it had been designed. Both Emily and Amy arrived to check out the maiden voyage of the mill. They stood by while Daniel poured corn into the hopper. The dried corn slowly dropped through the hopper, moving between the heavy stones. It wasn't long before powder began falling from the edges of the millstones into the collection tray under the edge of the stones. Everyone smiled as they watched the meal pile up on the tray. When Daniel stopped Rusty, they collected the meal from the tray and placed it in an old flour sack. Ten pounds of corn had produced one pound of cornmeal. They all celebrated, cheering and laughing. The mill could be an essential source of income for them. He also knew the best way to get the word out about the mill would be through Dolly Gordon.

❖

Daniel decided it was finally time to give Amy something she had wished for a few months back. She wanted to go back to Gordon Place to see her family, and now was the perfect time for it. Young Noah Gordon Brown was four weeks old and had never met his grandmother.

The Lanes and Browns gathered near the corral to begin the short journey to Amy's old home. They mounted their horses and stood by while Daniel opened up the Shimmering. Finally, along with Jake, they all went through the portal and found themselves on the trail just outside the edges of Dolly Gordon's home site. They walked their horses to the brick house where Amy's mother and family resided.

Dolly ran out of the house to greet them all. "Oh, what a surprise this is! It's so good to see you all! Step down and let me get a look at these children!"

They all dismounted, and Dolly stepped forward to hug Amy. "Oh, Amy! This baby is precious. Is it a boy or girl?"

Amy replied, "Granny, meet your grandson. This is Noah Gordon Brown."

Dolly cried tears of joy when she met young Noah. She took him from Amy's arms and held him in her own. She then realized she hadn't spoken to the others. "Oh, how are you, Tommy?"

"I'm jest fine, Dolly. It's good to see you."

"Oh, and Emily! Who do you have, here?"

Emily replied, "This is Alyson Catherine Lane."

Dolly remarked, "Well she's just as beautiful as can be! Hey Daniel! You alright?"

Daniel replied, "I'm doing well."

Dolly commanded, "Well, y'all all come on in. We'll have some refreshments."

Two of Dolly's men came over, collected their horses, and put them in the corral as everyone followed Dolly into the house. As they all sat in the parlor, Amy asked her mother, "Is Lucy back yet?"

"Oh, no. She's still in Nashville lookin' for a husband. Last I heard from her, she had her eyes set on a young officer in the Tennessee Militia. I still haven't heard anything about a wedding, though. How long can y'all stay?"

Emily spoke up and replied, "Well, Daniel and I can only stay for the day, We'll need to get back early tomorrow so Daniel can take care of the livestock. But, Tommy and Amy can stay as long as they like."

Amy said, "Well, we were thinking of staying for a few days if that's alright."

Dolly replied, "As far as I'm concerned, you can stay from now on. You're gonna have a hard time getting this precious little boy away from me!"

⸺◦○◦⸺

After lunch, everyone settled in, going their separate ways. Tommy and Amy walked up to the trading post to see John Jr. and Susan, while Daniel and Emily walked around the farm just enjoying the early spring weather and each other. Then, they walked over to the ferry to say hello to whoever was running it. When they arrived at the river, they found Mark and Luke; the Gordon twins were running the ferry. When Daniel reached the brothers, he asked, "What happened to your help?"

"Hey, Daniel!" they both said.

Then Luke said, "Awe, they run off. Guess this job wasn't stimulating enough for them. They headed toward Nashville to make their fortune."

Emily and Daniel lingered for a while, making small talk with the twins, then walked back toward the house. As they entered the clearing where the house lay, riders approached from the Southeastern trail. Ten Chickasaw braves rode up to Daniel and stopped. The man in the lead raised his hand, greeting Daniel, and said, "Hallito, Hoh-pah-e!"

"Hallito, Thomas!" replied Daniel.

Thomas Colbert was David Colbert's brother and Chief William's nephew.

"What brings you here, my brother?" Daniel asked.

Thomas spoke, "I bring a message from the three chiefs of the Chickasaw. They say it is time for Hoh-pah-e to meet the clans of our people."

Daniel asked, "Will you ride with me?"

Thomas replied, "No. We must guard your valley and Shobohli Eho while you are gone."

Daniel asked, "Where should I go to meet the clans?"

Thomas said, "Chief William's clan is near the place we call Rattlesnake Falls. Do you know this place?"

"I Do," replied Daniel.

Daniel recognized the falls' name as a former name for the waterfalls near Summertown, Tennessee, more recently known as Stillhouse Hollow Falls.

Thomas instructed, "Ride to the falls. Someone will meet you there and take you to the village."

CHAPTER 22

Emily packed her and Alyson's gear and then went outside, where her horse was waiting. Daniel helped her pack her horse and then said goodbye to Emily and Alyson. "Don't worry," He said, whispering in her ear. "I'll be home before supper."

Emily's eyes widened with understanding. She realized that even though Daniel's journey might take several days, he could return to her as if it were only a day. So, Emily mounted her horse with Alyson hanging on her back in the sling, then followed

Thomas and his braves down the trail to the Water Valley. There was no hurry. All that awaited her was feeding and caring for livestock. So, Thomas led them at a slow pace down the trail.

Daniel collected his horse from the corral, then mounted him and began riding toward the ferry. About halfway, he stopped and pulled out the scepter. Holding the scepter straight out, Daniel conjured the Shimmering to appear before him. He concentrated on the location of Rattlesnake Falls. He and Emily had been there a couple of times. It was on their way whenever they visited Emily's grandfather in Lawrenceburg. It was situated just off the highway. A small makeshift parking area rested at the top of the ridge that overlooked the waterfall. A trail wound through the forest and down the hill, leading to the waterfall's top and base. The one-mile trek down to the falls was made more accessible by boardwalks placed strategically in some more challenging terrain.

Daniel chose a spot at the bottom of the falls near a tiny creek that spilled away from a small pool at the base of the falls. He had no idea where Chief William's men would meet him, but he felt they could find him easily enough. The portal brought him through just in front of the pool. He checked the ground before dismounting because he wasn't interested in stepping onto a rattlesnake nest. Even though the weather was still relatively mild, he knew they didn't call this place Rattlesnake Falls without reason.

He finally dismounted, walked over to the pool, bent down, and drank from it. The water was cold, clear, and tasted sweet. Hoss and Jake helped themselves to the water while Daniel wandered around the pool, exploring. He noticed the pool was even smaller than the last time he and Emily had seen it. Time and erosion would wallow out the pool to make it more extensive in the coming years. Daniel meandered around for a couple of hours before someone finally showed. Two Chickasaw braves rode into the area. Daniel had seen them before but did not know their names. They both seemed to be about Daniel's age. The first was extremely well built and wore a look on his face that made Daniel believe he shouldn't overlook him as a mighty warrior. The other man was slightly built but just as capable in battle in Daniel's eyes.

The first man asked, "Are you Hoh-pah-e?"

Daniel replied, "I am Hoh-pah-e. What is your name?"

"I am Bearnard Colbert, son of Chief William. This is my brother, Brody. Our father has sent us to meet you. We will take you to our village."

Daniel replied, "Thank you. I look forward to meeting the people."

Daniel mounted and followed the braves as they led him west through the hills. The terrain was rough, with limestone outcroppings blocking them seemingly no matter which direction they traveled. They rode slowly up and down hills, winding through trees and wading through numerous small streams.

After two hours of riding, they topped a hill hiding a vast open space surrounded by hills, rocks, and streams. The valley was so large it put his Water Valley to shame. Permanent lodges were standing throughout the land, with one standing on top of a massive mound in the middle of all the others. Horses were running wild through the fields and wading through the streams. Children played together without a care. Women were working together, performing various tasks for the clan. Daniel's heart rose into his throat. This experience is what he had longed for his whole life. Books, movies, and replica villages were set up as tourist attractions; none of them sufficiently described what he was now experiencing.

Daniel followed Bearnard and Brody into the village, where they led him to the center, where Chief William resided. Willam walked out of his lodge and greeted Daniel.

"Hallito, Hoh-pah-e! It is good to see you."

Daniel dismounted his horse, walked over to William, and extended his hand, "Hallito, Great Chief! I am happy to be here."

William invited Daniel, saying, "Come, let us sit by the fire and eat together. We will speak of what we will do for the next days."

Several animal hide rugs were spread onto the ground near a fire where a stew was cooking. William pointed to what appeared to be a bearskin rug and invited Daniel to sit. William sat beside Daniel on another rug, and many men joined them around the fire. Women brought gourd bowls filled with stew for each of the men to eat. Daniel tasted the stew. It was delicious, made from meat he had never tasted before. He asked William, "What kind of stew is this?"

William replied, "Bear."

Daniel raised his eyebrows and said, "Wow! This is really good."

William smiled and nodded his head in agreement.

The two men exchanged conversations throughout the night, but mostly, they watched what the villagers were involved in. Many were singing and dancing around the fire. Some of the younger men and older boys played a game similar to Lacrosse. Women were constantly bringing Daniel something new to eat or to drink. He thoroughly enjoyed himself.

When the celebration finally ended, Daniel was escorted into a smaller hut so he could sleep. Blankets and animal skins were spread out on the ground. Daniel was so tired that he dropped to the ground on the soft hides and closed his eyes, ready for sleep. Jake joined him and lay next to Daniel. Heavy rain fell during the night. Daniel was so grateful that he and Jake had a dry place to sleep.

When morning broke, Daniel extracted himself from the comfortable bed. He walked out of the lodge and found many people preparing for travel. William walked over to where Daniel was standing and asked, "Did you sleep well, Hoh-pah-e?"

Daniel replied, "I did! Thank you for providing me a dry place to lay my head."

Then Daniel asked, "What will we do today?"

William replied, "We will travel today. We will go to meet the other clans at the home of my brother, George. Levi's clan will meet us there, too."

Daniel asked, "How long will it take us to get there?"

"It is nearly a day's ride to the great river that divides my land from his. We will wait there for George's ferry to take us across the river."

Daniel suggested, "I can get us all there faster, and we won't have to wait on the ferry."

William asked, "Do you know a shorter trail?"

Daniel answered, "Ittola Chuka."

The Chief raised his eyebrows in surprise. "You can go to another place through Ittola Chuka?"

"I can," replied Daniel. "I can travel from one time to another, or from one place to another. I can even travel to another time and another place at the same moment. As long as I can picture the place in my mind, I can travel there. Would you like to try it?"

William asked, "How can you take us to George's Stand? Have you been there?"

"I have. Many times during my time. My wife and I have traveled many places and seen many things."

William thought, then said, "I would like to try this. We will travel through Ittlola Chuka."

"Great!" replied Daniel. "When all the people are ready, I will take us through."

Once all the people had gathered together to begin their journey, Daniel stretched out the scepter to open up Ittola Chuka. The shimmering portal opened up before their eyes. Many of the people had never seen Ittola Chuka. Most had only heard stories about it. Daniel rode through the portal while Jake followed. Chief William and his warriors followed closely behind, and then all the other travelers walked through. A cold sensation entered their bodies as they walked through. Daniel heard the oohs and ahs behind him coming from the people. Once Daniel passed through, he stood by the portal, holding it open with his mind until everyone finished passing through.

The people were amazed once they came through to find that they were all standing in the middle of Chief George's Stand. George's clan, too, marveled how the people of William's clan had passed through Ittola Chuka. Then, the people all greeted one another and talked about the magic of Ittola Chuka.

Daniel, too, marveled. But not of the Shimmering. It was the stand itself that impressed him. The times that Daniel and Emily had traveled to Chief George's Stand, it no longer existed. Instead, there was an old plaque with a picture of how someone had imagined George's house to look. The house was indeed something to behold. It was like a plantation home, not an Indian village. Although George was a fundamentalist when it came to the ways of his people and the Black Hand, He was also quite the capitalist. His plantation spread out over thousands of acres. The land was more suitable for crops than his brother William's. George had fifteen hundred slaves at his disposal to work the fields where corn, tobacco, and cotton were grown. It was all awe-inspiring.

All the people settled in, waiting for Levi's clan to arrive. Levi also operated a stand that was only about five miles away. However, it was nowhere near as impressive as George's. They waited for two hours before someone finally spotted the approach of Levi's people traveling down the trail. Levi was quite surprised to see William's clan had already arrived. Typically, Levi would be waiting for his older brother because William lived so far away. When Levi approached William to greet him, he asked, "How did you get here so soon? I usually am waiting for you to arrive."

William explained, "Hoh-pah-e brought us here through Ittola Chuka."

Levi was shocked when he asked, "Daniel Lane has done this? He is truly Hoh-pah-e! He has been chosen by the one true creator!"

Everyone settled in for the festivities. They talked and visited with one another, eating and celebrating with each other. Finally, the chiefs gathered together and called the people to sit and listen.

Levi raised his hand to quiet the people, then began to speak.

We are honored to be here today. Our people have wandered without direction for many years because we did not have Hoh-pah-e to guide us. The one true creator could not find a man worthy of being called

Hoh-pah-e. Our father, James Colbert, did not believe in the one true creator. He did not believe in Hoh-pah-e. But he taught us how to survive and live alongside the white man. He taught us to farm and trade with the white man and fight side by side with the white man. But, now, the one true creator has delivered a white man to the Chickasaw people to be the next Hoh-pah-e. Daniel Lane is Nafkl to the Chickasaw! He is Hoh-pah-e!"

All the people cheered when Levi had finished.

George then spoke. "For many years, we have searched for the next Hoh-pah-e. My braves, Ilbuk Losa, have protected our lands and ways from the white man. We did not trust this white man who came into our midst. He was strange to us. Even odder than any other white man because he is not of our time. My son David Colbert has told me this. Daniel Lane is from a time not of our own. He has seen and done many things none of us ever will. He has traveled to places and times we will never see. But, since he entered our world, he and his woman have been a friend to the Chickasaw. He is a man of honor who we can trust to lead us. My son David told me this, and I saw it with my own eyes. Daniel Lane is Hoh-pah-e!

Again, the people raised their voices and cheered.

Finally, Chief William rose to speak.

"When I met Daniel Lane, he brought his woman to heal me. I was near death when she came. Our medicine men could not heal me, but she did. Daniel Lane is a man of compassion, not only for the Chickasaw but for all men. He is a brave man who came to the aid of David Colbert and his woman when other white men attacked and tried to kill them. Daniel Lane and David stood side by side and killed the white men who wanted to harm them. I believe that Daniel Lane will be a protector of all Chickasaw. He is an honest man who will judge our people well. Daniel Lane is Hoh-pah-e!

Again, the people stood and cheered even louder. They were pleased to finally have the one who had been missing from their people for decades and even centuries.

William once again raised his hands to quiet the people.

"When I was a boy, my mother's grandfather told me of Hoh-pah-e. Grandfather told stories of the places and things that Hoh-pah-e had witnessed. He told our chiefs about things that will happen in the years to come that are disturbing to not only the Chickasaw but other nations of the people as well. Daniel Lane has come to us from a time many years from now. He has witnessed what will become of our people. I ask that he now speak to us and tell what will become of the Chickasaw people."

Daniel's countenance turned low. He dreaded giving these people news that their time would be short-lived as a nation of people. Finally, he stood up and began to speak very somberly.

"People of the Chickasaw nation! I am truly honored that you have selected me to serve as Hoh-pah-e for the people. Allow me to say that I will serve you with a pure heart. I will never lie to you. If I don't know what to do, I will say I don't know. I have traveled here from very far away. Almost three years ago I traveled here through Ittola Chuka accidentally from two-hundreds years in the future. Your world will change greatly in the next two-hundred years. I am afraid the news I have for you is not good news."

The people moaned in wonder.

"For many years, the white man has come to this land from Europe across the great ocean of the Atlantic. Even your father, James Colbert, came from Scotland to find a new home in this land. And, even though he befriended the Chickasaw and taught them to farm and trade with the white man, he couldn't know what effect the white man would have on the Chickasaw people by their coming here. The Chickasaw have many white friends. Probably the greatest of these is David Crockett. Crockett will be a friend to the Chickasaw for years to come. But he will not be able to save you.

Last year, a treaty was signed between the Cherokee and the white men. The treaty is to pay five million dollars to the Cherokee to relocate from their homes to a place many miles west of here. Unfortunately, that treaty will not be honored. A few years from now, White soldiers will begin evicting the people of the Cherokee, Creek, Choctaw, Seminole, and other nations out of their homes. And yes, the Chickasaw will be forced out, too!"

The people began to shout and cry as they heard these words, but the chiefs remained stoic. They had already heard this news from their mother's grandfather many years ago. Daniel only verified what William, George, and Levi already knew.

Many cried out, "What must we do?"

Daniel beckoned the crowd to settle down, then spoke again.

"I'm afraid there is little you can do. I am sorry to deliver this news to you, but I said I would never lie to you. To fight against it would be useless. The white man has weapons which you cannot stand against. More and more of the whites come into this land every year and they will take away from you whatever they can. My advice is that you listen to your leaders and follow them. Many of you will die before all of this comes to pass, but many of you will experience the shame, the heartbreak, sickness, starvation and suffering like you have never known before."

Daniel shrugged as if he didn't know what else to say. Then, finally, he turned to the chiefs and said, "I'm sorry!"

William and his brothers consoled Daniel, saying, "We already suspected this. We just needed you to verify it."

Daniel asked, "What will you do now that the people know?"

William answered, "We will go on living as best we can."

Chapter 23

Daniel spent a week judging the clans of the Chickasaw Nation. Many disputes among the people had been unsettled. Although the chiefs had the authority to decide on the conflicts, they had chosen to curtail their people's disagreements until Daniel could come and decide on these matters. The chiefs knew Daniel would be unbiased in his decisions.

Daniel spent at least two days with each clan, listening to each case brought before him. Most were simple disagreements concerning family squabbles. Jealousy was prevalent among the clans. Land disputes were among the most challenging issues that Daniel was asked to judge. Most of these arguments occur in Chief George's clan. William and Levi's clans existed in a more communal presence. At the same time, George's clan was more about who could have the most. The most land, the most slaves, the most wives, and anything else.

Judging the people grew tiring for Daniel. Although he enjoyed spending time with these indigenous people, he longed to return home with his family. So when the week finally ended, Daniel paid his respects to each chief and bid them farewell.

Daniel opened the Shimmering, rotating his scepter counterclockwise, and then passed through. Daniel, Jake, and Hoss suddenly stood in front of his cabin. The same day, he had said goodbye to Emily and Alyson. Jake was happy to be home. He loped around the yard, barking and panting with delight. Emily, hearing Jake, walked out of the cabin and saw her husband standing before her. She ran out to meet Daniel, and they embraced.

Emily said, "I know it has only been a few hours since I saw you, but for some reason it seems much longer. How long have you been gone?"

Daniel replied, "Over a week. I think it was actually nine days."

Emily asked, "Can I get you anything?"

"No thanks! I just want to get back to doing what I want to do."

Emily suggested, "Why don't you take a day off. Let's go on a picnic. Maybe do some fishing."

Daniel replied, "Oh, that sounds good."

Daniel led Hoss back to the corral and unsaddled him, then released him into the pasture with the other horses. He then walked back to meet Emily, who had already packed a picnic supper and waited for him. They walked over to the bank of the Duck, where Emily spread out a quilt for them to rest. Daniel set Alyson down on the blanket and lay next to her. He sighed, a great sound of relief. Thoughts of the previous days were rushing through his mind. He felt guilty about the information he had expounded upon before the Chickasaw. Did he do the right thing? Should he have lied to them? He tried to imagine how they must have felt hearing of their nation's plight and how the lives they had known would soon disappear.

Daniel relayed to Emily all that had occurred during his absence from her. He had told Emily he had not been prepared for the question presented to him by the chiefs concerning their demise. He hadn't known that information about their imminent expulsion had been passed down to them by the previous prophet so many years ago.

Then Daniel said, "Something else occurred to me while I was gone."

Emily asked, "What is it?"

"When I took Tommy to the hospital in Columbia, things were pretty much like we had left them before we traveled here. Gus said that some how we had changed the timeline. He said that when he traveled through the Shimmering to go back home, he ended up in a place where slavery still existed. But I saw no evidence of that when I took Tommy and Amy through."

Emily asked, "So, why do you think that is?"

"I wonder if Gus might have discovered a portal leading to another dimension rather than traveling through the timeline. It doesn't make sense that our traveling through the Shimmering would cause the timeline to change. Your letter to yourself proves that we were supposed to find the Shimmering and travel through it. So somehow, Gus must have just stumbled into a parallel dimension of our world."

Emily replied, "That makes sense. So we don't need to repair the timeline, after all."

"Probably not," said Daniel. "However, I would like to do some checking around to make sure things go as we expect them to. But for now, I just want to fish."

A week passed quickly as Daniel and Emily enjoyed their time together on their homestead with only Alyson, Jake, and all the livestock to keep them company. Daniel decided one day to begin work on the new harrow. He selected two tall, straight Ash trees to cut down in the valley. Swinging the ax against the bulk of the conifer giants felt good to him. He felt alive and powerful as the ax made a "pop" each time it connected with the tree's base.

Emily hitched the fallen trees one at a time to Pepper's harness and hauled them back toward the corral so Daniel could cut them into beams. He first cut the trees into eight-foot lengths and peeled the bark. Then, using wedges, he split away the edges of the logs to square them off, creating eight-inch squared beams. Daniel used an adz to smooth off the edges of the beams to make them as square as possible. He also carved out two eight-foot-long planks that would join the beams together and smaller planks that he would use as a platform to stand on while driving the harrow.

Once all the lumber had been cut out, Daniel began constructing the harrow using the tines Mr. Brown had made. First, Daniel used a bit and brace to start holes into the beams, then used the lag screws to attach the tines to the beams. Once all the tines were attached, he joined the beams using the eight-foot planks. Daniel attached each plank to what would be the outer edge of the harrow and nailed them to each of the beams, spreading the beams two feet apart. Next, he nailed the smaller planks to the two middle beams to create a platform for standing. Lastly, Daniel installed eye screws on the front edge of the first beam to attach the mules' harnesses.

Daniel brought the mules out and harnessed them so he could try out his new harrow. First, he used the mules to flip the harrow onto its back. Daniel then hitched both mules to the eye screws on the front of the harrow and had the mules pull it into the field where they had plowed. Again, he used the mules to flip the harrow back over, then hitched them to the front again. Finally, Daniel stood on the platform and commanded, "Git up!"

The mules moved through the plowed dirt, dragging the harrow forward. The cultivated soil broke apart into smaller clumps of earth as the harrow traveled down the rows. Daniel's ride was a little rough at first, but eventually, he found his balance. Daniel checked the soil, looking behind him as the harrow pulled through the field. He was very pleased with the result of his handy work. Emily came out to check Daniel's progress as he made a trip back in her direction.

"Looks good!" she said. "That should make hoeing the rows a lot easier."

"I'm not done," said Daniel. "After this, I think I can make a planter to row up the dirt instead of us having to hoe it up."

As they walked back to the cabin together, Daniel sighed and said, "Hew!"

Emily asked, "You alright?"

Daniel slightly smirked, "Yeah, I'm just playing alligator."

"Alligator?" Emily asked.

"Yeah. I'm draggin' my tail behind me."

When Daniel finished harrowing the field a few days later, Tommy and Amy returned from their visit. However, they weren't alone. Amy's brothers, Evan and James, were with them. Daniel and Emily walked out to greet them all as they crossed Beaver Branch back into the valley. Daniel invited them all up to the cabin to visit. As they settled down on the porch, Daniel asked, "What brings you two to our neck of the woods?"

Tommy interrupted and said, "Daniel, I told Dolly about our mill. I thought she might be able to send some business our way. After tellin' her 'bout it, she suggested a partnership. I told her I'd have to ask you first."

Daniel asked, "What kind of partnership?"

"Well, she said if we was willin', she would furnish the grain, the labor and the transportation, while we just furnished the facilities, meaning the mill, a wagon to haul grain, and a place for her boys to sleep. Evan and James will operate the mill and transport the meal to Nashville where it will be sold to one of Dolly's contacts. Then, we'll split the money from the sell of the meal fifty-fifty. What do ya think?"

Daniel replied, "I think that's a great idea. Emily, what do you think?"

Emily smiled and replied, "I like it. When can we get started?"

———◇———

April 14, 1820

Daniel, Emily, and Tommy had decided what needed to be done to get the mill up and running. Evan and James would be responsible for operating the mill and transporting goods concerning the mill. The Gordon boys would start by making a trip to Nashville using Emily's wagon to buy grain from Mr. Baxter at the livery stables. They then transported the grain back to the Water Valley to grind at the mill. Once the grain was turned into meal, they would bag it up and transport it to Nashville to sell to Mr. Quincey at the dry goods store. While in Nashville, they would pick up the next load of grain from the livery and start all over.

For now, Emily was willing to allow the Gordons to use her mules. However, she wanted draft horses to be purchased to take their place as soon as they could manage it. She wasn't comfortable with someone using her mules when she wasn't there to watch. Daniel promised Emily he would look into buying a pair of draft horses to replace Pepper and Rusty soon.

Evan and James were set up to sleep in the hospital whenever they were in the valley. The young men left on Friday the fourteenth to begin their first leg of the journey. It would take them two days to make a round trip to Nashville and back. They left at first light, heading toward the Gordon Farm. If at any time one of the boys was needed at their mother's farm, she would replace them with any of her other four sons.

Daniel made one of his quick trips to Nashville while the Gordon boys made their first trip. Daniel first met with Mr. Quincey at the dry goods store to negotiate a price for Quincey to buy their cornmeal and wheat flour. He then visited Mr. Baxter at the livery and worked out a deal for them to purchase grain regularly at a discounted price. Both men seemed very excited to make their deals with Daniel. Before leaving the livery, Daniel asked Mr. Baxter, "Do you know anyone around here wanting to sell a couple of good draft horses or mules?"

Mr. Baxter asked, "Sumpin' happen to those mules of yours?"

Daniel replied, "No, Sir. We just need the mules around the farm, so I'm looking for something to haul the grain and meal for us without using my wife's mules."

Baxter thought momentarily, then said, "Well, why don't you try the Hermitage on the northeast side of town? That's Andy Jackson's place. He's got all kinds of horses. Maybe they'd be willin' to sell some to ya."

Daniel was familiar enough with the location of the Hermitage. He had visited the home of Andrew Jackson many times as a boy. So, before opening up the Shimmering, Daniel thought of a location near the Hermitage on the east bank of the Cumberland River. He opened the portal using the scepter and traveled through, immediately arriving at his destination. From there, he rode along a trail leading to the Hermitage. Daniel thought about the Civil War battles at Ft. Donelson and Ft. Henry on his way down the trail. He had pondered that he needed to check out some of the more major battle sites in Tennessee, wondering if he could discover any clues about Gus's accusation about their changing the timeline. He decided that maybe Ft. Donelson, Ft. Henry and Shiloh would be good places to begin his search.

After an hour's ride down the trail, Daniel arrived at the Hermitage. He turned Hoss onto a path leading up to the house. The large mansion that housed the Jackson family was not much different from what Daniel had remembered from his childhood visits. Six massive Greek columns stood in front of the structure, each as tall and straight as a pine tree. Several log structures were scattered around the mansion, where people busied themselves with various duties. Finally, a well-dressed black man walked out of the house to greet Daniel.

"May I hep ya, Suh?"

Daniel remained on his mount and spoke to the man. "My name is Daniel Lane. I'm looking to buy some horses and was told there might be some for sale here. Can you tell me, please, who should I speak to about it?"

"That'd be Massah Jeffry. He be duh boss. If you ride yo hoss right back there to duh barn, he be dare."

Daniel thanked the man, then rode along the path leading to the barn. Daniel could see slaves tending to the plantation everywhere along the path. In the distance, he observed at least fifty slaves working in the fields, preparing them for planting. A burly man about Daniel's age met him outside the barn doors as he rode up to the barn.

"Good day, Sir!" Daniel said. "My name is Daniel Lane."

The large man responded, "My name is Jeffry Hannah. I manage the farm for the Jackson family. What can I do for you Mr. Lane?"

Daniel replied, "I was told in Nashville that you might have horses for sale here."

Jeffry asked, "What sort of horses are you looking for?"

"I need a couple of draft horses to pull a supply wagon."

"Hmm!" said Jeffry. "Well, we've got a few Belgians that might suit your needs. Won't you step down and I'll show them to you?"

Daniel dismounted and tied Hoss to a hitching rail outside the barn. Jeffry led Daniel and Jake through the barn hallway, which served as a stable for the more important of the Jackson livestock. As they walked through the barn, horses would poke their heads through their stall doors, which kept them penned. When Jeffry and Daniel reached the back entrance of the barn, they walked through a gate leading to a large corral where twenty large horses were scattered.

Jeffry instructed, "These are the Belgian mares. The studs are kept in a different pen. Do you have a preference?"

Daniel quickly thought about it. If he chose one stud and one mare, he could raise Belgians. He could breed two mares to a jack donkey and raise draft mules if he chose to. Then Daniel asked, "How much for the studs and how much for the mares?"

Jeffry replied, "A stud will cost you a hundred. Mares are fifty each."

Daniel knew his cash was beginning to run low. He needed to be careful with his purchases until the mill began to produce an income. He then asked, "Are any of the mares pregnant?"

Jeffry replied, "Yessir! They've all been bred within the last three weeks. I can't guarantee which ones are pregnant of course, but I know for a fact that they were bred. "

Daniel began walking among the herd as they nibbled on short clumps of grass scattered around the pen. Occasionally, he would walk up to a mare and rub her nose or the side of her neck to get close enough to check her teeth. He found three or four young mares to suit his needs.

"How old is that mare with the two front socks, there?"

Jeffry replied, "She's four years old."

Daniel asked, "Has she ever foaled?"

"Yessir! She had a pretty little colt last time."

Daniel walked through again and then pointed at another horse. "How about this one? Is she a filly?"

"Yessir! This is her first season."

Daniel walked back over to Jeffry, then said, "I'll take the four year old with two front socks and that filly. But, I want the right to bring them back and have them bred again next year if they turn out not to be pregnant this time."

Jeffry reached out his hand to seal the deal and said, "We can oblige you with that. I'll draw up a bill of sale and you can take your horses with you."

Daniel followed Jeffry into a small room in the barn that served as Jeffry's office. Jeffry pulled out a pen and paper and wrote a bill of sale for the two horses. Once the bill was signed and Daniel had paid him a hundred dollars, Jeffry led Daniel back out to the pen and had two slaves catch and halter the two horses Daniel had selected. Daniel met them at the front of the barn where Hoss was still tied. He shook Jeffry's hand and said, "It's been a pleasure, Mr. Hannah!"

Jeffry replied, "Thank you, Mr. Lane. Safe travels to you."

Daniel mounted Hoss and led the two Belgians away from the Hermitage plantation. Both the mare and filly towered over Daniel's barrel-chested bay stud. When he had reached a safe distance out of view of anyone, Daniel opened up the Shimmering and led the horses and Jake back through. He suddenly found himself walking through the Water Valley along the bank of the Beaver. When he reached his cabin, Emily and Alyson walked out the door and saw him approaching.

Emily admired the two Belgians as she moved closer. "Well, looks like you got a couple of nice mares."

Daniel replied, "That one is still a filly, but they're both supposed to be bred."

Emily smiled and said, "Looks like our herd just keeps getting bigger and bigger."

CHAPTER 24

D aniel awoke to a clap of thunder. He thought he had heard rain at night, but now it was falling in sheets. Rain like this always exposed the weaknesses in Daniel's craftsmanship. Slow drips began to fall from the roof as he and Emily watched from the safety of the bed. Jake, however, was not so lucky. One of the leaky spots found him as he lay on the floor. Jake whimpered, got up, and found a new spot under the table.

Daniel was in no hurry to begin the day with the rain falling as hard as it was. He chose to lie in bed a while longer and mull over his decisions over the past few days. One thing that bothered him was how readily Daniel had used the Shimmering for his convenience. He felt guilty about it. He had always wanted to live a simpler life, yet he was using the portal to avoid that simpler life whenever it suited him. Daniel decided there in bed that it would need to stop. He would only use the Shimmering for Chickasaw business or in case of a medical emergency, with one exception. He needed to discover whether or not they had changed the timeline by traveling through the Shimmering as Gus had conjectured. After his travel back to his century when Tommy needed surgery,

Daniel began questioning Gus's theory. He had seen no evidence of slavery still existing in the twenty-first century. However, he felt he needed to investigate further to be sure.

Daniel's mind moved to other matters. He thought of the Gordon boys, who were undoubtedly traveling in this horrid weather. Daniel hoped that the canvas top of Emily's wagon would hold up and keep the grain dry as they traveled along the trail. If the grain were to get too wet, it would be useless to them. It would most likely mold and be unfit for man or livestock.

Emily finally stirred from her sleep as Alyson woke, ready for her morning feeding. She and Daniel got out of bed and dressed to begin their day. As Emily prepared breakfast, Daniel donned the canvas raincoat Emily had made for him. He collected his hat and stepped out into the rain. Daniel turned just before closing the door to see if Jake was following. He wasn't. Jake was dry and determined to stay that way as long as possible.

The rain didn't appear to be letting up anytime soon. Regardless, Daniel needed to check the livestock and gather the eggs and milk. It was part of the lifestyle that he and Emily had chosen. Sometimes, life could be difficult, but today's rain was more inconvenient than a hardship. Things seemed to slow down on days like this. There was more time for reflection, with no need to hurry to finish a job better suited for a dryer day.

Daniel checked on the horse pens and found the horses huddled under trees scattered throughout the enclosure. When they saw Daniel approach, they waited to see if he would add fresh hay to the racks for them to eat. Unfortunately, the spring grass was already growing and plentiful enough for the horses, so Daniel did not put hay in the stands. They would have to browse the pasture instead.

Daniel then walked to the hog pens and found them all content to root around in the mud, searching for roots and nuts. They looked up when Daniel walked by, then returned to poking their noses into the fresh mud.

When Daniel approached the goat pen, he found them huddled under the shelter, trying to stay dry. They called out to Daniel in unison, "Maah!" as he walked closer. He opened the gate to the shed and walked in, pushing against the huddled masses of goats. Some of the goats stood up on their hind legs, with their front legs resting on Daniel for support. Daniel worked his way slowly through the pen, finally reaching his destination. He separated one of the does from the other goats and put her on the milking stanchion. He washed the mud from her teats, then stroked them, releasing the milk in her bag. Daniel found milking to be relaxing, almost therapeutic. The rhythmic sound of the milk hitting the pail wiped his mind's problems away.

When Daniel had finished milking, he placed a wooden plate over the mouth of the bucket to keep the rain out of the milk. He then exited the goat pen and walked over to the chicken coop. When he walked into the coop, he found many hens foraging for food in the muddy soil. Occasionally, one of them would find an earthworm that had surfaced to the top, trying to avoid the overly soaked ground. Once spotted, several hens would fight over the small wiggling creature until it was torn into several smaller sections and devoured.

Daniel searched through the nesting boxes and collected the morning's eggs. He placed fourteen fresh eggs into the pockets of his canvas coat, then exited the coop. The rain was still falling tremendously as he walked back to the cabin. Daniel stepped up to the door and was surprised when Emily opened the door for him.

"Saw you coming through the window." she said.

"Thanks!" said Daniel as he handed her the milk pail.

They both walked back into the cabin, where Emily set the milk on the table, and then Daniel unloaded his pockets full of eggs.

"Breakfast is ready," said Emily.

They both sat down to enjoy their meal together. Emily asked, "Whatcha thinkin' about?"

Daniel replied, "Lot's of things. The rain, the Shimmering, the mill. My mind is all over the place this morning."

Emily suggested, "Maybe you need a day off. You can't do much today, anyway. Just relax and let your mind go."

Daniel smiled at her, nodded, then said, "Sounds good."

⸻ ◆ ⸻

The rain finally subsided around mid-afternoon. Daniel sat on his front porch stool, whittling on a stick. He wasn't carving anything in particular. Daniel was passing the time while deep in thought. It was nice to relax for a change, but Daniel found it difficult to relax with all he had on his mind. The stress began to wear on him. He finally concluded that he could only solve one problem at a time. He needed to prioritize things in order of importance. The rain had stopped, so that was one thing he didn't have to deal with. However, the ground was so soaked he couldn't get any planting done until it dried out some. The Gordon boys would handle most of the mill duties, so he didn't need to concern himself with that. The Shimmering was his most important task right now. He needed to settle his mind about whether or not they had changed the timeline. Daniel decided to explore the Civil War battlegrounds to verify that nothing had changed to cause the South to win the war.

Just as he had decided what to do next, Evan and James Gordon drove across the Beaver Branch and up to Daniel's cabin. Daniel asked, "How'd it go?"

James spoke, "No problems other than the rain. I think the grain is in good shape, though. We covered it with an extra tarp to keep out the moisture."

"Good!" said Daniel. "Let's get it unloaded."

Daniel followed the wagon as Evan drove it back to the mill. The three of them unloaded the grain into the mill house and covered it again with the tarp in case it rained again. Daniel opened one of the sacks and asked, "Wheat?"

Evan replied, "Yeah. We talked to Mr. Quincey and he said they needed more flour than anything else. For some reason they haven't been able to keep up with the demand for flour."

James said, "Alright if we start milling in the morning?"

Daniel replied, "That's fine with me. By the way, we bought some new draft horses for you to use. Emily is pretty particular about her mules. So, I went to Nashville and bought some Belgians."

Evan asked, "How'd you get over there and back before us?"

Daniel replied, "I took a short cut by way of Leipers Creek and I traveled quickly. I bought a mare and a filly from the Hermitage."

Evan asked, "Did ya see Andy while you were there?

Daniel said, "No, I just dealt with the stock manager.

General Jackson wasn't there."

Daniel led the Gordon boys to the corral, where the Belgians mingled with the other horses. The mare and the filly towered over the other horses in the pen. Daniel had them put the mules back in the pen with the other animals. Rusty and Pepper kicked up their heels as they ran into the field to join the horses. When they noticed the two Belgians, Rusty and Pepper, curiously and cautiously approached them. The mules quickly discovered they were no longer the largest ducks in the pond. The Belgians were just as large and powerful as the mules.

Once satisfied that the animals would be okay, Daniel and the Gordons returned to the cabin. Emily had supper waiting on the table as they entered the cabin. Evan and James made themselves at home, helping themselves with the chicken and dumplings, green beans, and cornbread Emily had prepared. Jake walked over and lay his head on Evan's leg, hoping to gain some sympathy and a nibble of the chicken and dumplings. Evan rubbed Jake's head but never offered Jake anything to eat.

After supper, the Gordons retired to the hospital, where they found their beds made and waiting for them. They shucked off their boots and plopped down on their beds without undressing. They were so tired from the day's events that they quickly fell asleep.

Daniel abruptly woke during the night to the sound of horse whinnies. Daniel leaped out of bed and quickly dressed. He grabbed his rifle as he and Jake ran out the door. The Gordons were quickly on Daniel's heels as he ran toward the corral. They found the horses and mules running in circles away from something when they reached the pens. Emily soon joined the trio, running toward the corral, wearing Alyson on her back.

Suddenly, a woman screamed a blood-curdling scream. Only, it wasn't a woman. Daniel saw it in the dim light of the moon. A mountain lion was chasing the horses and mules around in circles. The men scattered throughout the pen, trying to herd the livestock away from the cougar. The animals ran toward the corral near where Emily was waiting. She held up her hands to slow the horses down, returning them to the next corner of the lot.

Another scream was heard, but this time, it was the scream of a man. Emily searched the area to her left. She saw Evan on the ground with the cougar on top of him, biting and scratching viciously at Evan's outstretched arm. Emily quickly scanned the pen, looking for Daniel, but he was not visible in the low light. She then turned and grabbed a bucket, and dipped it in the water trough next to the gate. She ran toward Evan and the cougar and doused them with the water. The cougar once again screamed and ran away. Emily then saw Daniel to her right and called out to him. "Daniel! Shoot it! Shoot it!" as she pointed toward the fleeing cat. Daniel saw the lion running away and raised his rifle. "Boom!" it reported. The big cat jumped in the air and twisted around several times before falling to the ground dead.

Daniel quickly checked the cougar to ensure it was dead before checking Evan. Emily was already at Evan's side as he lay on the ground. His arm had been badly mauled and was bleeding. Emily ripped off a part of her nightgown to use as a bandage and wrapped Evan's arm in it to slow the bleeding. James arrived just behind Daniel to find his younger brother bleeding and in severe pain. "What happened?" he asked.

Emily replied. "The cougar got him."

"Why is he wet?" asked James.

"I threw a bucket of water on the cat as it was on top of Evan."

Daniel said, "That was quick thinking. You probably saved his life."

With saddened eyes, Emily looked at Daniel and said, "He may not be out of trouble yet."

"What do you mean?" asked James.

Emily asked Daniel, "Did you get a good look at that cat after you shot it?"

Daniel answered, "No, not really."

Emily instructed him, "Go over and take a closer look. Let me know what you see."

Daniel and James walked over to the cat and examined it. Then, they heard Emily say, "Don't touch it with your bare hands."

Daniel used the barrel of his rifle to poke at the cat, moving it around to examine it. Suddenly, Daniel realized what he was supposed to be looking for. The cougar had a foam mixed with blood oozing from its mouth. "Dang it!" whispered Daniel under his breath.

"What is it?" asked James.

"Come on." said Daniel.

The two men walked back to Emily and stood before her and Evan.

Emily asked, "Well?"

Daniel defeatedly looked at Emily and asked, "Rabies?"

Emily nodded her head. "I suspected it with how the lion acted when I threw the water at her."

James fearfully asked, "What's rabies?"

Daniel replied, "Hydrophobia!"

James' eyes widened with the realization and gravity of the word. "You mean he's gonna die?"

Emily stood and tried to calm James, "No. Not necessarily."

James cried as he replied, "But there ain't no cure for hydrophobia! Everyone who gets bit, dies!"

Again, Emily tried to soothe James, saying, "James, there is a treatment for rabies, and we have access to it."

Emily looked at Daniel to observe his demeanor. Daniel nodded in agreement. Daniel was finding it most challenging to keep his gift a secret. Every time he turned around, there seemed to be another need for him to use the Shimmering.

Emily instructed Daniel, "You'll need to take the head with you so they can verify whether or not it is rabies. Make sure you don't touch it."

Daniel picked up an ax leaning against the outside of the fence and found an oilcloth sack nearby. He walked out to the spot in the corral where the cougar lay and chopped off the head of the big cat. He collected the head into the oilcloth and tied it up, careful not to touch any part of the cougar's head.

Just then, Tommy showed up. "What's going on?" he asked.

Emily explained the situation and told Tommy what they were about to do. She then turned to James and explained, "James, we're about to tell you something secret. Very few people know about it. At least white people that is. Daniel has been given a gift by the Chickasaw. He has the ability to travel through time. Daniel is going to take you and Evan into the future where they have the ability and the medicine to possibly cure Evan. You will see things that you never thought could exist. You need to be careful. Let Daniel do most of the talking. You need to pretend that you are Mennonite. That will explain to the people you encounter why you are dressed strangely and your ignorance as to their ways. Do you understand?"

James stared at Emily with his mouth open. "I think so."

Emily said, "Good! Now you three need to get going!"

James and Daniel helped Evan to his feet and escorted him out of the corral. When they reached the cabin, Daniel quickly went inside and retrieved his scepter.

"What's that?" asked James.

Daniel replied, "It's the scepter the Chickasaw gave me that lets us travel through time."

Daniel used his free hand to help hold Evan, then began swirling the scepter clockwise in front of him. The Shimmering opened up to the astonishment of James and Evan.

Daniel said, "Let's go!"

As he led the Gordons through the portal, they felt a rush of cold wind enter their bodies. Then, immediately, they found themselves standing behind the largest stone building either of the Gordons had ever seen. The ground they stood on was very hard. The area was dimly lit with lights that hung from tall poles. There were wagon-like things with black wheels scattered throughout the area.

Daniel led them to the emergency entrance of Maury General Hospital. The glass doors swung open automatically. Evan and James looked at everything they encountered with curious eyes. Daniel led them to the front counter, where a receptionist sat. She wore a mask over her nose and mouth as she said, "Gentlemen, you'll need to put on a mask to be in here."

Daniel's brow furrowed as he asked, "Is something wrong?"

The lady replied, "Due to COVID restrictions, no one is allowed in the hospital without wearing a mask."

She passed through a hole in her glass window three paper surgical-type masks.

While Daniel and the Gordons struggled to put theirs on, Daniel asked, "What's COVID?"

The receptionist looked up in shock and asked, "Where have you been the last month? It's been all over the news. COVID 19, also known as the Corona Virus has been killing people all over the world. No one is sure where or how it started, but some believe it began in China. It's much like the flu but seems to be more

deadly."

Daniel replied, "Well, we live off the grid over in Water Valley. We don't get much news there."

After Daniel and the Gordons finally put on their masks, the woman asked, "Now, what can I help you with?"

Daniel replied, "My friend Evan here was attacked by a mountain lion about an hour ago. We think it might have been rabid because of how it reacted toward being doused with water. I brought the cat's head with us just in case."

"Oh my!" replied the woman. "Let me get some information and we'll get him back to see a doctor right away."

The woman began asking various personal questions, which Evan found he could not answer. He had no driver's license. He didn't have a social security number. He didn't even know his address. So when she asked for his phone number, he asked, "What's a phone number?"

Daniel tried to help the woman fill out her forms as best he could without telling her any factual information about themselves. Finally, the woman was somewhat satisfied she had enough information to admit Evan into the emergency department. A nurse came out to meet them from behind an automatic door. "Evan Gordon?" she announced.

All three men stood to move toward the nurse. When she saw them, she instructed, "I'm sorry, but only one family member per patient. " James looked at Daniel and said, "You go. You know more about this than I do. I'll wait out here."

Daniel nodded in agreement and followed Evan and the nurse to the back while James sat in the waiting room in front of a box on the wall playing moving pictures. James was amazed at the technology that existed here in the future. The room he sat in had a wall of dark windows. He could see what Daniel had called "cars" from the windows, moving up and down a pathway at incredible speeds. Occasionally, one of the cars would pull up to the hospital with red lights flashing and an awful screaming sound coming from it. Then, two people would get out and open up the back of the car, remove a rolling bed with someone strapped to it, and roll them into the hospital.

James was tired from the long day, but everything around him was so exciting. He couldn't fall asleep with so much going on.

After an hour or so, Daniel and Evan came out to meet James.

"Well?" asked James.

Daniel replied, "We won't know for some time yet. They have to send the cougar's head to a laboratory to check it for rabies. That can take some time. Meanwhile, they gave Evan a shot to help him fight off the disease. He'll have to come back for more injections over the next two weeks. Right now all we can do is hope and pray that we got him here in time."

James asked, "Are we gonna stay here for two weeks?"

"No!" said Daniel. "I'll bring him through the Shimmering when it's time to come back. We'll head back home for now."

Daniel led the brothers outside to a secluded spot in the parking lot. He took out the scepter, opened the Shimmering, and led Evan and James through.

CHAPTER 25

Emily sat in her chair beside the fireplace, rocking Alyson to sleep. Daniel was not there at the moment. Emily thought she heard him stirring outside. Jake lifted his head slightly and lowly murmured a rumbling growl. Emily didn't move from her seat. Instead, she waited, staring at the door of the cabin. She heard footsteps on the porch. They didn't sound like Daniel's. Besides, Jake would not have reacted the way he was had Daniel been on the other side of the door. The door latch slowly lifted itself as Emily watched in terror. Who could this be, and why would they enter her home unannounced?

Suddenly, the door burst open. A dark being stood just inside, filling the doorway. Jake began to bark furiously. He stood between the being and Emily, trying to ward off the intruder. Through the dim light of the fireplace, Emily began to recognize the one standing before her. The creature was dressed all in black. His hair was wild and long. His eyes showed bright red. He bared his razor-sharp teeth at her as he growled an unsettling growl. His hands reached toward Emily. They were longer than usual. His fingers were bony, crooked, and elongated. The creature's skin was covered in long hair like an animal's fur. It was Evan. He was changed, but it was he.

Emily screamed with terror as the creature swung his bony arm at her. He struck Alyson, causing her to fly out of Emily's arms. The baby cried uncontrollably as she fell to the floor. Emily, too, was crying while she screamed for help.

Jake leaped toward the being to rescue Emily from imminent attack. Instead, the creature swung an arm at Jake and tossed him aside like yesterday's garbage. Jake's body hit the floor with a thud.

The being then turned back to Emily and grabbed her, raising her from the floor with one hand. She screamed again as he lifted her toward his face. Saliva dripped from his mouth, anticipating receiving her in his blackened canines. Emily closed her eyes, wishing it all would be over. She could smell his rancid breath as he slowly moved her closer and closer to him. Emily let out one last blood-curdling scream.

"Emily!"

Emily suddenly awoke. She stared up into her husband's eyes. She panted, trying to catch her breath. Tears had formed in the corners of her eyes.

"Are you alright?" Daniel asked.

"Oh, Daniel! I had a terrible dream! It was horrible!"

Daniel asked, "What happened?"

Emily explained, "It was Evan. He turned into some kind of creature. He looked like a werewolf. He came after me. He knocked Alyson out of my arms and she hit the ground. Jake tried to save me but Evan threw him aside too. He was lifting me toward himself like he intended to eat me or something. That's when I woke up. It was the worst dream I've ever had!"

Daniel wiped her hair away from her face and said, "It's okay. You're okay."

Emily finally caught her composure and asked, "When did you get back? How's Evan?"

Daniel replied, "Just a few minutes ago. Evan is pretty beat. They gave him a couple of shots and drew some blood. We won't know until the test results come back whether or not he was exposed to rabies. He and James went off to bed."

James woke around noon and looked over at the other bed where Evan was sleeping. Evan seemed restless. He tossed a lot and couldn't seem to get comfortable. When James walked over to Evan's bed, he found his brother sweating profusely. James reached down and felt Evan's forehead. His skin felt like it was on fire.

James quickly left the hospital room to search for Emily. He banged on the cabin door and called out, "Emily!".

Emily came to the door and found James in a frantic state.

"What's wrong?"

James replied, "It's Evan! He's burning up with fever! You gotta come quick!"

Emily pulled off her apron and followed James back to the hospital room. She walked into the room and found Evan writhing in pain. So Emily went to the table where her medical bag was sitting and mulled around until she found her thermometer. Emily put the thermometer under his tongue and waited a couple of minutes. When she pulled the thermometer from Evan's mouth, she read the mercury line and found he had a temperature of 103.5. Emily rushed back to her cabin, poured a pan of water, and added a few drops of peppermint and lavender oil. She carried the pan back to the hospital and wiped Evan's body with a small towel dipped into the water and oil mixture. She bathed his head, arms, and chest, trying to bring his temperature down. She and James tried several times to get Evan to drink fresh water to avoid dehydration.

Emily heard Alyson in the distance. She had woken from her afternoon nap. Emily told James to keep bathing Evan in the water and oils while she was gone. She gathered Alyson and a few of her favorite things, her blanket and cornhusk doll, and then walked her over to Amy's to get her to babysit.

When Emily returned to the hospital, she found Evan was awake. He still ran a fever but was at least coherent. While James watched his brother, Emily returned to the cabin and made a vegetable broth for Evan. She chopped some onion, carrots, celery, tomatoes, mushrooms, and garlic and placed them in a pot of water. Emily added ginger, thyme, bay leaves, salt, and pepper. She brought the water to a boil and let it simmer for several hours.

Meantime, she went outside to find Daniel. He was out in the field checking to see how wet the soil was. She watched him as she walked closer to his location. Daniel would stoop down, gather a handful of dirt, then crumble it between his fingers. He did this at several locations in the field until he realized that Emily was approaching.

"What's up?" asked Daniel.

Emily replied, "It's Evan! He's in bad shape. He's running a high fever and is incoherent most of the time. I think we need to let Dolly know."

"Sure thing!" Daniel said. "I'll head on over and bring her back."

Emily asked, "Are you taking the short cut?"

Daniel returned, "Should I?"

Emily replied, "I think so. There might not be a lot of time. Bring her back quickly."

Daniel nodded in agreement as he joined Emily on the short walk back to the cabin.

Daniel asked, "Where's Alyson?"

"Amy has her."

Daniel said, "So Amy knows about Evan?"

"She knows he's running a fever, but not just how bad Evan is doing. So I'll run over there after you leave and let her know how he's doing."

When they returned to the cabin, Daniel walked down to Beaver Branch and washed the mud off his hands. He then retrieved his gear before heading to Dolly's house. He didn't bother saddling a horse. He decided there was no need for pretense with Dolly. She was sharp and probably already suspected he could control the Shimmering.

Daniel took his rifle, tomahawk, and the quiver holding his scepter. He stepped outside into the yard and opened up the Shimmering. Jake stepped up next to Daniel. When Daniel looked down and saw Jake at his side, Daniel said, "Let's go, Jake!"

They stepped into the portal and instantly found themselves standing in front of Dolly's house. Daniel looked around to see if anyone had seen them arrive. No one was in sight. Daniel walked up the steps of the house and knocked on the door. A moment later, Lucy Gordon opened the door and greeted Daniel.

"Hello, Mr. Lane."

"Hi, Lucy. Is your mother in?"

Lucy replied, "No, sir. She just left to walk up to the trading post. She should be back soon. Would you like to wait inside?"

Daniel replied, "No thanks! I'll walk on over and find her there."

Lucy asked, "Is something wrong?"

Daniel paused, then spoke, "Why don't you walk with me? This concerns all of you."

Lucy quickly grabbed her wrap and joined Daniel as he walked along the path leading to the Gordon's trading post.

Lucy anxiously asked Daniel, "Is something wrong with Amy? Is she okay?"

Daniel evaded the question by saying, "Why don't we wait until we see your mother. I'll answer all your questions then."

Minutes later, Daniel and Lucy stepped into the small log structure that served as a trading post and the living quarters for John Jr. and Susan Gordon. Daniel opened the door to allow Lucy to enter first. As she entered, Lucy announced, "Mother? Mr. Lane is here to see you. He says it's urgent."

Dolly stepped toward them with John Jr. and Susan close behind. She looked at Daniel with fear and asked, "Who is it, Daniel? Is something wrong with Amy or the baby? One of the boys?"

Daniel replied, "It's Evan, Dolly! He was attacked by a cougar last night. He's in pretty bad shape. Emily suggested that I come and get you."

"How bad is pretty bad?" asked Dolly.

Daniel replied, "Well, the lion bit him in the arm and tore him up pretty bad, but that's not the worse part. We think the cat might have been rabid."

Dolly gasped and asked, "Rabid? You mean rabies? Hydrophobia?"

Lucy, John, and Susan all gasped in unison at Dolly's question.

Daniel nodded his head. Dolly nearly passed out when he did. John Jr. caught her before she hit the floor. Daniel took her by the hand and said, "Dolly, I was able to take him to the hospital where Emily used to work. They have started him on treatment that could cure him. When we got him home, we put him to bed. When James woke up, he found Evan burning up with fever and called Emily over to check on him. Emily sent me to fetch you."

Dolly replied, "I didn't think anything could be done for rabies."

Daniel said, "In this time, there isn't. But, from my time and Emily's time, there is. It isn't a sure fire cure, but sometimes it works."

Dolly asked, "Your time? How can you get back to your time? I thought that whole time travel thing was just an accident."

Daniel replied, "It was at first. But, recently the Chickasaw made me a prophet for their nation. I have been given the ability to travel wherever and whenever I need to. So, I took Evan and James forward to the year 2020 so Evan could be treated for his injuries."

Dolly's family was dumbfounded by Daniel's revelations. Lucy was the first to speak, "Mother, what is he talking about? What does he mean by his time and our time?"

Dolly explained, "There is a Chickasaw legend about a place near here where time travel is possible. Daniel found it accidentally when he came here a couple of years ago. When was it, Daniel?"

"December 21, 2017."

"Right!" Dolly said. "Six months later, Emily and Tommy came through and found Daniel. They decided to stay here and make their home. I suspected when he arrived that he may have come from a different time than our own."

"How's that?" asked John.

"Because he was dressed differently than anyone from around here. Plus, I already knew someone else who had traveled through Ittola Chuka to get here."

"Who?" they all asked.

"Gus! Gus accidentally found the same time portal and traveled here from the year 1973. He was just a sixteen year old boy when he came through. Scared and all alone. So, Daniel, have you come to take me to see my son?"

"I have, Dolly."

Dolly asked, "So, how does this work?"

Daniel replied, "I'll open up a portal and we will walk through together. When we get to the other side, we'll find ourselves standing in my front yard. Are you ready?"

Dolly looked at John and said, "Make sure the boys know what's happened. Y'all stay here and take care of things for me. I'll be back as soon as I can."

She then looked at Daniel and said, "I'm ready!"

They all followed Daniel outside and watched as he took out his scepter and held it in front of himself. The scepter vibrated, and suddenly, a shimmering light appeared before them. Daniel took Dolly by the hand and led her and Jake through. A cold blast of air entered Dolly's body as she entered the portal. Then, suddenly, she found herself standing in front of what she assumed was Daniel's cabin.

CHAPTER 26

Daniel led Dolly to the entrance of Emily's hospital. He opened the door and allowed Dolly to walk in ahead of him. Dolly found James and Emily at Evan's bedside. Evan opened his eyes and tried to rise when he saw his mother standing over him. Dolly placed her hand on his chest to keep him lying down. Finally, Evan gave up and asked, "Mother, what are you doing here?"

Dolly replied, "I heard you weren't feeling well, son. I wanted to come and check on you."

Emily entered the room holding a wooden tray with a bowl of the vegetable broth she had made. She sat the tray in front of Evan and prepared to feed him when Dolly said, "I'll feed him if you like. You've probably got other things to do around here."

Emily said, "If you'll excuse me, I think I'll go pick up Alyson from Amy's and let Amy know you're here."

Emily left the hospital room and walked up to Amy's cabin. Along the way, she noticed the scent of honeysuckle blooming in the valley. She could hear tree frogs chirping in the distance and crickets singing among the rocks next to the Beaver Branch. Emily looked up to the sky and saw a bald eagle circling the treetops. She heard the trickling water of the Beaver as it rolled past her over rocks and fallen tree limbs. She allowed herself to relax for a moment. All nature was singing around her, temporarily escaping her problems and responsibilities. Emily was at peace.

When she arrived at Amy's cabin, she found Amy, Alyson, and little Noah sitting on the front porch. Amy was singing a light little tune that Emily didn't recognize to the children.

Fare ye well, sings the whippoorwill.
Fare ye well, early mornin' sings.
Daylight comes, and the sun will rise again
Mornin' light brings the songs of spring.

It was a lonesome-sounding song, much like Emily had heard among the people of the Appalachian Trail in East Tennessee and Kentucky. However, it was beautiful, and Amy had a lovely voice.

I will rise to the screamin' jaybird
Chirpin' frogs and hummin' bees
This is life on the lonely mountain
Winds blow by through the weepin' trees.

As Emily came closer, Amy noticed her and stopped singing. Emily said, "Please don't stop. That's beautiful. Did Dolly sing that to you as a child?"

Amy replied, "No. I just made it up to sing to Noah."

Emily, impressed, said, "Oh, Amy, that's beautiful. You have a lovely voice."

Amy blushed as she said, "Thanks!"

Then Amy remembered her brother and asked, "How's Evan?"

Emily replied, "Maybe a little better. Your mother is with him now."

Excitedly, Amy asked, "Can I go see them?"

"Sure. I came to pick up Alyson so you could go down and visit with your family."

Emily picked up Alyson and carried her back to their cabin while Amy walked alongside them carrying Noah. Amy was both excited to see her mother and concerned for Evan. She realized Evan must not be doing well if Emily and Daniel arranged to bring her here to see him.

As they neared Emily's cabin, Emily broke away from Amy. Amy continued to the hospital while Emily searched for Daniel, who would be somewhere around the cultivated fields. Emily walked past the corral and saw Daniel and Tommy standing in the field, digging around in the dirt. When Emily approached them, she asked, "How's it looking?"

Daniel replied, "Not bad. We should be able to start planting tomorrow as long as the rain holds off."

Tommy asked, "How's Evan?"

Emily replied, "Not too good. Amy just went up to check on him and to see Dolly."

Tommy said, "I think I'll go own over thar and check own um."

Tommy walked away, and Emily and Daniel stood there alone, looking at each other with sadness and fear in their eyes.

Daniel asked, "What do you think?"

Emily replied, "I don't think his chances are good. He was bitten by a rabid animal, introducing dangerous toxins into his body. Then, the doctors injected him with more serum, trying to build immunity to the toxin. His body isn't used to the elements that our bodies have been introduced to throughout our lives. It's like Columbus bringing sickness to the natives of San Salvador. His body won't be able to endure it. It may just kill him faster.

Dolly awoke from her sleep next to Evan's bed the following day. James had made a cot on the floor under the window at the front of the hospital. He remained asleep while Dolly rose from her bed. Dolly walked to Evan's bed to check on him. He looked worse. His fever was back, and his eyes were sunken with dark circles around them.

Dolly called out, "James!"

James slowly began to wake.

"James! Wake up!"

James finally realized it was Dolly calling his name. "What is it, Mother?"

"Go and get Emily! Evan is getting worse!"

James jumped to his feet, ran outside to the other cabin door, and began beating on it, calling, "Emily! Emily!"

Finally, Daniel opened the door and asked, "What is it?"

"Mother says Evan is worse. She wants Emily to come. Quickly!"

Emily heard what James said and replied, "I'll be right there, James!"

Emily quickly dressed and instructed Daniel, "Watch Alyson, please."

She darted out of the cabin and ran next door to the hospital. She opened the door to find Dolly bathing Evan with peppermint oils and water while Evan's body rocked back and forth, trying to avoid her touch. He threw up his arms defensively to keep her from touching him. His whole body was racked with pain. He didn't want anyone to touch him. Emily tore some strips of cloth from a roll of bandages and used them to tie his arms to the bedpost. Then he began to kick, so they tied his feet, too. Evan began to scream and growl in pain, still rocking his body back and forth and side to side, looking to escape.

Dolly screamed, "What's happening, Emily?"

Emily replied, "I think his body is rejecting the treatment he received. The injections the doctor gave him are supposed to help him build up an immunity to the virus that the cougar infected him with. But, because

Evan isn't used to 21st century medicines, his body is reacting differently. Instead of building up immunity it's just making him sick more quickly. I'm afraid there's nothing we can do."

Dolly looked solemnly at Emily and asked, "So, he's gonna die?"

"Yes. I'm afraid so. But it won't happen quickly. It will be a slow painful death."

Dolly stared at her young son as he lay tied to the bed, suffering in anguish.

A moment later, Dolly asked, "Would you mind leaving me with my son for a while, alone?"

Emily replied, "No, Dolly. We'll be right outside if you need us."

Emily asked James with her eyes to follow her out of the cabin. James complied and walked out behind Emily. They found Daniel sitting with Alyson on the front porch of their cabin. James and Emily walked over to join Daniel and the baby without saying a word. Daniel sensed that there was nothing to be said, so he remained silent.

Not long after, Emily started to rise so she could cook breakfast. When she stood, she was suddenly startled by a "BANG!". Emily looked at Daniel questioningly as he jumped to his feet. Daniel handed Alyson to Emily as he ran to the hospital cabin next door. He threw open the door and looked inside to find Dolly standing at the foot of Evan's bed, holding a rifle with a smoking barrel.

Dolly turned to look at Daniel with tears filling her eyes. Daniel carefully removed the rifle from Dolly's grip and held her up with his free arm so she didn't collapse to the floor.

Evan no longer writhed in pain. He no longer fought against his fetters, which entrapped him to the bedposts. He lay still with a bullet hole in his forehead, with no more suffering.

Dolly spent most of the day sitting beside her second eldest son's bed. She quietly cried to herself from time to time, but never out loud. Whenever Emily, James, or Amy came in to check on her, she replied, "I'll just sit here for a while."

Finally, about an hour before dusk, Dolly walked out of the hospital and said, "I want to take my boy home."

Emily said, "Amy and I can prepare his body to travel home."

Dolly nodded without a word, walked to Emily's porch, and sat down.

Emily and Amy returned to the hospital cabin and began preparing Evan's body for travel. First, they stripped away his clothing and washed his body from head to toe. Next, they wrapped his body in a blanket and tied it up with leather lacing. Then, they took all of Evan's clothes and the bedding outside to burn. Next, Emily doused the bed and walls of the cabin with whiskey, hoping the alcohol content would be enough to kill any of the rabies virus that might still exist within the dried blood on the surfaces. Next, Tommy and James came to retrieve the body from the cabin and placed it in the back of Daniel's wagon. Then, they hitched the two new Belgian horses to the wagon and readied them for transport through the Shimmering. Dolly and James climbed aboard the wagon to drive it home.

Daniel opened the Shimmering with his scepter, then signaled James to drive on through. Tommy, Amy, Noah, Emily, Alyson, Daniel, and Jake followed the wagon on foot. The procession slowly moved until they arrived in front of Dolly's brick home.

Lucy came running out of the house to greet them, then realized that it would not be a happy occasion from the look on everyone's faces.

Lucy asked, "Mother?"

Dolly stared ahead without acknowledging her daughter.

James instructed, "Lucy, go and find all the brothers. Evan is dead and needs to be buried."

Lucy burst into tears as she ran to the trading post to find John Jr. and Susan.

Nathan greeted everyone as he approached from the corral. James instructed him, "Nathan, we're going to need a casket built. Can you see to it?"

Nathan responded, "Who is it, Masta James?"

"Evan," James replied.

"Oh Lordy! I sho is sorry. I'll git um started right away, suh."

They carried Evan's body into the house and laid it to rest on the table in the parlor. Amy went upstairs, found Evan's best suit, and brought it down so they could dress him for the burial. Dolly turned to James and Daniel and asked, "Daniel, can you please take James to Nashville so he can bring his sisters back here for the funeral?"

Daniel replied, "Absolutely! Anything at all that you need, just ask."

Daniel and James went outside, and Daniel opened up the Shimmering once again to take them to Nashville to retrieve James' sisters, Belinda and Cynthia.

Lucy, John Jr., and Susan arrived just as Daniel and James left from the trading post. Tommy asked Lucy, "Where are the other brothers?"

Lucy replied, "Micah and Luke are at the ferry today. I think Mark is out in the fields with Titus, the foreman."

Tommy replied, "I'll run and git Micah and Luke. Can you send someone to fetch Mark?"

Lucy nodded and said, "Yes."

Within thirty minutes, Mark, Luke, and Micah returned to the house to comfort their mother and each other. Lucy instructed the slave cooks to start preparing food for all those arriving for the funeral. Titus had two of the field hands dig a new grave for Evan. He would be buried next to his younger brother, Joshua.

⸻◦⸻

The next day, just before noon, James and Daniel pulled up in the wagon, and Cynthia and her family followed behind in their Surrey. Just behind them were Belinda and her family. All the remaining members of the Gordon family had arrived to lay their dear brother to rest.

Evan's body had been placed in the newly built casket, which remained in the parlor. All the family and friends were given one last time to pay their respects before the coffin was removed from the house. Everyone shed tears as they passed by the casket and as they greeted one another. Then, Micah, James, Luke, Mark, Tommy, and Daniel raised the coffin to their shoulders and carried it out of the house and down to the family cemetery.

The farm was at a standstill. All the slaves gathered to pay their respects to the family while remaining about thirty feet away from the family and the grave. As the casket was set to rest just above the grave, John Jr. stood before his family and read from the Bible, Psalm 23.

Amy began singing "Amazing Grace." Her beautiful voice echoed through the trees surrounding the cemetery until she neared the final line of the first stanza. "I once was lost, but now I'm found. Was blind but now …". Amy's voice cracked, then failed.

Then a powerful, clear baritone voice erupted from the crowd, finishing her line, "I see!"

The slave then sang the second stanza. "Twas grace that taught my heart to fear, and grace my fears relieved, how precious did that grace appear the hour I first believed."

Then suddenly, a chorus of black angelic voices joined in on the third stanza, "When we've been there ten-thousand years, bright shining as the sun, we've no less days to sing God's praise than when we first begun."

CHAPTER 27

Things were returning to normal in the Water Valley. Daniel and Tommy were nearly complete with planting their seventy-five acres of corn. Emily and Amy had almost finished planting their vegetable garden, and James had recruited his brother Micah to help with the mill. Babies were being born, too. Emily's mare, Dimples, and all four Indian ponies were pregnant and nearing their foaling periods. The sows were farrowing new litters, and the does would be kidding soon, too.

Daniel was glad the planting was nearly completed. He loved the work, but other things were pressing on his mind. Daniel was still curious about the timeline. He was almost sure that Gus was wrong about their having changed the timeline. Daniel felt Gus must have accidentally found another dimension that led him to believe they had changed the timeline. Daniel wanted to be positive, though. He felt the only way to be sure was to check out some of the Civil War battles in Middle Tennessee and ensure they were historically accurate.

That night, after supper, Daniel decided to discuss his plans with Emily. He felt she could look at things from a different perspective and give insight in ways he might not have thought about. So, as they sat by the fire and watched the flames flicker, he broached the subject with her.

"I've been thinking lately about what Gus said."

Emily was only half listening as she rocked Alyson by the fire. "Hmm?"

Daniel repeated, "I've been thinking about what Gus said. You know? About the timeline?"

Emily looked up and asked, "What have you been thinking about it?"

Daniel replied, "I've been thinking that maybe I should test his theory."

"And, how would you do that?"

Daniel said, "I'm thinking about going to some of the Civil War battles to make sure they turn out like they are supposed to according to history. If something is wrong, I'll try to fix it somehow."

"How do you think you can fix it?"

Daniel said, "By offering information that will give the union an edge if need be."

Emily asked, "Don't you think that's a little bit dangerous? Going back in time, or forward in this case, and sticking your nose right in the middle of a war?"

Daniel replied, "Well, I wouldn't be in the battle. I would just observe from a distance. Kind of like a scout. I wouldn't be involved in the battles, just relaying information to the ones in charge."

Emily asked, "When do you plan on taking this little trip?"

Daniel answered, "I thought maybe after the planting is finished."

They both sat in silence for a while. Then, Daniel said, "I promised you I wouldn't travel through the Shimmering without discussing it with you. I'm keeping that promise. If you're not okay with this, I won't go."

Emily thought to herself, "*Yeah, but if I'm not okay with it, and you don't go, you'll just sit around here and mope until you get your way.*"

After a long stint of silence, Emily said, "Daniel, I don't know if you've thought about this or not but, you do realize you could go on any trip you want and I would never know. You simply have to come back to the moment in time that you left and I would never know that you had left."

"I know, Emily. But I won't do that. I made you a promise and I will keep my promise. I will never lie to you and I will always keep my promises to you."

Emily smiled at his statement and replied, "Alright then. Under two conditions, though. Take Jake with you for backup, and be back here before dark on the day you leave."

Daniel said, "I will. I will be back before dark. I promise!"

Emily remarked, "That's what you said last time. Remember?"

Daniel smiled and said, "Yeah, but I didn't know I was going to travel back in time then. This time I know what I'm doing."

Daniel decided to leave the next day. Since he promised Emily that he would be back before dark, it didn't matter if he finished the planting or not. He would be back in plenty of time to get it done.

He rose early, just before dawn. He couldn't sleep anyway, so he gathered his gear as quietly as possible and kissed Emily while she lay sleeping in bed. She woke to his touch.

"Leaving already?"

Daniel replied, "Yeah, I couldn't sleep so I thought I might as well get going."

"Be safe!" Emily replied.

"I will."

Daniel stepped out of the cabin with Jake in tow. They walked down to the corral, saddled Hoss, and led him out. Daniel opened up the Shimmering by rotating his scepter clockwise. His time and destination were outside Fort Henry on February 5th, 1862.

In May of 1861, Tennessee governor Isham G. Harris commissioned State Attorney General Daniel S. Donelson to the rank of Brigadier General. He directed him to build two forts along the rivers of Middle Tennessee to protect Nashville from Union invasion. Donelson found two suitable sites, but they were both within the borders of Kentucky. Since Kentucky was considered a neutral state, he continued his search just inside the Tennessee border along the Cumberland River. After himself, the first fort was named Fort Donelson and constructed along the Cumberland's western bank.

Once construction had begun, Donelson continued his search and found a location twelve miles away on the eastern bank of the Tennessee River. Fort Henry was named after Tennessee Senator Gustavus Adolphus Henry Sr., who served as a Confederate States Senator from 1861 to 1865.

Daniel landed outside of Fort Henry on the afternoon of February 5th. Torrential rain was falling, making it difficult for Daniel to see the fort. He dared not get too close for fear that Confederate troops might mistake him for a Union scout.

He knew that General Grant would be moving his troops from the north into two different divisions. One under the command of McClernand would move toward the fort from the east bank of the Tennessee River, while C. S. Smith's division would overtake Fort Heiman on the Kentucky side, then turn its artillery upon Fort Henry.

Daniel rode toward McCernand's division, hoping to find General Grant with them. The rain made it difficult for Daniel to see much, but he, in turn, hoped it would make it difficult for anyone to see him as well. He relied much on the keen hearing of his companions, Hoss and Jake. Finally, as they topped a hill, Daniel saw Grant's army in the distance. Unfortunately, the division was nearly at a standstill due to the muddy conditions through which they were traveling.

Daniel chose a less direct route through the trees, hoping to arrive more quickly and unobserved. When he neared the front of the division, he watched from the trees the Union soldiers struggle through the mud. Mule teams hitched to cannons, and ammunition transports were stuck two feet deep in the mud. Many men were called out of formation to help move the artillery forward. Daniel quietly moved past them in the trees, hoping to catch sight of General Grant.

About half a mile later, Daniel caught a glimpse of several officers gathered near the division's rear. The familiar profile of General Ulysses S. Grant with his short-cropped beard was in the center of them all. Daniel dismounted the big Bay stallion and led him out of the trees, with Jake walking beside them. They only reached the tree line about twenty feet before two sentries stopped him.

"Who are you and where do you think you're going?"

Daniel replied, "My name is Daniel Lane and I'm here to see General Grant. I have some information for him."

"Concerning?" asked one of the sentries.

"Fort Henry, Fort Donelson, and his ironclads making their way down the river." Daniel replied.

The sentry commanded, "Wait here!"

Daniel stood by with the other sentry as the first went to speak with the General. Daniel noticed that the sentry didn't break in on the discussion but waited to be recognized by one of the officers. Minutes dragged on as Daniel and the sentry waited. Finally, a junior General who served as Aide de Camp waved the sentry over to receive the message he wished to deliver. Then, Daniel observed the aide walking over to General Grant and relaying the message. Grant looked at Daniel standing in the distance, and Jake stood beside him. The General noticed his frontier garb and the antique weapons that he carried.

General Grant turned away from the aide and continued with his duties. The aide, in turn, walked to the sentry and gave his orders. The sentry turned to Daniel and the other sentry and beckoned them forward.

They walked forward until they reached General Grant's position. The General looked up from a map and asked Daniel, "Who are you, sir and what is your business here?"

"General Grant, my name is Daniel Lane. I came here to observe your operations and give any guidance that will ensure your victory."

"And, just how do you propose to do that?"

Daniel continued, "General, what I have to say is for your ears only. If you would allow me five minutes of your time. Your sentries and the aide here are welcome to keep their weapons pointed at me while we talk, if you like. I only ask that what I say be heard by you alone."

The General felt he had no reason to fear Daniel. He had a whole division of troops here to protect him. What could one man and a dog do to harm him with these odds? He made the order, and then he and Daniel stepped away from everyone else.

"Well, sir!" Grant said, "What do you have to say?"

Daniel began, "Well, General, let me begin by telling you I know what is about to happen. I know when, where, and how you will overtake Fort Henry and Fort Donelson. I know that you will then move down the Cumberland and Tennessee Rivers and then win a bloody battle at a place called Shiloh. Sir, you will continue this war for another four years until Robert E. Lee surrenders unconditionally in Richmond. You will become President of the United States of America in 1869 and will serve two terms."

Grant asked, "Can you tell me how many fingers I'm holding behind my back?"

Daniel snickered and replied, "No, Sir. I'm not a psychic."

"Then what are you, Mr. Lane?"

Daniel replied, "The Chickasaw call me, Prophet."

"Prophet! Hogwash! More like lunatic! I don't have time for this nonsense. I have a war to fight."

Daniel interrupted, "General, let me show you something."

Daniel positioned Hoss between the Union soldiers watching him and the General. He removed his scepter from its quiver and opened the Shimmering so the soldiers couldn't see it. Daniel announced, "I'll be right back, General."

Daniel walked into the Shimmering, and it closed immediately. He then appeared a few paces behind the General and said, "Here I am, General."

General Grant spun around and found Daniel suddenly standing behind him. "How did you do that?"

The soldiers never saw Daniel change his position. Instead, they noticed that the General was now facing the opposite direction while talking to the stranger.

Daniel said, "Sir, I have been given this mysterious power by the Chickasaw nation. I can travel anywhere instantly. I can travel through time. This is how I got here today to see you from my time in 1820."

The General asked, "To what purpose?"

"Something ocured in my time that made me suspicious that the timeline had become disrupted. I just want to make sure that things are the way they are supposed to be."

Grant asked, "How can you be sure?"

Daniel replied, "Sir, I was born in 1987. I accidentally traveled back in time from 2017 to 1817. The things that you are fighting for now will have an effect on my world in the future. Slavery will be no more. It isn't perfect, but Black men, White men, Asians and men of all races are allowed to live freely. If you don't win these battles and this war, we could forever be burdened with the bonds of slavery. I can't let that happen."

Grant asked, "Alright! What should I do?"

Daniel said, "Just allow me access to you in the event that I see something going wrong. I am a historian and this war is one of my specialties. I know what is supposed to happen and when. If something goes wrong, I will let you know."

Grant held out his hand and said, "I am at your service, sir!"

Daniel shook his hand and replied, "And I at yours."

Grant waved his officers over to him and instructed them, "Men, this man will from now be known as our special scout. He will be given full access to me. If you see him, allow him to see me straight away. His name will be the Prophet!"

CHAPTER 28

On the morning of February 5th, General Grant called Daniel to his tent. When Daniel arrived, Grant asked him for information concerning their military presence. Daniel gave his report to the General.

"By now, General, you should have received a report that C. S. Smith and his division have taken Fort Heiman in Kentucky."

"I have not as of yet," said Grant.

"You can send your infantry to attack Fort Henry with Smith providing fire from Fort Heiman. Flag officer Andrew Foote's navy of ironclads and timberclads will be in position by 12:30 p.m. to attack the fort with little resistance because most of their canons are underwater along with much of their powder and ammunition. So, Tilghman will flee with his army to Fort Donelson. Your men will pursue them, but because of the heavy rains they won't be able to catch them in time. Our next step is to prepare for battle at Fort Donelson."

Grant said, "Our intelligence tells us that there are mines in the rivers around Fort Henry."

Daniel replied, "They are correct. However, your boats won't have any problem with the mines because they won't float. They are leaking and will sink to the bottom. Since the rain has caused the river waters to rise so much, your ironclads will move right over the tops of the mines."

General Grant replied, "Very good Mr. Lane. Thank-you for your report. This will make my job as commander much easier if the information you provide me is accurate."

Daniel said, "General, what I'm telling you is what history has told me, but one thing you should keep in mind. My friend, David Crockett once told me, 'history and fact seldom coincide.'"

Grant replied, "I understand."

He then called for General Orville E. Babcock, his Aide de Camp, who entered the General's tent and awaited orders. "Orville, have a scout sent back to Fort Heiman and make a report of the situation there. Then, if Smith has overtaken the fort, have him fire on Fort Henry straightaway."

Babcock replied, "Yes, General!" then stepped out and called for a scout.

A young man of about twenty came to attention in front of Babcock as the aide commanded, "Brody, the General has requested information concerning Fort Heiman. He wants it immediately! If the fort has been seized, have General Smith begin his attack against Fort Henry by way of artillery. Understood?"

"Yes, Sir, General!"

The young man ran for his mount and sent his horse running forward before he ever attempted to stride the saddle. Instead, he hopped alongside the horse and jumped into the saddle in one motion like a pony express rider. He left the clearing at full gallop, then disappeared into the trees north of camp.

Brody made the ride in twenty minutes. He pulled up just outside the fort to see which army might be occupying the fortress. When Brody saw the stars and stripes of the Union flying high above the walls, he continued his ride to the front gate. Sentries stopped him at the entrance and asked who he was and what he wanted.

"Corporal James Brody, Union scout for General Grant. I have a message for General Smith."

The sentries opened the gate and allowed Brody to enter. Brody rode into the fort and was directed to General Smith.

General Smith had set up temporary headquarters in a small log cabin within the fort's walls. The corporal dismounted his steed and walked to the door of the cabin. Another sentry opened the door and allowed Brody entrance.

Brody stood at attention until General Smith recognized him.

"What is it Brody?"

"Sir! General Grant sends his compliments on your capture of Fort Heiman and sends orders to commence artillery fire on Fort Henry."

General Smith replied, "Tell the General thank-you. We will begin firing as soon as my men can ready the guns. Right now the canons are pointed in the wrong direction. By the time you reach the General we will begin our attack."

"Thank-you, sir!"

Brody left General Smith's headquarters and mounted his horse again, heading back to General Grant's location. He galloped his horse through the trees along the river bed, careful to remain out of sight in case Confederate troops might be nearby. He arrived at General Grant's tent twenty minutes later and reported to his aide, General Babcock.

General Grant told Babcock, "Keep the infantry moving forward. We'll try to capture as many of the rebels as we can while fleeing the fort."

Babcock replied, "Yes sir, General!"

General Foote moved his gunboats forward toward Fort Henry. The high waters of the rivers allowed him to take his four ironclads, Cincinnati, Essex, St. Louis, and Carondelet, and three timber clads, Conestoga, Lexington, and Tyler, up a chute of the river, bringing them closer to the fort. Fortunately, the bow guns of the gunboats committed severe damage to the eleven guns within the walls of Fort Henry.

Commander Henry Walke of the Carondelet fired first against the fort and immediately took out one of its heavy guns. His men cheered, then prepared the bow gun to fire again.

Walke checked the locations of his compatriots through a porthole. The other ironclads were having similar success. Carondelet fired again, causing more damage to the tiny fort that had little to protect it.

The big guns of Fort Henry fired back. The chute of the river where the gunboats rested was quickly filled with smoke and fire. Foote had his boats continue their attack against Fort Henry. They took out two more of the fort's canons. Henry fired back against the gunboats, hitting the Essex and damaging it. Steam spewed from its boilers. Many of the men abandoned the ship to avoid the unbearably hot steam billowing from the boat. Most of the men were caught with no escape and subjected to severe scorching of their skin, dying from their injuries. The direct hit left thirty-two men dead.

While the artillery battle ensued, the rebels retreated from the fort heading to Fort Donelson, leaving the gunnery crews behind for protective distraction. General McClernand and his troops pursued the rebels, trying to cut them off before reaching Fort Donelson, twelve miles away. However, the Confederate soldiers did get away safely to Fort Donelson because the rain had made such a mess of the terrain.

Daniel stood beside General Grant as report after report came in concerning the battle at Henry. Everything that Daniel had told him was coming to fruition. When a dispatch reached the General's tent and was read, Grant looked at Daniel and grinned. Finally, as the day ended and the last communication was received, General Grant looked at Daniel and said, "I don't know how you do what you do, but, Sir, you *are* a prophet."

CHAPTER 29

Daniel and Jake returned home after Fort Henry was seized. Daniel felt General Grant had enough information to take Fort Donelson as well. Grant was a capable military leader. Daniel felt they needed little help to win the battle at hand. So, Daniel went back home to his family and his homestead. He would check on Grant later.

Grant prepared his army for the next battle. He had ten thousand reinforcements brought in by steamboat—the U.S.S. Pittsburgh ironclad was brought in to replace the Cincinnati, the St. Louis, and the Essex, which were disabled during the battle at Fort Henry.

Because the terrain was still soggy from the torrential rains the previous days, Grant took his time in moving forward against Fort Donelson. Major General Henry Halleck, Grant's superior, had little confidence in Grant when he hesitated to attack Fort Donelson. Grant wired Halleck and stated, "Fort Henry is ours. ... I shall take and destroy Fort Donelson on the 8th and return to Fort Henry."

Grant's prediction was too optimistic. However, he continued to prepare his troops for the impending battle. On February 12th, Foote moved his gunships into position to take Fort Donelson and allow the ten thousand new troops to disembark and be positioned for the battle. Grant was aboard one of the ships when the fighting broke out. The Confederates tried to clear a path to Nashville. Nathan Bedford Forrest led his cavalry against Union forces on the right flank, hoping to clear the way. However, because Grant's officers hesitated during his absence, the rebels were able to push back on the right flank and killed many of the Union soldiers who were overwhelmed.

Grant's officers weren't the only ones who were hesitant. Brigadier-General Buckner of the Confederates attempted to move his brigade from the fort to begin the trek to Nashville. But, when he heard artillery fire in his direction, he lost his nerve and moved his men back into the fort.

Snow fell overnight, making conditions even more difficult for both sides. Temperatures dipped down as low as ten degrees. Many of the Union soldiers had abandoned their blankets and coats during the previous battle, causing several to die from exposure.

With reinforcements arriving and Union gunboats present, the Confederates were done by February 15th. On the morning of the 16th, General Buckner sent word to Grant requesting terms of surrender.

Buckner and Grant had a previous history. They served together in California during a bleak time in Grant's career. Grant lost his commission as an officer and was broke. Buckner loaned Grant money so Grant could travel back home.

Buckner thought their previous friendship might prove beneficial to him and his army's surrender. However, Buckner was sadly mistaken. Grant sent his reply to the request for terms:

Sir: Yours of this date proposing Armistice and appointment of Commissioners to settle terms of Capitulation has just been received. No terms except unconditional and immediate surrender can be accepted.

I propose to move immediately upon your works.

I am Sir: very respectfully, your [obedient servant]

U.S. Grant

Brig. Gen.

Buckner was appalled at Grant's response. Nevertheless, Buckner had no choice but to agree to Grant's terms or lack of terms. He surrendered more than seven thousand of his army, ammunition, and badly needed supplies to the Union General. Buckner was imprisoned at Fort Warren in Boston until August 1862, when he would be released as part of a prisoner exchange.

April 16, 1820

Daniel returned to his home just as Emily set the table for the evening meal. James and Micah were already in the cabin, looking forward to whatever Emily had prepared. Emily had killed two older hens from her flock that no longer lay eggs. She roasted the birds over the fire and seasoned them with salt, pepper, and a little sage. The cabin smelled wonderful as Daniel entered. Emily opened a Dutch oven and pulled out several sweet potatoes she had baked. She placed a loaf of freshly baked bread on the table and invited everyone to "dig in."

When Emily saw Daniel enter the cabin, she smiled, walked over, and hugged him. "Glad you made it back."

Daniel asked, "What did I miss today?"

"Not much," replied Emily. "Tommy worked on the planting, and Micah, and James worked at the mill."

Daniel turned to James and asked, "How much did you get done?"

"We got about half a load finished. We should be able to take a load to Nashville day after tomorrow."

Daniel replied, "Sounds good. Is there anything you need?"

James replied, "Well, I was thinking if we had a frame of some sort to hold the flour sacks while they were being filled, it would make it much easier. Then, it would only take one man for the job. One of us could stay at the mill while the other drives the freight wagon. We can swap out every trip so neither of us gets too bored."

Daniel said, "Sure. You should be able to fix something up easy enough."

Emily asked, "How did it go with you? How long were you gone?"

Daniel replied, "Oh, about three days. I met General Grant."

Emily said, "Really! How did that go?"

Daniel said, "Pretty well. It wasn't as hard to convince him as I thought it might be. I gave him a little demonstration and he was all in. He's the only one that knows, though."

Jake came over to Emily while she sat at the table with the others. He nudged her with his nose. Emily gave him a leg bone from her plate. Jake held it in his mouth, looking at her while wagging his tail for a moment. Emily patted his head, and then Jake left the table and found a spot near the fireplace to gnaw on his bone.

⸻◦⸻

Daniel rose and began his chores the following day, like any other day. After breakfast, he and Tommy worked to finish planting corn in the seventy-five-acre field. Because of the soil preparation they had made using the new harrow, planting went relatively quickly. Daniel decided to hold off on building a planter for sowing the cornfield until next season. He had too many other things on his mind for now.

James and Micah worked together at the mill. They found some lumber and built a frame for holding the meal bags while they were being filled. After an hour of sawing and hammering, they tried out the new frame.

They set the frame underneath the grinding wheels so that the flour or cornmeal would be funneled into the meal sacks without someone there constantly scooping it into the sacks. It worked well and made the work easier for one man to handle the mill by himself.

The Gordons had ground enough wheat to fill the wagon by the end of the day. Micah to James, "You know; we could run a load to Nashville every day at this rate. We'd have to buy another wagon and some more horses, but we could do it."

James replied, "Hold on, little brother. Let's take care of it one day at a time. We're just furnishing the labor. Remember? Daniel is the one who has to furnish the horses and wagons. He might not be so keen about forkin' out more money just yet."

The days were getting longer, which meant longer hours working in the field. Tommy and Daniel parted ways just before dusk to eat supper with their families. Daniel met with James and Micah on his way back to the cabin.

"How'd it go today?" he asked.

James replied, "We finished up a load of flour. We can leave first thing in the morning to deliver it."

Daniel said, "Sounds like that frame idea of yours worked."

Micah said, "Yep! It works a lot better than two men trying to scoop flour into the sack together. It's less messy, too."

When they entered the cabin, they all said, "Mmm, something smells good!"

Emily had prepared boiled cabbage, fried catfish, cornbread, and beans, with peach pie for dessert.

Daniel said, "I see you went fishing today."

Emily replied, "Amy and I did. We caught a big mess of fish."

Everyone was quiet as they ate their meal. Because it was so delicious, everyone barely spoke a word. Then, just as Emily began serving the pie, she asked Daniel, "Are you leaving again in the morning?"

Daniel replied, "I think so. But I'll be back before supper. I wouldn't want to miss another meal like this one."

Emily smiled as she dished out an extra-large piece of pie to Daniel.

CHAPTER 30

Morgan roused from a deep sleep. First, his head pounded a beat—boom, boom, boom, boom. Then, it became louder in his ears after a while—boom, boom, boom, boom. Then, a high-pitched whistle rang in his ears that matched the booming in his head.

"*What is that*?" he thought to himself.

He closed his eyes, trying to relieve the pressure on his brain. It was no use. The booming beat and the whistle only grew louder. Then he heard voices in the distance. Singing! Men were singing!

Morgan struggled to get to his feet. He stood, leaning over and looking at his feet while trying to gain his balance. Morgan saw his haversack lying next to him. He reached over, grabbed the strap, lifted the bag to his shoulder, and stood up straight as best he could.

Daniel appeared in a clearing just north of Grant's army's marching. He knew the General would be on his way to Savannah, Tennessee, by the river. Daniel hung back and admired the soldiers as they marched forward singing. He would find Grant later.

In the distance, Daniel saw a man stumbling toward the soldiers. He seemed to be injured. He was dressed in a Union Army uniform, but it was different. It looked brand new. Unlike everyone else's uniform, it wasn't tattered, torn, or worn-looking. It was barely even dirty. Daniel continued to watch from a distance as three men left the formation to meet the injured man.

The sergeant looked in the distance and at who his men were pointing.

"Henry, you and Hawlsey follow me. The rest of you men stay in formation."

Sergeant Bob Sikes and the two privates trotted out to see who was trying to catch up to their unit. Just as they reached Morgan, he tumbled to the ground, exhausted.

"Looks like he's bleeding, Sergeant!" observed Henry.

"Yeah, I can see that, Henry. See if he's been shot."

Hawlsey and Henry both looked Morgan over, thoroughly searching for bullet wounds.

"No, Sergeant! But he's covered in little pieces of glass."

"Glass?" asked the sergeant.

Morgan was able to speak now as he breathily said, "I had an accident. I went through my windshield."

"Windshield?" asked the sergeant. "What's a windshield?"

They all pondered momentarily, then Hawlsey offered, "Maybe he meant window."

Morgan again said breathily, "Yeah, window. Glass."

Then, Sergeant Sikes noticed the bars on Morgan's uniform.

"Captain, we'll get an ambulance up here to pick you up so we can transport you to our next location."

Morgan said, "No. I don't need an ambulance. Just put me in a car."

"A cart?" asked Henry. "I don't think we've got any carts. The closest thing would be the ambulance, Sir."

The sergeant told Hawsey, "Jim, go back to the line and fetch the ambulance for the captain."

"Yes, Sergeant!"

Then the sergeant asked Morgan, "Sir, where were you going when you had the accident?"

"Shiloh. What day is it, anyway?"

Henry spoke up, "Saturday, Sir. April 5th."

"Oh good!" said Morgan. "I haven't missed it then."

"Missed what?" asked Sikes.

"The battle at Shiloh." Morgan replied.

Daniel curiously watched as the man was loaded onto a wagon and then joined the formation as it traveled toward Shiloh. He needed to find Grant first but would return to find this stranger when time afforded.

⸻◆⸻

When the Army of the Tennessee arrived on April 5th, the medical corp split off and began to set up tents to use as hospitals to care for the wounded. Doctors holding the ranks of Major and Captain spouted off orders to the enlisted men who served as orderlies. Tents measuring about twelve feet squared were erected, and make-shift tables were set up inside the tents to serve as the surgery. Other smaller tents were set up throughout the camp for sleeping quarters.

Morgan was impressed by how in character everyone seemed to be. He had never been to a re-enactment that was so formal. Usually, all involved were content with being regular people, hanging out until the show began. However, the men here acted like they were *really* in the military and preparing for an actual battle.

Daniel watched from afar while the new Captain helped prepare the hospital. Finally, he moved closer to hear what was said.

As Daniel looked on, Morgan soon found a Major who seemed to be in charge and asked, "Major?"

The Major replied, "Yes." He turned and saw Morgan with a look of puzzlement.

"Major, I'm Morgan Turner. Where would you like me to set up?"

The Major answered, "Captain Turner. You must be one of the new surgeons. Glad to meet you. Uh...you are a surgeon?"

"Yes, sir!"

"I'm Major Timothy Tremble. Where did you study, Captain?"

"Vanderbilt, Sir."

"Vanderbilt? Why aren't you fighting for the south?"

Morgan replied, "Well, Sir, I wanted to be on the winning side."

Tremble replied, "I see. But, Captain, you look like you've been in a fight. Are you alright?"

"Yes, Sir. I had an accident early this morning. I'm feeling fine, though, Sir."

"Good." said the Major. "Well, why don't you set up with the rest of the surgeons on the north side of the surgeries. When you're settled, come and help us set up the surgeries."

"Yes, Sir!" Morgan said as he saluted and went to find the other surgeons' tents.

Daniel caught up with the Captain as he moved toward the area where Morgan would set up his quarters for the weekend.

"Excuse me, Captain."

"Yes?" replied Morgan.

"My name is Daniel Lane. I am a special aide to General Grant. You're new here are you not?"

Morgan replied, "Not really. I grew up coming here as a boy. But, this is my first year to come as a member of the medical corp."

Daniel asked, "You say you used to come here as a boy? Where did you grow up?"

Morgan answered, "Just down the road aways in Columbia."

"Really?" asked Daniel. "I'm from Columbia, too. Where did you live in Columbia? I was a mail carrier. I might have delivered your mail at some point."

"I grew up over on Carter's Creek Pike. My family has a farm there. The Turner Farm."

Daniel thought, then asked, "Tell me, when was the last year you came here as a boy?"

Morgan rolled his eyes back, trying to recall the last time he had been there. "I think I was sixteen, so that would have been 1950."

Daniel raised his eyebrows, realizing that this man was from the future. Somehow, he had found an opening to the Shimmering and traveled one hundred years into the past.

Daniel began to speak again, "Captain . . ."

"Ah, call me Morgan."

Daniel replied, "Right. Morgan, how did you get here?"

Morgan replied, "I drove my old Chevy. It was raining something awful. When I came down the Trace, it really rained hard. I lost control of the car and ran off the road. I went through the windshield and the last thing I remember was I was going head first into a tree. Funny thing is, when I woke up, there wasn't a tree. Come to think of it, my car was missing, too."

Daniel asked, "Where were you when you ran off the road?"

Morgan said, "I was just getting ready to leave the Trace at the Waynesboro exit."

Daniel said, "Morgan, I need to tell you something you aren't going to believe."

"Oh yeah? What is it?"

"This isn't a re-enactment of the battle of Shiloh."

Morgan replied, "It's not? Well which re-enactment is it?"

Daniel said, "It's not a re-enactment. You managed to find a time portal that took you one hundred years into the past. You're about to be a part of the real Battle of Shiloh."

Morgan chuckled and said, "Right! And, Elvis doesn't wear blue suede shoes. What makes you say such a thing. Time travel? There's no such thing as time travel."

Daniel said, "Morgan, the same thing happened to me. Only, I did it from 2017. I traveled back in time two-hundred years to the year 1817. There are these places located along the Natchez Trace that are called Ittola Chuka, by the Chickasaw. Each one opens at different times of the year and if someone walks through, they travel either back or forward in time. When the battle starts tomorrow you'll see. The wounded who come in here won't be carrying scratches, or cuts, or simple powder burns because they got to close to the wrong end of their weapons. You're going to be dealing with gun shot wounds. You're going to be doing amputations, and you're going to see young men come in here missing half their bodies. They're going to be screaming in pain and all you're going to be able to give them for pain is some Laudanum or maybe some whiskey."

"That's funny, Mr. Lane. But I've got too much to do right now than to be drawn in by your practical jokes. So I'll see you around."

Daniel said, "Just a minute." Daniel pulled an arrowhead from his shirt pocket and handed it to Morgan. "This was given to me by one of my Chickasaw friends. I want you to have it."

Morgan looked at the arrowhead and noticed how new it looked. Most of the arrowheads he had seen before were chipped or broken somehow. Morgan took the arrowhead and shook his head in unbelief as he turned and walked away. Daniel wasn't surprised that the young man didn't believe him. He, too, was in denial when he first came through the Shimmering.

Daniel continued riding north along the Hamburg-Savannah Road. He then turned right, easterly on the Browns Landing Road until reaching the Tennessee River. The road then turned Northerly and followed the river's path until he reached Pittsburg Landing. Daniel found where Grant's headquarters were being erected, off to his west. Unfortunately, Grant had not yet arrived. He was brought in by boat because he injured his foot when his horse rolled over.

Daniel dismounted and found a place under a Chestnut tree where he could bivouac. He tied Hoss to one of the lower-hanging limbs and unsaddled him. Jake found a shady spot to relax as he panted from the long walk. Daniel unrolled his bed and lay on it to rest before things got chaotic.

—◦—

April 6, 1862

Colonel Everett Peabody had been sending patrols along the Confederate lines south of Pittsburg Landing for three days. Then, on the 6th at 6:00 a.m., his patrols returned with the news that nine thousand Confederate troops were being readied for attack. Peabody's superiors believed that the Rebels were still at Corinth, Mississippi. Peabody's patrol proved otherwise.

One hundred seventy-four steamboats traveled down the Tennessee River carrying forty thousand men under the command of Major General Don Carlos Buell to reinforce the Union ranks. Grant was still in Savannah, Tennessee, when he received word that the Confederates were attacking. Grant ordered General Halleck to hold until Buell's army could arrive.

General Albert Sidney Johnston of the Confederate Army wanted to turn the Union army away from Pittsburg Landing so they could cut off their supplies and reinforcements. But instead of hitting Grant's left flank, they attacked the right flank, engaging General William T. Sherman's army. Sherman thought it was simply a skirmish until it continued for an hour.

Union troops were stretched thin all the way to Shiloh Church by 8:45 a.m. when Prentiss had his untested forces fall back. The Union soldiers abandoned their camps, leaving food and other supplies behind. Rebel soldiers stopped temporarily, collecting the supplies and eating because they were starving. For an hour, Johnston struggled to get his troops back on track to pursue the Union troops who were fleeing.

Daniel had to leave his camp when the battle started. He gathered Jake, Hoss, and his belongings and pulled them back to the Union hospital. When Grant finally arrived, he mounted a horse, even though he was still injured, and began riding up and down the lines, encouraging his men to fight. His encouragement helped because they managed to push the Rebels back three hours later so that the Union Army held the Western two-thirds of the Confederate army.

When Johnston and his army pushed back on Grant's left flank at the peach orchard, Johnston got hit in the leg with a musket ball. He died of his wound at 2:45 p.m.

Daniel knew the battle would be bloody, but he had never experienced anything so gruesome as he did at the hospital. Men were brought in with limbs missing from canon fire. Others were bleeding badly from gunshot wounds. Daniel watched as Morgan and the other surgeons worked quickly on each injured soldier brought to their tables.

Daniel was impressed by Morgan's ability to stay calm under pressure. His skill was unmatched. Daniel thought, *"He can suture faster than Aunt Sally can knit one and pearl two!"*

Daniel noticed that each surgical tent had a pile of human limbs outside. They were tossed outside after having been amputated from many of the unfortunate soldiers who had been maimed. After a surgeon finished with one patient, the patient was removed, and the table was doused with water for a quick cleaning. Conditions were horrible at best. There was no time to worry about sanitation. Morgan and the others only had time to try to stop someone's bleeding, either by stitching or amputation.

Men screamed and cried from fear, pain, and the realization that their lives would never be the same if they survived.

When Daniel saw that Morgan was handling things well enough, he left to find a quieter place to observe. He ended up about half a mile to the North. He thought he would probably be safe here. Daniel could watch some of the battles and the hospital. However, he wanted to watch Morgan in case something went wrong.

The fighting continued through the afternoon. Finally, General Hurlbut withdrew his army from the left flank, allowing the Rebels to close in around Wallace and Prentiss' troops. Their men fought bravely from a position that would later be called the Hornet's Nest because of the sound of metal whizzing through the air from the troops who used dense thickets as cover.

At 5:00 p.m., Wallace and Prentiss tried to retreat as well. Wallace took a bullet to the head and died. Two thousand Union soldiers were captured.

CHAPTER 31

APRIL 7, 1862

Lighting had ceased during the dark hours of the early morning, but the dawn brought more cannon fire. Morgan had managed to steal a few hours of sleep just as the barrage began again. Daniel saw Morgan exiting his tent and left his place of rest to catch up with Morgan.

Daniel waved to Morgan and called out, "Morgan!"

Morgan looked back to see who had called his name. When he recognized Daniel, Morgan quickly trotted over to him. "You were right!" he said. "I thought I was just here for a re-enactment. So how did I get here? I've got to get back!"

Daniel put up his hands to calm Morgan. "Don't worry. I'm going to get you back home. But, we need to leave now. Get your things and meet me back at my camp. Be careful, though. That canon fire seems to be getting closer."

Morgan ran back to his tent to gather his haversack and belongings. Daniel trotted out to his campsite and began saddling Hoss and packing his gear. When he loaded all of his gear onto his horse, Daniel looked back to see if Morgan was coming yet.

Morgan ran out of his tent and ran toward Daniel when cannon fire erupted next to him, destroying his tent and propelling him ten feet into the air. Morgan toppled to the ground and lay still. Daniel feared that he was too late to get Morgan back home. Daniel quickly mounted Hoss and rode at a gallop to where Morgan was lying.

Daniel dismounted and checked on Morgan. Morgan had cuts on his face and hands. He was unconscious but breathing. Daniel splashed some water on Morgan's face from his canteen. He still didn't wake. Daniel decided the best thing to do would be to get Morgan back to his own time and let the doctors care for him.

Daniel draped Morgan onto the back of Hoss, then slowly and carefully led him away from the battle. Once he felt he was at a safe distance, Daniel opened up the Shimmering and led Morgan, the horse, and Jake through. Daniel took Morgan forward to the date on which Morgan had wrecked his car on his way to Shiloh. Daniel didn't know the exact location, so he arrived at the Trace near the road to Waynesboro. When they exited the Shimmering, the rain was pouring tremendously.

As Daniel led his horse down the shoulder of the road, an ambulance could be heard with its siren blaring, heading farther down the road. Daniel topped a hill and saw the ambulance had stopped beside an old Chevy Bel Air. The car had collided head-on with a large oak tree, and the front windshield was shattered. Police were there, and they all seemed to be searching for something.

When Daniel arrived, one of the officers informed him they were searching for the driver of the wrecked car. Daniel told the officer, "I think this is the man you're looking for. I found him down the road, dazed and confused. He said he had had a wreck; then he passed out."

The officer noticed both Daniel and the body draped over the saddle were wearing strange clothing. He didn't say anything about the garb but waved over the two men from the ambulance to come and take care of the unconscious man. They brought a stretcher over to where Daniel waited and carefully removed Morgan from the back of the horse.

The officer asked Daniel, "Do you know this man?"

Daniel replied, "No, sir. He did mentioned something about being from Columbia before he passed out, though. He's wearing a bag around his shoulder. Maybe it's got some identification in it."

The officer turned back to the ambulance driver and said, "Hold up! Let me see what's in that satchel he's wearing."

The driver took Morgan's haversack and handed it to the police officer. The officer rummaged through it until he finally found Morgan's wallet. He opened the wallet and found Morgan's driver's license.

"Morgan Turner, Columbia, Tennessee."

He looked further and found an I.D. Badge from Vanderbilt Hospital.

"It says here that he's a doctor at Vanderbilt."

The officer turned back around to tell Daniel, but when he looked up, Daniel, the horse, and the dog were all missing.

⸺⬦⬦⸺

April 7, 1962

Morgan had been asleep for two days. When he woke, his head throbbed, and his whole body ached. Two young ladies stood over his bed when he opened his eyes. They both wore huge smiles on their faces, and tears ran down their cheeks.

One of them spoke, "Hey, there! How ya feelin'?"

Morgan slowly began to recognize the familiar face. It was Maggie, his longtime girlfriend. He looked at the other face hovering over him. His sister Lacy was there, too.

"Where am I?" he asked.

Maggie replied, "You're at Waynesboro Community Hospital. You've been unconscious for two days."

Morgan tried to sit up, then gave up.

"How did I get here? What happened?"

Lacy answered, "The police found your car wrecked on the highway and called for an ambulance. They brought you in. Your car hit a tree head on."

As Morgan began to remember, he said, "I was on my way to Shiloh for the re-enactment. It was raining furiously. I lost control of the Chevy and ran off the road."

Maggie said, "Sorry you didn't make it to the re-enactment. I know how much you were looking forward to it."

Suddenly, Morgan's eyes opened wide with realization. "But I did make it! Only it wasn't a re-enactment. I was there for the real thing. Union soldiers picked me up and took me by officer's ambulance to Shiloh. I helped set up the hospital tents. The fighting began and we were overwhelmed with injured soldiers. It was worse than I could have ever imagined. I worked all day of the 6th until after dark. When I woke up in my tent the next day, Daniel said he would take me home. Daniel! Where is Daniel?"

Maggie tried to calm Morgan, "Morgan! Calm down. Who is Daniel?"

"Daniel told me about my situation. He explained that I had traveled through time. I was at the real battle at Shiloh. It wasn't a re-enactment. I was going to meet him. He was going to bring me home. But then, . . . I don't remember anything else."

Maggie soothingly said, "Morgan, it must have been a dream. You wrecked your car before you made it to Shiloh. The police said they found you lying not far from your car. From the looks of the windshield, they thought you must have hit your head pretty badly. You're lucky to be alive."

Morgan said, "But, Daniel . . ."

"There was no Daniel. As soon as you were found on Saturday, they brought you here to the hospital. We got here about an hour after they called your dad. We've been here ever since. It was all just a dream."

Morgan questioned himself aloud, "But Daniel said he could travel through time. He said he came from the year 2017."

Lacy spoke up, "Really Morgan? Time travel? Even if you did meet this Daniel guy, do you think he could really travel through time?"

Morgan slowly replied, "No. It must have been a dream."

———◆◇◆———

April 8, 1962

While making his rounds, Morgan's doctor, Dr. Chandler, stopped in to check on him. Dr. Chandler was a bald older man with glasses on the end of his nose.

"Well, Dr. Turner. How are you doing this morning?"

Morgan put on his best happy face and said, "Great! I'm ready to get out of here."

Dr. Chandler checked Morgan's eyes by shining a light to observe his pupils' reactions. He checked Morgan's chart at the end of his bed and wrote something at the bottom of the page.

"Well, I think we can get you out of here today. I recommend a few days of rest before you go back to work, however."

Morgan replied, "That sounds good to me."

Chandler said, "Okay then, you can go ahead and start getting dressed when you feel up to it. I'll get the paperwork started so you can leave."

Morgan replied, "Thank you, Doctor."

Once Dr. Chandler left the room, Maggie gathered Morgan's things together, preparing to go home. She collected his clothes from the closet and lay them on his bed. When she saw his haversack lying on a chair in the corner of the room, she also picked it up and moved it to the bed. However, as Maggie picked it up, something fell out and hit the floor.

"What was that?" she asked, looking around on the floor for anything that might have fallen from the satchel.

There it was, hiding underneath Morgan's bed. Maggie got down on all fours and retrieved the item to examine it. She stood back up and asked Morgan, "Where'd you get this? I've never seen it before."

Maggie opened her hand to show Morgan the arrowhead she found under his bed. Morgan's eyes lit up as he realized what he was seeing.

"That's the arrowhead I got from Daniel! He gave it to me the day before the fighting started. See! I told you he was real! It wasn't a dream! Daniel does exist!"

EPILOGUE

Daniel sat on his front porch admiring the sun as it sank in the western sky. A slight breeze drifted past him, touching his face as he stared into the distance. He reminisced about his adventures living in his little valley with his friends and family.

Tommy and Amy now had four children. Noah was sixteen and a big help to Tommy and Daniel on the homestead. Noah doted after his three younger sisters, whom he adored. They loved their older brother with all their hearts. He protected, taught, and treated them more like his children than younger siblings.

Alyson, too, was now sixteen. She was an only child but managed to never be lonely because of Noah and his sisters. Emily taught Alyson everything she could about healing, remedies, and anything related to the medical field. Alyson hoped to leave the valley someday and attend school to become a doctor.

Jake was gone. Daniel thought about him and all the adventures the two of them had shared. Daniel couldn't have asked for a better friend and traveling companion. Jake died at the ripe old age of fifteen in the summer of 1830. Daniel laid him to rest next to Gus up on the grassy knoll behind their cabin under the large Hickory tree.

Emily came out of the house to check on Daniel. She noticed how melancholy he seemed.

"Whatcha thinking about?"

Daniel replied, "Oh, nothing. Everything."

Emily asked, "Have you finished writing your book yet?"

Daniel said, "I did. I just finished it a little while ago. It's just the way I remember it. I guess I'll take it to Nashville and see about getting it published tomorrow or the next day."

Emily asked, "What about Morgan?"

"What about Morgan?" Daniel asked.

"Have you been to see him lately?"

Daniel replied, "Oh, it's been a week or so since I last saw him."

Emily asked, "Have you talked to him?"

"No, I'm not sure I should. Beside, he might not even remember me."

Emily said, "Oh, he'll remember you all right. You should go."

"What, now?"

"Now!" said Emily.

———◆———

October 1, 1973

A shimmering light opened up behind the hospital, revealing a portal into the past and the future. Daniel stepped out into the dim night light and searched the parking lot for a red 1972 Cadillac Coupe de Ville that he had seen many times before. There it was, parked in the exact same place it always was. This time, Daniel walked over to it and stood, waiting for its owner to arrive.

Daniel knew the exact time he would arrive. He had been here many times but never approached the owner. Tonight would be different.

Daniel looked out of place wearing his buckskin britches and linen shirt. The only thing he carried with him was the scepter draped over his shoulder in its quiver.

It was time. A man walked out of the back doors of Maury General Hospital at exactly 8:20 p.m., the same time and place he had every time Daniel had watched him.

The man walked straight to his car, not thinking about anything except getting home to his wife and children. Suddenly, he noticed a strange man standing beside his Coupe de Ville. Morgan Turner slowed his pace as he cautiously moved toward his car. As he approached the man, he noticed how he dressed oddly.

"May I help you?" he asked.

"Morgan?"

Morgan asked, "Do I know you?"

"It's me, Morgan. Daniel."

Morgan's eyes lit up with the realization that the man who had helped him so many years ago was now standing before him.

"Daniel! Is it really you? I thought I would never see you again. How long has it been?"

Daniel replied, "For me, it's been sixteen years."

Morgan asked, "What brings you back here?"

"Oh, I've been coming here to keep an eye on you for a while now."

"Well, why haven't you talked to me before?"

Daniel replied, "Who says I haven't? I have come to this exact date and time many times over the years. But, I want to ask you something. Have you been going back to the Trace? Are you trying to find it?"

Morgan tried to act dumb by replying, "Find what?"

"You know what. The Shimmering. Like I said, Morgan, I've been watching you. You need to stop looking. If you find it, you might find yourself in a place and time you can't get back from and I might not be there to rescue you again."

Morgan said, "I won't go back again. I just wanted to know if it was real or not. Everyone told me it was a dream. That, it never happened."

Daniel said, "It doesn't matter what others tell you,

Morgan. It happened. Just as sure as I'm standing here, now. It happened!"

About the Author

About the Author

Michael L. Clark lives in Pensacola, Florida, with his wife Cindy. Clark's debut series was inspired by his many trips down the Natchez Trace. The stops along the Trail mentioned the people who once lived on the trail but gave limited information about their lives. Clark began to wonder about their stories and imagine traveling back in time to live among them and learn more. That desire sparked the idea for his first novel, The Shimmering, which has since evolved into a series of time-traveling Historical Novels.

His fourth novel, Ambush at Horse Creek, is the first of many books he calls The Young Americans series. Each story depicts a young person growing up in a historical situation. Ambush is about a teenage boy who rides for the Pony Express.

His latest series, The Red Raven, is based on pirates who operated during the early 18th Century.

Books by This Author

The Shimmering

The Diary of Gus Childers, The Shimmering Book 2

The Prophet, The Shimmering Book 3

Ambush at Horse Creek

The Red Raven

Raven's Destiny, The Red Raven Book 2